A SIP OF YOU

A SIP OF YOU

SORCHA GRACE

Praise for A TASTE OF YOU: THE EPICUREAN BOOK 1

"With a deliciously sexy hero, a heroine with unforgettable spice, and mouthwatering sensuality, Sorcha Grace's *A Taste of You* will have you begging for seconds. Absolutely delectable."
—J. Kenner, *New York Times* bestselling author of RELEASE ME, CLAIM ME, and COMPLETE ME

"More than just a taste of sexy here. Scorching hot flames have burned up dinner! Witty and fun, *A Taste of You* by Sorcha Grace is a satisfying, sensual read not to be missed."
—Raine Miller, *New York Times* Bestselling Author

"Fans of Sylvia Day and E.L. James will find a lot to like about the mysterious William Lambourne and will root for a heroine who deserves a second chance at love. An intriguing start to a saucy new trilogy."
—Roni Loren, National bestselling author of FALL INTO YOU

"Yummy! Imagine Christian Grey with warm chocolate and you have William Lambourne. Add a complex heroine who gives love another try and you have *A Taste of You*. This steamy romance will take you through twists and turns and have you cheering for love to prevail. I can't wait to read what's next for William and Catherine!"
—Aleatha Romig, Author of the bestselling CONSEQUENCES series

A SIP OF YOU

To M, S, and D—You still know why. XOXO.

ONE

"You doing okay back there, Miss Kelly?" Anthony's voice got my attention as I blinked out my window at the view of Chicago's Northwest side. We were speeding up the Kennedy toward O'Hare. Traffic was light, and the big black SUV seemed to glide effortlessly in an open lane. I glanced down at my fingers entwined tightly in my lap, and loosed my white-knuckled grip.

"It's Cat, Anthony." I caught his smile in the rearview mirror. He hadn't forgotten that I'd asked him to call me by my first name. In his small way, he was trying to take my mind off this trip and help me relax. He'd taken on an impossible job. I was nervous and giddy all at the same time.

"Of course, Miss Cat. We'll be at the executive terminal in less than ten minutes."

"Great." But my voice sounded tinny and false. How had I gotten myself into this?

William. No one but William Maddox Lambourne could have convinced me to go back to California. Well, maybe Beckett could have, but not likely. I'd moved from Santa Cruz to Chicago barely nine months ago and I'd had no plans to go back. Ever. Until this morning, when William told me the incredible news that his brother, presumed dead for nearly twenty years, might be alive.

It was the stuff soap operas were made of and I still couldn't quite get my head around it, but the look of desperation on William's face had been achingly real. He'd only had to say the words *come with me* and I was lost. I would have done anything for him and when he'd added that he needed me at his side, which was a first, I knew I'd go. In that instant, my petty hang-ups about going back to California were set aside in favor of supporting William during whatever shit storm was brewing out west. So here I was.

William had sent Anthony to drive me to O'Hare and from there we were taking a private plane to California. Like everything else he did, William traveled in style. I, Catherine Kelly, connoisseur of cheap seats in coach, was about to fly on a billionaire's private jet to his vineyard in Napa Valley. It seemed so utterly ridiculous—but it was so fabulously exciting too.

This entire day felt surreal. This morning I had woken up in William's arms at The Peninsula Chicago after the best night—and the best sex—of my life. Last night, when we'd come back together after our break-up—a break-up that had totally leveled me and gutted me to my very center—everything had changed, and I was still riding high from our reunion. Images of my sexy striptease, William's stormy eyes on me, and his hot mouth on my body were still very fresh in my head. I'd cried at the orgasm he'd given me. Yes, cried. I'd never felt anything as intense before and it had been fucking amazing.

And then there'd been the sweetness of sharing jelly beans, of talking for hours, which had been amazing too. Finally, William had started to open up to me and I felt closer to him now than I ever had.

After everything I'd been through in the past few years, I never imagined I could feel this way about someone again. William and I had only known each other for a short time, and yet he'd already changed my world completely and I had fallen for him. Hard.

We'd been standing in my kitchen late this morning, kissing, his tongue tasting sugary and sweet from Beckett's cupcakes. We were getting ready to spend a lazy Saturday together. I glanced down now at the watch William had placed on my wrist, a gift he had brought me from London several days ago. Anthony must have seen me and thought I was checking the time because he called out, "Almost there, Miss Cat. Just a few more minutes."

"Thanks, Anthony," I answered back.

But I wasn't concerned about the remaining minutes of our drive. The Patek Philippe on my wrist was excruciatingly accurate and my insides knotted and fluttered as I remembered William's instructions for me to think about his touch at 11:42 every morning. He had very specific ideas about my regularly checking my new expensive timepiece and, as he'd shared them, he had tickled my neck with hot kisses and trailed his hand down my body, palming my breast then cupping my sex, feeling through my clothes the inferno that blazed between my legs whenever he put his hands on me. But then his phone rang and that call had ruined everything. And now, in a few hours, I'd be back in California. Back home. Well, not exactly home, but only a hundred and fifty miles away.

I leaned my head back against the seat cushions, closed my eyes, and sighed.

Mentally, I went over my checklist one last time. It had been a hectic afternoon. I'd had to pack, find a dog sitter for Laird, and make sure my condo was taken care of. Thank God for Beckett, who never let me down. Since I worked freelance, work was coming with me. This trip was open-ended, so I hadn't even known how much to pack. I'd argued that I needed more time to get ready, but William assured me that everything would be taken care of.

He was good at taking care of details. He was good at taking care of *me*, when I let him. I ended up bringing just one bag with a pair of jeans, a few T-shirts and light sweaters, two cute dresses, and lots—and I do mean *lots*—of lingerie. It was in the sixties and seventies in Napa, and with the temperature in Chicago hovering in the twenties, the warmer weather sounded welcoming.

I'd changed into jeans and a hot pink sweater, but I still wore the ivory bra and panties William had given me this morning. I wanted to have a part of his gift close to me. Even in the back of the heated SUV, my hands were freezing and I'd forgotten my gloves, as usual. I wouldn't need them in Napa and I just hoped those were the only items I'd forgotten.

On the seat beside me were my purse, my laptop bag, and of course my camera bag. Leaving my cameras behind would have been like leaving a necessary appendage—I needed them like I needed my arms and my legs—so I'd brought both my digital Canon PowerShot and my vintage Leica.

This trip wasn't exactly great timing for me and I sighed again. I'd just finished shooting Fresh Market's spring campaign, and I still needed to edit my shots of asparagus and cherries. Thanks in part to Beckett's brilliant food styling, my latest work for Fresh Market would be featured online, in stores, in mailings, and on billboards all over the Midwest. Every detail had to be perfect. I was hoping I'd have some time to work over the next few days, as the final images needed to be submitted by the end of the week. But the reality was I had no idea what the next few days would look like, so now I was stressing about work a little too.

"Miss Cat, we're here," Anthony said. He angled the SUV toward a sign that read "Signature Flight Support." I'd flown in and out of O'Hare a few times, but I'd never been to this section of the airport.

We approached a nondescript, beige, two-story building. There were no cabs lined up here, no angry traffic cops, no people running with their luggage pulled behind them. There were signs for a few companies that provided air charter service, but we headed for an area marked simply as "Private."

"It looks pretty empty," I said.

"It was probably busier earlier in the day." Anthony glanced back at me and flashed a smile again. He looked formidable in the *Men in Black* suit William's male employees seemed to prefer, especially with his ever-present earpiece. He even had a military-style shaved head and, I suspected, a military background in something covert and deadly. He drove for William, but I knew his job entailed much more than just chauffeuring around Chicago's *former* most eligible billionaire bachelor—or his new *girlfriend*. Yes, as of last night, William and I were officially a couple.

Anthony nodded at the windshield. "Those are Mr. Lambourne's jets up ahead."

"Jets?" *Plural*? I leaned forward and watched as Anthony drove right onto the tarmac and toward the two planes. Behind them was a hangar, whose doors were partially closed. I could hear the engines roaring to life, and mechanics in bright orange vests scurried about performing what I assumed were last minute checks on both aircraft.

Just then a man ducked out of the plane on the right, and my breath caught in my throat. I'd know William anywhere. There was something about the way he moved, the way he stood, the power and hard lines of his toned body. His commanding presence was all the more noticeable because he was so damned handsome. Movie-star good looks, with the killer smile and charm to match. I'd seen other women eye him hungrily—hell, I'd been one of them—and some had even propositioned him almost openly right in front of me.

His thick, dark hair blew around his face like a tarnished halo, his vivid blue-grey eyes scanned the tarmac, and I felt a jolt the moment his gaze landed on the SUV. I doubted he could see me inside, but I felt like he was looking directly at me. My belly fluttered and my breathing shallowed. There wasn't a woman alive who could resist William Lambourne. And I, who knew what he could make me feel, what he could do with his mouth and his hands and that sculpted body, wetted my lips with the tip of my tongue in anticipation. I felt like the luckiest girl in the world.

But it wasn't just my body that warmed upon seeing him, my heart swelled too. I was in love with William—something I'd just realized yesterday. It was what fueled our reunion last night and everything since, but I still hadn't found the right moment to reveal *those* feelings to him. Yet.

Anthony pulled to a stop, and William watched the SUV with a hooded look. I noted his stance was wide, like a fighter's. I could tell he felt defensive, and I wanted nothing more than to take him in my arms and comfort him. "He really does need me," I muttered under my breath as I gathered my stuff. And that thought assuaged some of the reservations I still couldn't shake about making this trip.

My hand was on the door handle, ready to open it so I could sprint into William's arms, when Anthony opened it for me and helped me down. The wind whipped about me, wrapping my coat around my legs and blinding me with my hair across my eyes. It was freezing, the windchill obviously well below twenty degrees.

"I'll take those for you," Anthony said over the wind. I gave him my laptop bag but held on to my purse and camera bag. William waved at me. I started for the plane, and Anthony followed with my gear. I climbed the stairs, my gaze never leaving William's, and finally I reached the top step and he took my hand.

"You're here." He squeezed my fingers. "Finally."

"Am I late?" For once, I thought I was actually on time.

"No, but I can't stand being apart from you." He slid his arm around my back, and I felt the warmth of his skin even through my layers.

I was thankful for his touch. His big hands steadied me—and also shot heat and arousal through me. He seemed to know exactly the effect he had on me as he pulled me just inside the door, out of the bitter cold, and crushed me against him. "I'm so glad you're here."

"Me too." Our mouths locked, and he kissed me with an intensity that showed me just how much he'd hated being away from me these past few hours. Despite the chill, he was warm. My hearting racing, I dropped my purse and camera bag and threaded my fingers through his curls.

When we came up for air, I was almost dizzy. "It's only been a few hours since we were together, but it feels like days since we last kissed."

"It's all my fault," William replied. "But let me try to make it up to you."

His lips found mine again and this time his kiss was deeper, more demanding. He tasted so good, and I felt jolts of electricity every place his hard, strong body came in contact with mine. I'd never had this kind of chemistry with anyone before—not even with Jace, my late husband. But it had been like this with William since the moment I met him. I had flashes of us together—him pushing me against the shelves of the freezer at Willowgrass as his tongue, tasting of cinnamon and bourbon, invaded me for our first kiss. The sweet richness of chocolate and the ecstasy of his mouth on me while I writhed on the floor of my kitchen, completely naked and open to him the first time he made me come. And I'd never forget the taste of champagne and chilled grapes mixed with my own taste on his lips as he thrust inside me, filling me until I shattered again and again on his bed. For me, the experience of kissing William was forever linked with food and sex and was like a drug I could never get enough of.

Finally, he broke the kiss. I noted his eyes had darkened. We were standing in the plane's doorway and poor Anthony was standing on the steps behind me, waiting for our make-out session to conclude. I flushed with embarrassment as William tugged me farther inside the cabin. It was easy to forget just about everything—and everyone—else when we were together.

Here the roar of the wind quieted. The lights in the cabin were soft and cast a warm glow, and it took a moment for my eyes to adjust. And then it was all I could do not to sputter in amazement: I was engulfed in total luxury. I glanced around and, knowing William was used to this sort of thing, I gave Anthony a have-you-*seen*-this look.

"Pretty nice, huh?" Anthony nodded, stopping behind me and setting my laptop case on the large, plush seat closest to us. Then he moved away to stow the rest of my stuff.

"Do you like it?" William asked with a smile, his hand on my back again, gently stroking me like he needed to have his hands on me at all times. I was already his, but I loved his possessiveness just the same.

"Like it? I don't know what to compare it to. It's incredible," I answered as I looked around in awe.

The cabin reminded me more of a living room than any airplane I had ever seen. The floor was carpeted in light beige and the walls were a slightly bolder shade of that same color. On my left was a rich brown leather couch with coordinating throw pillows. Across from it were two wide leather armchairs and a dark wood desk equipped for either a business conference or work. In fact, a laptop was already open on the desk.

Behind the chairs were a large sectional and a coffee table facing a big flat-screen TV. A smaller flat-screen with its volume muted and a stock market ticker scrolling across it was built into the plane's back wall. Beyond was a door, indicating the plane had yet another room. Everything looked luxurious, polished, and totally posh.

"Thank you, Anthony," William said as Anthony finished with my bags. "I'll see you in a few hours."

"Yes, sir." He disappeared through the cabin door.

"Is he coming with us?"

"He'll travel on the other plane. Was the drive here alright?" William asked as he removed his hand from my back. I missed his warmth immediately.

I wanted to ask about the other plane. I hadn't realized this trip would be more than just the two of us, but I left that for the moment. "The drive was fine." I smiled at him and waited for him to offer to show me around, but he wasn't looking at me. In fact, he looked distracted. He seemed alternately fascinated by the floor and then by the stock report. I cleared my throat. "What's through the door?"

"Hmm?" He blinked at me, seeming to remember I was there. "The bedroom and a bathroom. Take a look. I need to speak with the pilot."

Without another word, he turned and headed to the cockpit. *He's definitely distracted*, I thought as I made my way back to the bedroom. I opened the door and almost laughed. I couldn't believe this plane. It was like something out of a movie. The bedroom boasted the same color scheme and opulent finishes as the rest of the interior, and I had to wonder if there were decorators for private jets. Probably.

Inside the bedroom, the requisite bed was more than large enough for two. The space was small and spartan yet richly appointed, as was William's style. Everything looked *very expensive*. Across from the bed was the bathroom. I peeked inside and wasn't surprised to see it was modern in tone like William's penthouse.

This was majorly impressive. Was I completely lame if my instinct was to snap a couple of pictures and text them to Beckett? He'd be so jealous, but he was the perfect person to share this with. I'd told Beckett I didn't want to get too wrapped up in the whole billionaire thing, and he had promised to keep me grounded.

I sent a quick text and then took one last awe-filled look around. I'd always flown cramped and uncomfortable in coach, even on overseas trips with Jace for surfing events. Once we'd been bumped off a flight from San Francisco to Sydney and the airline had moved us up to business class on the next flight. We thought we were living large when we reclined our seats all the way and took advantage of the open bar. But I never in a million years imagined taking a shower or sleeping in a bed on a plane. I stepped back into the bedroom and ran my hand over the luxurious duvet. I wondered if I would be joining the Mile High Club on this trip. I'd never done that. A curl of desire spiraled through me. I sincerely hoped so.

When I returned to the main cabin, William introduced me to the captain and co-pilot, who greeted me warmly and told us we were ready to depart. When they retreated, William took me in his arms again. "Every time I see you, you're more beautiful. Have I told you I don't deserve you?"

"Yes." I grinned. "But you can tell me again."

"I don't deserve you. And you are *very* beautiful. I intend to tell you that every day. Plan on holding to me to that."

Then he kissed me deeply. As always, the feel of his body pressed to mine made me heady with desire, but I was looking for something else too. I was thrilled that he was thinking about us together every day, but what I really wanted right now was to recapture the connection we'd shared last night. I wanted us to talk for hours again, and I wanted him to open up to me even more. I wanted to know him in every way and I wanted him to know all of me too. I *loved* him and was just waiting for the perfect moment to tell him.

I kissed him back eagerly, but he pulled away. Disappointment rocked through me as, again, I got the feeling his mind was somewhere else.

"Is everything all right?" I asked.

"Now that you're here, everything is fine. I just want to make sure you feel welcome," he said, lifting a highball glass of amber liquid from the table. He'd already drank some of it; I could taste the bourbon on his tongue.

"Can I get you something to drink?" he asked. "The bar is fully stocked."

"What, no flight attendant?" I joked. "What kind of plane is this?"

"Well, I like my privacy," he said with a smile that faded far too quickly, "but I'll try to make sure the accommodations are more to your liking next time. In the meantime, I guess I'll have to wait on you, hand and foot." His words sounded so seductive, and my throat went dry, but I kept things light between us for the moment.

"You'll do, I suppose." I smiled, but then saw he wasn't even really looking at me. Something about William was definitely off. I couldn't tell if it was because he was nervous about what he'd find on the trip—probably, but he hadn't said anything more about his brother. Or maybe he just didn't like flying, or maybe it was something else entirely. It was still so hard for me to read him.

"In all seriousness," I said when he placed his hand on the small of my back and guided me to the seats before the table. "This is amazing. I never even imagined planes like this existed, and you have two."

"I have five, actually. But only two are making this trip."

Before I could respond to that revelation, William reached over and buckled me in. His arm grazed my breast as he did so, and my nipples tightened in anticipation. He glanced up at me, his eyes more grey than blue. Even distracted, he didn't miss anything and could tell when I had even the smallest response to his touch.

"Some of my staff and my security team are flying out on the other plane. I don't like traveling with an entourage, but it's usually necessary, so I deal with it." He sighed as he took another sip of the bourbon. "Do you want a drink?" he asked again. Had he forgotten he'd already asked me that?

"No, I'm fine," I said.

He buckled himself in and pressed a button to signal the cockpit. "We're ready to go."

"We've been cleared for departure, Mr. Lambourne," came the reply. A moment later the jet began to taxi.

I hadn't realized how quickly a smaller plane would move. It seemed to whip down the runway. William reached over and tightly grasped my hand in his. I glanced at him and noted the tight set of his jaw and the strained look on his face.

"Are you sure everything is okay?" I asked as the engines roared even louder.

He nodded, tight-lipped. The plane leapt into the air and for a moment we seemed to hang and glide, and then we made our way up and up. Still, William gripped my hand in an almost painful clench.

"Positive?" I asked. He didn't respond, and I sighed. He could be incredibly frustrating sometimes—a lot of times. I knew letting me in and telling me what was going on—in his mind, in his heart, in his life—was never going to be easy for him. But he knew how important honesty was to me and to our relationship. "You know I'm here for you, right?" I said. "If you want to talk about anything..."

He glanced at me, then released my hand and reached for his drink.

So I guessed that was a no. Hopefully at some point I would find out more about the phone call that brought us here and about Wyatt's mysterious reappearance. Wyatt was William's older brother, or he had been until he and William's parents were presumably killed in a plane crash when William was only eleven. Not long after we first met, I'd done a little Googling of my own and read about the plane crash. I knew what lengths William went to in his attempt to figure out what happened to his family. The plane wreckage had never been found, but apparently that wasn't unusual for a plane crash in Alaska. So I knew some, but I wanted the details and to know what William knew.

I had so many questions and William had promised me answers, but it didn't appear those answers would come now. He was too wound up, too tense. A few minutes later, there was a ping and William rose. I watched him as he made his way carefully to the bar near the big flat-screen and freshened his drink. The flight felt pretty smooth to me, so his careful walk seemed a little overdone. Or maybe that bourbon hadn't been his first.

"Are you sure you don't want anything?" he asked. "I had the galley stocked before we left. The lobster club sandwich is very good and so are the spring rolls. Or how about sparkling water? I've got fresh limes." He seemed to be rambling a bit now. I cut him off.

"I'm not hungry right now. Thanks."

I watched as he reached in his pocket, popped a pill in his mouth, and then took a deep swallow of his drink.

I was concerned now, but I tried not to let on how much. "That must be your secret medicine," I said, my tone teasing. "Now I know what gives you all that stamina and vitality."

He laughed, but it didn't quite reach his eyes, which were more guarded than ever. "Come here," he said, taking a seat on the couch across from me. I unbuckled my seat belt and made my way to him. William took my hand and pulled me down beside him. It was soft and comfortable, and I curled my legs under me. William's hand continued to stroke mine.

"So you're not Superman, after all," I said quietly.

"Far from it. That was Xanax. I hate flying, but it's necessary. And then, so is the Xanax."

I nodded, squeezing the fingers that still stroked my hand gently. Of course he hated flying, and I couldn't believe I just realized it. His whole family died in a plane crash. His mother and father and older brother were gone in an instant. It was amazing that he ever set foot on a plane. *He* was amazing.

"I know this has to be unbearable for you," I whispered. *Please let him open up to me now,* I thought. *William, let me in.*

"The Xanax makes it bearable, but you, Catherine, you help more than you could possibly know."

"I want to know," I said. "Maybe talking to me would help."

His eyes grew tender, and he pulled me into his lap. I could feel the tension in his tightly coiled body, but he seemed to relax slightly when we touched. His hands stroked up my arms to cup my face and then he leaned forward and kissed me gently. I tasted the bourbon again. It had a smooth, smoky flavor that was earthy and elemental, much like the man himself. The sweet kiss deepened when I responded, and he pulled me closer, pressing me against him so we were one. His lips touched mine tenderly, but there was something else there too—something desperate and dark. And something temptingly erotic. My toes curled as my body came alive with desire. I wanted more. More of his mouth, more of his hands, more of everything.

But instead of giving in to temptation, William pulled back and sighed again. "Thank you for coming, Catherine. I know this wasn't what we had planned for today. It means the world to me that you would drop everything to be with me. And I know I owe you explanations. I promise they'll come. Soon." He raked a hand through his hair, closing his eyes briefly in what looked like pain. "It's such a fucked-up, sordid story," he said, eyes still closed as though he was seeing it in his mind. "I hope it doesn't change anything, but I know it might." His eyes opened and his gaze met mine again. I could tell that whatever this was, it was weighing heavily on him.

"William, I can't believe…" I started to utter a protest, as I couldn't think of anything he might reveal that would change the way I felt about him, but he cut me off.

"It can wait. It will take a while to tell you all of it anyway, and now isn't the time." He gently set me back on the couch, and I had to resist the urge to climb back into his warm, welcoming lap.

He stood. "As I said, it's just the pilots and the two of us, no flight attendant. Are you certain I can't get you something?" But he wasn't really looking at me as he spoke. Again, he was distracted and so far away.

"I'm really not hungry," I said again. "Maybe later." I accepted I wasn't going to get the answers I wanted right now, but that didn't silence all the troubling thoughts that were starting to swirl around in my head. I tried to stay focused on William and his needs, as he was so obviously out of sorts. "Why don't you go lie down?" I suggested. "Relax."

"That's a good idea," he said and started for the bedroom without even a backward glance. I'd never seen him like this. It was fascinating in one sense, but it concerned me too. I waited for William to look back at me, for him to motion for me to follow him into the bedroom—I was hoping to join the Mile High Club, after all—but he opened the door and shut it without a single acknowledgement or invitation to join him. And that was *really* not like William.

What exactly waited for us in Napa?

TWO

I looked around the empty cabin, feeling uneasy. It was a little creepy to be alone on a plane like this and I almost wished Anthony had flown with us. I didn't like being by myself in the empty cabin, but there wasn't much I could do at this point. The flight was just over three hours, and I was apparently going to be entertaining myself for most of it. I thought about pulling out my laptop and doing some work, but the idea didn't appeal. Instead, I grabbed my tablet and my headphones and scrolled through the movies I'd downloaded. I curled up on the sectional, throw pillows tucked around me, and started a movie. After about fifteen minutes, my stomach rumbled and I decided maybe I would have a snack after all.

Leave it to William to stock his plane with the kind of food I'd expect from one of the Michelin-starred restaurants he favored. I spotted the lobster club sandwich and the spring rolls he'd offered, and there was also a cucumber and shrimp salad, Asian beef with noodles, crème brûlée cheesecake with fresh berries, and toffee-covered macadamia nuts. No airplane peanuts for William. There was even popcorn, but it was wasabi ranch flavor, which I'd never tried, and I didn't want to sample it now. I decided on a fruit salad and a sparkling water and, with another look at the closed bedroom door, returned to my movie.

I'd unwittingly chosen a romantic comedy—or perhaps the choice was more deliberate on the part of my unconscious than I wanted to admit. The story reminded me of how I'd met William outside Willowgrass on the night I'd been scoping out the restaurant for the *Chicago Now* shoot. One of these days I was going to have to call Jenny Hill and thank her for breaking her wrist so I'd been able to take the assignment. It had turned out to be a lot more than a good career opportunity. I never would have thought that less than a month later, I'd be in love again—with Stormy Eyes, the handsome man I literally fell for that night—and watching a movie on his private jet.

I still found it hard to believe that a girl like me was with a man like William Lambourne. He had everything. He was gorgeous, with all that thick mahogany hair, those stormy blue-grey eyes, and that ripped body. And he was rich. I still had difficulty fathoming the extent of his wealth. His penthouse was the kind of place someone like me only read about in magazines. I had no idea how many business ventures he was involved in, but WML Capital Management seemed to have more than its share of *global interests*. Hell, we were going to his vineyard on his private jet, and the watch I was wearing was worth more than my yearly income. And though he could be infuriatingly bossy and demanding and downright thickheaded at times, he was also sweet, caring, sensitive, and passionate about so many things, including food. I'd eaten more with William and in front of William than I had with any other man in my entire life. And I'd loved every bite of it.

But he had his drawbacks too. If I was being romantic, I'd say he was mysterious, but really he was incredibly secretive. He'd already amassed a track record of withholding information from me when he felt like it. Important information about things like his socialite ex-girlfriends or spontaneous overseas trips, and, of course, about his family and the accident that had claimed their lives. The reason for this trip fell under the "Secretive" category, but I was letting it slide because of how obviously upsetting the situation was. Plus, I had reason to believe he was going to change his mysterious ways. It couldn't just be sex between us. I needed more, and I knew William wanted more too. We'd talked about that.

An hour and a half later my movie ended, and I was bored and annoyed, flipping through an old magazine I'd found. Apparently even flights on private jets weren't exciting past the first few minutes. The co-pilot had come out earlier to check on me, which was nice. When I'd told him William was sleeping, he hadn't seemed surprised.

"He usually sleeps," he'd said. "He hates to fly."

I'd wondered if the co-pilot knew about the Xanax too. Sometimes it seemed like everyone knew William better than me.

"It should be a smooth flight. We'll be there on time, if not a few minutes early," he had said before shutting himself back in the cockpit.

"Great," I'd said, trying to sound enthusiastic.

In truth, a ball of dread formed in my belly when I thought about returning to California. I didn't know how I was going to avoid being reminded of Jace and the life we shared there together. Santa

Cruz seemed like forever ago, but parts of it were still so raw they might have happened yesterday. And those parts still ripped at old and tender wounds. I pushed all of that out of my mind and focused on the real reason for the trip: William. We were going to be spending our time at his vineyard in Napa and that was far, far away from anything that could hurt me. But it would have been nice if William had been here to distract me from my worries.

I shivered, noting that, just like a commercial airliner, it was too cold. I checked the cupboards and couldn't find a blanket. Now would have been a great time for a flight attendant to appear. But I was on my own, and I wasn't helpless. The blankets were probably stored in the bedroom. Quietly, I opened the door and tiptoed inside. I stopped in my tracks, staring at William in shock.

He was out. I'd rarely seen him sleep, much less sleep so deeply. I moved closer so I could see his face, which was turned toward me. His strong features were slack, but his brow was drawn with tension. Despite his light snoring, I didn't think his slumber was peaceful.

He stirred a little when I closed the door, but then he quieted again and his breathing became regular. One arm was thrown up over his head, and a blanket was twisted around his legs. He wore a T-shirt and boxer briefs, the black clothing and the swirl of his dark hair like a stain on the white sheets. His body was perfect, his biceps making the T-shirt's sleeve bunch, and the lines of his flat abs were visible where his shirt had pulled up slightly. He was a fallen angel asleep in his winged chariot, and I couldn't resist him.

What the hell? I thought. Why should I resist him? He was *my* fallen angel. I quickly stripped down to my ivory bra and panties, which were embellished with delicate lace. I felt almost virginal in them, especially with William wearing all that black. I climbed in bed beside him; it was plenty big enough for both of us.

"Catherine," he murmured, shifting slightly onto his side. I pulled the blanket up to cover us and spooned behind him. Did the man ever get cold? The heat radiating from him immediately warmed me. Neither of us had slept much the night before, and I felt my body relax and melt into his. He sighed and pulled my arm tighter around him. This was home, I thought. Even though I was in-between worlds—somewhere between my first home and my new home— William was my anchor now. I snuggled into him, putting my head behind his shoulder and breathing in his strong, masculine scent. My eyes drifted closed and, wrapped in his warmth, I fell asleep.

*****

A quiet buzz made my eyelids flutter, and I blinked awake, momentarily confused by my surroundings. I was moving, and yet I was lying still in a comfortable bed with the softest sheets and blanket enveloping me. And I wasn't alone.

William.

My eyes closed again, and I felt him reach to answer the phone. The room was silent except for the distant droning of the plane's engines until William said, "Very good," and hung up. Even half-asleep I marveled that he sounded awake and collected. The mattress beneath me moved as I felt him turn to face me. I managed to open my eyes and give him a sleepy smile, but I was so relaxed and warm that I struggled to keep them open. They fluttered closed, and I imagined I was drifting on a cloud, thirty thousand feet in the air.

William's finger stroked my cheek. "Wake up, beautiful girl," he murmured.

With difficulty, I opened my eyes. He was smiling at me, his own eyes soft and grey.

"We'll be landing soon."

"Hi," I whispered, wanting to keep the intimacy of the moment. "I hope you don't mind that I joined you. I was cold and kind of lonely out there by myself." I snuggled closer to him. "And it looked so warm and inviting in here, even if you were dead to the world."

"Mind?" He laughed gently, his hand cupping my cheek. "Of course I don't mind. I can't think of a better way to wake up. I love you in any bed I'm in, Catherine."

My heart sped up at this and a thrill of longing raced through me. I loved that he used the word *love* with me, even though neither of us had confessed feeling that yet. I knew I loved him, and I knew I was going to tell him on this trip. Even if William wasn't saying he loved me, it still felt special when he used the word to describe us. Maybe if I started to use it more, it would make revealing my feelings easier. "Good, because I love being here with you too."

His mouth nudged mine open, his lips playful and searching. His hand trailed down my arm and came to rest on my lower back, pulling me closer. His mouth closed over mine, our tongues entwining as his hands explored my body. If I had been warm before, I was burning up now.

He trailed kisses along my jaw, moving to nuzzle my neck and glide his mouth over my collarbone, toward my breasts. "There's just one problem."

"What's that?" I asked, my voice breathless, my nipples already beginning to harden in anticipation of his skilled lips and tongue.

He reached for my bra clasp. "You're wearing too many clothes."

The front closure of my ivory bra snapped open, and slowly, William pushed the lacy material away. His fingertips brushed against my flesh as the material parted, and I felt my skin flush and tingle with awareness. My breathing was already shallow and my heart rammed in my chest. Being with William was always exciting, but sex at thirty thousand feet was the height of sensual decadence. I'd been thinking about us together like this all day, and my body was more than ready for him.

I moaned as his lips skated over my bare skin. His breath was hot and his tongue moist as it darted out to tease one of my nipples. My breasts were heavy, aching for his touch. He sensed I didn't want gentle right now and his mouth closed on one of my hardened peaks and sucked, making me gasp. My hips lifted in response, and I ached to get closer to him. It seemed like I could never get close enough.

His hands fondled and stroked as his mouth worked on me, teasing and tonguing until I was writhing. Then he stopped. "You have magnificent tits."

What? It took me a moment to focus on his words, and even then I could only moan. Why was he stopping?

"I love your breasts." He kissed them, stroking them lovingly.

There was that word again: love. "I'm glad you love them."

"I'm being serious." He propped his head on his elbow and studied me carefully. So I guessed we were going to have a conversation about my breasts now. I was amused and also very turned on.

He cupped my right breast and tested its weight. "You fit my hand perfectly." His fingers stroked my sensitive skin. "And your areolas...very nice. They're naturally rosy."

"My areolas?" I laughed again. "That sounds so clinical." I cleared my throat. "I'm impressed with your knowledge of female anatomy, Mr. Lambourne," I said in my most professional voice.

He ignored my teasing, though I swore I saw his lips curve slightly. "Yes, your *areolas*, Catherine. As I was saying, before you interrupted, they're naturally rosy, and they turn a dusky pink when you're turned on." His gaze met mine. "Like now." His gaze flicked back to my breasts, and he circled the pad of his thumb over my erect nipple. I had difficulty concentrating on his words. I was wet for him, my lace-trimmed ivory panties damp against my sex.

"You know how I can tell when you're about to come?" he asked. "Your nipples get rock hard just before." He tongued my left nipple, sucking and licking it while his hand massaged my right breast. I felt hot desire coiling in my core and the heavy liquid heat pooled until the pressure made me feel as though I'd explode. His lips pulled harder, demanding more, and I winced. My breasts were more tender than normal, and his skilled mouth and tongue were delivering an irresistible combination of pleasure and pain that already had me shuddering with pleasure.

"Are you okay?" he asked. I should have known he would notice my reaction. He was so attuned to my every need and desire.

"More than okay," I said, my voice breathy. "I'm going to get my period soon, so I'm a little extra sensitive." I don't know why telling him this made me blush, but it did. "But it's good. So good. Don't stop."

He paused and glanced up at me. "That will be new for us. I'll have to remember to exploit this sensitivity in the future. I bet if I do this," he nipped at my already tortured point, "you'll feel it all the way down here." His leg parted mine and his thigh brushed my sex, where my clit was pulsing. He nipped me again, and my hips arched off the bed and I moaned. I clamped my legs about his, and I rocked against him, trying to ease the building ache.

"I can make you come," William murmured, his voice deep and husky. "Just with my mouth, just on your breasts. I don't even have to touch your clit."

My hips were moving rhythmically now as he worked me with his hands. He nuzzled against my neck and whispered, "Do you want me to keep touching you like this, Catherine?" His voice sounded dark, breathy, and erotic.

I already felt my orgasm building. I gave a short laugh. "It's like high school. No going past second base, right?"

He made a low growl in the back of his throat and moved so I could feel his hard cock against my leg. He was just as worked up as I was. "I don't know what kind of high school you went to..."

I smiled at the censure in his tone.

"And I don't want to think about some horny, fumbling teenage boy touching you like this in the back of his mother's station wagon." His mouth closed on my aching breast again, and I gasped.

"A station wagon?" I teased when I could breathe again. "Give me some credit."

"I don't care what kind of car he had. He couldn't make you feel like this." He sucked long and hard, and I felt a pull in my core. "Could he do this to you?"

"No," I moaned long and loud as I pushed my breast into his hands.

"You're close now, aren't you?"

"Yes." I was so close, edged closer as his fingers plucked and stroked and his mouth on my right nipple tongued and sucked. Everything inside me coiled into a tight ball in my core. I writhed against William, seemingly out of control. I felt the hard, steady pressure of his leg against my soaked panties. I panted, inching closer and closer...

He gave my sensitive, swollen right bud one last quick bite, followed by a long hard suck, and I crested over the edge, my body exploding into a shuddering orgasm so intense I couldn't hold back my cries. Wave after wave of pleasure rippled through me, and I rode each one higher and higher until finally I spiraled slowly down and managed to open my eyes.

William lifted his head and gazed down at me. Every inch of me tingled and sparked, and in the soft warmth of the plane's bed I could feel my skin gleaming with a light sheen of perspiration and a pale rosy warmth. My nipples were, amazingly enough, still rock hard and flushed dark pink. He was right.

"You glow after you come," William said, looking into my eyes. "Like a deep, perfect blush. So beautiful. I could watch you come all day."

I turned lazily to face him, and we lay on our sides, smiling at one another. I moved to press against him, feeling the hardness of his cock against my belly. I was only getting started. "Thank you for that," I murmured, finally finding my voice. "I didn't know...I mean, I've never..."

His brow lifted. "You've never come like that before?"

I smiled. "Not exactly." I loved to have them played with, but a nipple orgasm was a first for me. Only with William. I giggled. "It felt amazing. *You're* amazing. I loved it." I loved *him*. This was what I had been wanting on this trip—the same closeness and intimacy we'd shared last night at the hotel.

I kissed him lightly, then more deeply as I drew my hand between our bodies and against the flat plane of his abdomen, then down to his thick erection. It was barely contained in his black boxer briefs, and I teased my fingers under the waistband and closed my hand around him. He pulsed against my palm as I ran my hand up to the smooth tip and down to the wide, veined root.

"Now, let me do something for you," I said, still stroking him. "And I'm going to stick with the high school theme."

His expression was amused and also a little wary. "I have no idea what you're thinking. Should I be nervous?"

William nervous? This was new. He'd used anticipation to heighten my arousal several times. Now I wanted to see if I could have the same effect on him.

"Now it's your turn to trust me, William. It'll be fun." I sat up.

"Fun?"

"You'll like it. Just lay back, and close your eyes. Don't look."

He studied me for a moment longer, and I feared he'd refuse. He didn't like surprises or any situation that veered off plan. His eyes were sharp and blue now, narrowed and serious. "Okay." He rolled onto his back. "I surrender. Do what you will with me."

A giddy feeling swept through me, but I tamped it down. "Oh, I plan to. To begin, I don't think we need these." I slid his boxer briefs down, pausing so he could lift his slim hips and then tugging them slowly down his sculpted legs. When they reached his ankles, he kicked them off and onto the floor. "Keep your eyes closed," I said, glancing at his face and then back to his impressive erection. There was nothing about William's body that didn't impress me. From his broad chest to his trim waist, he had the kind of body I'd expect to see in a calendar of hot firemen—only I had the X-rated version before me, with his beautiful cock jutting up, eagerly waiting for me.

"Very nice, Mr. Lambourne," I purred. "I promise I won't leave you in this painful state for long."

He threw an arm over his eyes. "I'm not promising to keep my eyes closed for much longer, and the anticipation is killing me."

I was counting on the anticipation playing a part in this little seduction. Resisting the urge to stroke him once more, I slid off the bed. "Give me just a minute." I padded to the well-appointed bathroom, still marveling at its size. It was practically as big as my bathroom at home and nicer than it too.

"Catherine?"

"Coming!

I opened cabinets and drawers until I found what I needed. In the mirror, I caught a reflection of myself. My brown hair was mussed about my shoulders, and my eyes looked huge and soft green against the pink glow of my cheeks. When I returned, William still had his arm thrown over his face, and I smiled as I sat beside him. "This will be a little cold at first."

"What?" His body tensed, and I couldn't stop a smile.

"Relax." I poured a large blob of expensive-looking lavender hand lotion into my hand. I allowed it to warm for a few seconds and then wrapped my wet palm around William's engorged shaft. He jerked and then stilled, his body at attention. I stroked him, working the thick, rich lotion in, tightening my grip as I slid my coiled fingers over the impressive length of him.

"Catherine." His hips moved, pushing his cock into my hand. "Are you jerking me off?" He was smiling, but the tightness in his voice indicated he was very worked up. I continued my rhythmic movements

"Uh huh."

William's fingers clenched and unclenched the sheets as I stroked him. Without ceasing, I maneuvered myself between his legs and cupped his heavy balls with my other hand. I bent and trailed kisses along his inner thigh, letting the coarse hair on his leg tickle my cheek and my bare breast. He hissed in a breath, and I saw his fingers curl and uncurl again. I had him all but squirming. Which was majorly turning me on.

His cock swelled in my fist, filling it almost completely. The veins were thick and pulsing now as my hand worked the engorged flesh. Slower then faster. William surrendered to my efforts, his hips rocking and his hands clenching and unclenching. He moaned, sounds of ecstasy even he, the god of control, couldn't suppress. I felt his body tensing, his pleasure mounting. I was enjoying this—having the chance to watch him for once. His jaw clenched and his hand fell away from his eyes, which were tightly shut.

"I'm close." His voice was taut and controlled, and in that moment he opened his eyes and focused solely on me.

"Just let go." I closed my hand tightly and sped up my movements.

"Oh God, Catherine." His voice was husky with need and, with our eyes locked, I watched his face, wanting to see him go over the edge as I milked him. His entire body rose up, and I knew he was there. Suddenly his hand joined mine, and we pumped his shaft together until his back bowed and he released. His expression was beautiful in that moment—ecstasy and agony combined.

Finally, when his body began to relax, he sighed. It was a long, contented sigh. "That was fucking amazing. I can't remember the last time someone gave me a hand job. Thank you." He leaned up and pulled me into a deep kiss, his tongue softly tangling with mine.

I pulled away first and laughed. "You're welcome. You've never come like that before?" I asked, blinking with mock innocence.

He gave me a smirk. "Sometimes you're very naughty, aren't you?" He pulled me into his arms and kissed me deeply again—a playful kiss, but laced with emotion too. I leaned into him contentedly. I could stay here forever, in our own private world, far, far away from all the stresses and realities of real life. He pulled back slightly and murmured, "I loved your hand." A frisson of desire zinged through me in response to just the tone of his voice. It amazed me that I never seemed to get enough of William. The more he satiated me, the more I craved him. His hand cupped my sex. "But I love this more." He stroked my cleft, and I felt my damp panties press against the tender flesh. There was that word again—*love*. I moaned quietly, pushing harder against his hand.

"I wish we had more time, but..." He drew away and studied his right wrist and the cheap drugstore watch I'd given him this morning when he returned the Patek Philippe to me. "We are either about to land"—he glanced at his Rolex on his left hand—"or we have just enough time to get cleaned up before we land."

I slapped his chest playfully. My Walgreen's watch was black, plastic, and chronically fast, and William liked to tease me about what Beckett called "Cat Time," my habit of running ten minutes late for just about everything. But he was wearing my watch and, even if the time was wrong, it meant a lot to me that he still had it on. I would have been happy to snuggle back under the covers with him, but he sat up and pulled me with him. "Hop to it, *girlfriend*." He grinned at me. We were both still getting used to our new relationship status, and terms like *boyfriend* and *girlfriend* were novelties to us both. William rose. "We're almost in California."

THREE

About thirty minutes later, William and I were strapped in as the jet landed at Napa County Airport. The Xanax must have worked because William didn't crush my hand when he held it this time, and he was able to chat a little, mentioning that the airport was about thirty miles from his estate in St. Helena.

Estate. I wasn't sure what differentiated a regular house from an estate, but I knew *ordinary* didn't apply to anything related to William. I'd find out soon enough.

I held William's hand eagerly as we exited the jet and blinked into the setting sun of early evening in California. It was only a little after five o'clock here, and the sun was low on the horizon, about to dip below the brown landscape of mountains.

I had the overwhelming sense that I was home as soon as I saw the mountains and felt the cool breeze in my hair. It was chilly, but it didn't cut through me like the biting wind in Chicago. And there was a smell too, of green grass and trees and sunshine. I'd forgotten that smell, but I recognized it now and it permeated everything underneath the more powerful odors of jet fuel and exhaust.

William led me down the steps pushed against the side of the plane, and I noted the larger jet had already arrived. George Graham, William's assistant, and several other members of William's team were lined up in two clusters on the tarmac a little distance away, waiting for us. I felt a bit like a visiting dignitary and smiled at the idea of approaching George and curtseying. Since he didn't seem to possess a sense of humor, he probably wouldn't get the joke. George was short and stocky with clipped silver hair and a military bearing and I didn't think I'd ever seen him smile.

When we touched the asphalt, George came forward immediately, and I noted his *Men in Black* suit was perfectly pressed despite the long flight. "Good evening, Mr. Lambourne." George nodded to me. "Miss Kelly." Unlike Anthony, who was friendly, I was perfectly happy to have George continue calling me *Miss Kelly*.

"A word, Mr. Lambourne."

William shot me an apologetic look. "Give me just a minute." He kissed me lightly on the cheek and stroked my upper arm, then stepped away with George. They walked as they spoke, heading toward the second group of two or three people. I stood there alone, feeling momentarily uncertain, and then moved toward the first group, where Anthony smiled at me and William's executive assistant, Parker, stood scrolling through a Smartphone. As I approached, she glanced up, gave me a quick smile, and asked, "Is there anything I can get for you, Miss Kelly?"

"No, thanks. I'm fine," I said, distracted by watching William and George reach the second group of people, who were only a few feet away from us. With the roar of the jet engines, I couldn't make out anything that was being said.

"Just let me know if you change your mind, Miss Kelly." Parker added.

"Please, it's Catherine. And I don't need anything, thanks," I replied as I kept watching. I didn't recognize anyone in that group, and then I spotted a beautiful, statuesque, dark-haired woman. I didn't recognize her either, but she was hard to ignore. She wore a tight black skirt and a matching jacket, with four-inch stilettos accenting her already long, lean legs. Generous cleavage swelled at the V of her jacket, and she had the famous California tan I missed seeing when I looked in the mirror. Her wide, dark brown eyes were fastened unapologetically on me, and she didn't look away when our gazes clashed. I didn't recognize her, but William obviously did. He enfolded her in a warm embrace then kissed her on the cheek.

Jealousy stabbed through me and I had to look away. I'd spent years with Jace on beaches all over the world, surrounded by women in bikinis who were more than happy to attempt to entice a famous surfer. But I never worried about Jace and I'd never felt even so much as a twinge of envy when he talked to one of his fawning, flirty fans. But everything between William and me was so new. I never thought I was a jealous person, but I'd already had moments of jealousy with him and now I was having another one. I needed to get a grip, but I had a thousand questions, most importantly: who the hell was this woman and who was she to William?

I returned my gaze to William and watched as he seemed to linger beside her. She was perfectly comfortable touching him, stroking his shoulder and placing her hand possessively on his forearm. In fact, she seemed to touch him as much as possible, even making certain her breast rubbed against his arm when she stood beside him. I shifted impatiently, waiting for William to walk back or call me over and introduce us, but after a few moments, it became clear that wasn't going to happen. After yet another embrace, she moved away, leaving William to exchange a few more private words with George.

What the hell was that? I thought as I clenched my hands by my sides. My heart was racing and I felt nervous and jittery all over. How could William be so solicitous, so attuned to my every need in the bedroom and then forget something basic like introducing me, his girlfriend, once we arrived? I stood awkwardly and unsure on the tarmac, my face heated with embarrassment and anger.

I tried to be discrete, but I kept looking over at her. She was tall and willowy—I'd bet money that she was a former something, actress or model. I could totally see it.

I tried to reassure myself. William had brought me. He'd said he needed me. Not an hour ago, we'd been pleasuring one another on his private plane. It was me he'd had his mouth and hands on just minutes ago. It was my hand that had made him come. I clenched my hands again and willed all these ridiculous insecurities away. It felt like the Art Institute all over again—my worst first date ever—but instead of Chicago ice princess socialite Lara Kendall, a brunette California version was staring daggers at me from just a few feet away. Great. William still hadn't spilled the details of his previous relationship with Lara and that still irked me, though he'd made it clear there was nothing and had never been anything serious between them. He'd probably tell me the same thing about this woman. If I asked. But I wasn't sure I wanted to.

With nothing else to do but stew and imagine the worst, I stood in place, alone, and peered about the airport, inhaling the sweet, familiar air and staring at the mountains in the distance. I'd missed the jagged landscapes of California. Illinois was so flat, the vistas unrelieved except by an occasional glimpse of the lake. But as much as I longed for this home, that ball of dread was rolling around in my stomach. I remembered leaving California. Vividly. It felt like another life, and like I'd been another person. And I had been. I was Cat Ryder then, not Catherine Kelly. So much had changed in the last year.

Finally, William looked as though he was wrapping up. He nodded to George and then strode to me. "Come on," he said with a smile, taking my hand and squeezing it. "I have something to show you."

As we walked toward the small terminal, he pulled me close to him, close enough that I could smell the lavender body wash from his quick shower on the jet after our fooling around. I smiled back at him, his anticipation contagious, but as I looked over my shoulder at the plane we'd just exited and at his people now scattering across the tarmac, I couldn't help but feel that making this trip was a big mistake.

*****

"Your luggage is already on the way to the house," William said once we entered the terminal. Another one of the perks of traveling like the super rich, I supposed.

"What's it like, this house of yours?" I asked as we walked through an empty waiting area. William's penthouse was majorly impressive, so I had no idea what to expect in St. Helena. He didn't answer, so I kept chattering. "You haven't mentioned anything about it and I'm so curious." I was trying to keep things light and cheerful and I really was excited, but I was also doing everything I could to not ask about the sexy brunette in his welcoming committee. He just smiled and led me to the exit.

We stepped outside and William paused, then veered me toward a stunning vintage silver Porsche convertible parked at the curb. I looked up and his smile had broadened into a wide grin

"Wow," I said as I stopped and admired the car.

William walked to the passenger side and opened the door for me. "Get in," he said.

I did and he waited until I pulled my legs in and buckled my seatbelt before he closed the door. *He's being so sweet*, I thought as I watched him round the front of the car. He was still all smiles, his gait easy. He seemed more relaxed here, more comfortable, while I was trying not to let on that I was anything but.

Once he was in the driver's seat, he turned and asked, "Will you be warm enough? I'd like to keep the top down, but I'll put it up if you want."

"I'll be fine," I smiled. "Top down. Definitely." I was wearing a sweater, and after witnessing William's welcoming committee, I could use a little cooling off.

"Excellent choice. Ready?"

I nodded. William smiled again and then started the engine. The car turned over with a purr and we pulled away. The clear sky was streaked with the colors of the setting sun as we sped out of the airport, and my heart felt too full when William took my hand and entwined his fingers with mine.

The wind was whipping my hair around my face and I wished I had a ponytail holder, but it wasn't too loud to talk. "So this is a Porsche, right?" I asked. Of course it was a Porsche, but I also couldn't help but notice that he seemed particularly proud of it and I wanted to know why. As wealthy as he was, I hadn't seen him act so attached to a *thing* before, so this was new.

"Yep," he answered. "This is my California car."

"It's the perfect car for here," I said. "When did you get it?"

"It was my father's, actually."

I swallowed my surprise and attempted to act nonchalant. William so rarely talked about his family. I knew there was something special about this car.

He nodded and continued, "It's a 1969 Speedster. My mother gave it to my father for his fortieth birthday. I was about five and I remember what a big deal it was. My father loved this car. He kept it at our lake house and only drove it in the summers. It was put in storage after they died."

My heart clenched. This was why I came to California. This was the side of William I wanted to see. "Why did you get it out of storage?"

He shrugged. "I wanted to drive it. I wanted to drive it my whole life. After I bought the vineyard in Napa, I had it restored and shipped out here." Then he smiled. "It *is* the perfect car for California."

And he looked perfect in it. His dark hair whipped back from his face, showcasing his strong cheekbones and straight nose. He had the most beautiful profile of any man I'd ever met, especially with the golden light of the early evening flickering across his skin. He looked a whole lot more comfortable and relaxed driving the Porsche than he ever did behind the wheel of his black Range Rover in Chicago.

William squeezed my hand again before releasing it to grab the gear shift. "Hang on. It's about a forty minute drive." He shifted, and the car jumped smoothly forward.

I laughed from sheer pleasure, and he laughed with me. Neither of us had forgotten the reason we were in California. Wyatt was never far from my thoughts or, I'm sure, William's, but already he seemed happier here. I'd never seen him smile or laugh so much. Maybe it had been a good decision to come with him after all. I started to relax a little too.

The drive was amazing, even for a native Californian like me. I'd been to Napa before, but I never paid much attention to the rolling hills and green square fields, divided into rows and rows of grapes. I wanted to grab my camera and shoot a few landscapes, but I knew I'd have time for that later. William threaded his fingers through mine or rested his hand on my thigh when he didn't need to shift, and his touch helped keep me warm.

Finally, William turned into a drive lined with trees. "We're almost there," he said. The drive was long and straight, slightly uphill, and the trees formed a canopy overhead until we finally emerged. Set among lush bushes and more trees was a very large Mediterranean-style stucco house with a vivid red tile roof. "This is home," William said.

I glanced at him, surprised. This house was the antithesis of everything I'd known of William so far. In Chicago, his penthouse, his office, everything about him was sleek, modern, and minimalist to the point of being cold and impersonal. This place was the exact opposite.

He was looking at me, so I cleared my throat and tried to think of something to say. "It's beautiful."

"Welcome to Casa di Rosabela."

The house had a name? Was I in the Twilight Zone? William owned a house with a name. I don't know why this surprised me, but it did.

"It was built in the 1920s," he said as he slowed the car and pulled around the circular drive to stop in front of the door. "I didn't name it. The Italian man who built it and established the vineyard here named it for his wife."

"That's so romantic."

"It is, isn't it?" He climbed out of the car and though I unbuckled my seatbelt and reached for the door, he was there before I could open it. He helped me out, then rested his hand lightly on the small of my back and guided me toward the house.

I couldn't help but stare at the house and manicured grounds and marvel. I wondered how much something like this went for. Ten million? Twenty million maybe? Caught up in my astonishment, I missed half of what William was saying and finally tuned back in when he led me through the front door. "It's eleven-thousand square feet with about thirty acres dedicated to grapes plus an olive orchard."

I nodded, mutely, as he led me by the hand into a large open living room. The floors were tiled and the high ceilings had exposed wooden beams. Huge windows overlooked the sloping vineyard with its perfect rows extending as far as I could see. Beyond them, in the last light of dusk, sat majestic hills, stately sentinels of all they surveyed.

The entire place was meticulously and very expensively decorated in what I'd call *California chic*, traditional but with a clean modern flair, and complimented by a gorgeous art on just about every wall. I didn't know where to look first. William led me on a tour and I saw the screening room, the gym, and the small tasting room, and peeked at the outdoor area, fully equipped with a pool, fireplace, outdoor kitchen, and dining area. William told me there were two guest casitas and buildings for the work of the winery. It was late, and he promised to show me those tomorrow.

"And this is the best room in the house," William said, pulling me by the hand. He had yet to release my hand and had smiled and studied my reaction to everything in the house. But for the first time, he seemed to look for my approval. He led me around the corner and through an arched doorway. "This is the kitchen."

I laughed. I'd half expected—maybe wanted—him to show me the bedroom. But, of course, William's favorite room would be the kitchen. And I could see why he loved it. It was a real chef's kitchen, equipped with all the top-of-the-line appliances Beckett was always going on about. But unlike William's sterile kitchen in Chicago, this one was warm and vibrant with colorful painted tiles, rich wood cabinets topped with dark stone counters, and gleaming copper pots of all sizes hanging from a big iron pot rack. Still no refrigerator magnets or silly pictures of bicycle-riding chefs, but this room felt warm and welcoming in a way his penthouse kitchen never could.

"What do you think?" he asked. "Do you like my house?"

I didn't know what to say. It was overwhelming. I knew William was rich, but knowing something intellectually was different than being surrounded by it, by such unimaginable wealth. And it was so unexpected. This place was so different from what I'd known of William so far. My head spun. William was still looking at me and his hand tightened on mine.

"It's incredible," I told him. "I love it—really, really love it. I feel…I don't know…comfortable here."

"Good. I want you to feel at home. Tomorrow I'll show you the vineyard. I'm focusing mostly on whites, including champagne, but I have a small area for reds and our first bottling of a very special rosé is finally ready. I can't wait to show you the barn and the wine cave tomorrow too." He sounded so excited, which made me smile.

"Wine cave? Is that like a bat cave?" I laughed. "I don't know much about wine."

He brought my hand to his lips and kissed it. "I'll teach you." His gaze moved away from mine, and he smiled and nodded. I turned to find a petite Hispanic woman standing in the doorway. "Catherine, this is Fernanda, my cook and housekeeper."

I reached out to shake her small hand. Her eyes were large and deep brown. "Nice to meet you," I said.

"We've been expecting you, Miss Kelly." She nodded at William. "It's good to see you again, Mr. Lambourne. I've prepared everything as you requested."

"Thank you, Fernanda." William smiled at me. "I'll be cooking dinner for us."

"Ring me if you need me, Mr. Lambourne." Then she turned and walked into what I guessed was the pantry.

William took my hand again. "One more room, Catherine." From the velvet tone of his voice I had a feeling I knew where we were going. Finally.

He took me up a set of stairs and guided me down the hall to the master suite, which was more like the master wing. The rooms—plural—were huge and luxuriously furnished in rich, dark tones, and the bedroom contained the biggest bed I'd ever seen.

"Is this a bedroom or a small country?" I joked as I bounced on the bed with my feet dangling off the edge.

William gestured to the closet. "Your luggage has already been unpacked." He opened the door, then pulled me up and led me inside a closet that was bigger than my living room. The few clothes I'd brought hung in the front, but there were also clothes I'd never seen before. I glanced at William, and he couldn't contain his grin. "I told you I'd make sure you had everything you needed."

I gaped at him as I ran my hand over the racks of clothing, feeling the sensuous fabrics. There was a small, thoughtfully planned wardrobe here—everything from jeans to two evening dresses—and though it didn't favor my favorite color, black, it seemed to suit me. I wondered if William had picked out all of this himself and if so, when. I didn't know about this. "These are all for me?"

"Of course they're for you," William said, but I was hardly listening. I moved into the closet and stared at racks of shoes and a whole section of drawers filled with lingerie. Really top notch lingerie, the kind I drooled over.

"William…I-I…this is too much," I managed.

"Nothing is too much for you. And I told you I'd take care of everything." He gave me a tender kiss on the lips and cupped my face with his hands. "Relax. Freshen up. Come down when you're ready. Dinner will be at eight."

I nodded, my heart pounding and my head spinning as I watched him leave.

As soon as I was alone, I flopped back on the giant bed. *Holy shit*. For a few moments I was simply too stunned to do more than lie there. And then I seriously needed to talk to someone.

I grabbed my cell and called Beckett. He answered on the second ring, and I heard music in the background. "Is this a bad time?" I asked.

"Of course not! I've been dying to talk to you. Are you in Napa?"

"Yes. And get this, Beckett." I told him about the private jets and our fooling around at thirty thousand feet.

"Cat, I would seriously hate you if I didn't love you so much."

I laughed. "I would hate me too, and I haven't even told you about the house yet."

"What are you waiting for?"

"It's incredible, Beckett. I've never seen anything like it. It's a mansion—like a straight-out-of-the-rolling-hills-of-Tuscany kind of mansion."

"Listen to you, auditioning for HGTV or something."

"I'm not even done." I sat up and folded my legs, Indian style. "The views are amazing. I knew Napa was gorgeous, but I had no idea. And the art. I'm afraid to get too close to it. It's everywhere and it must be worth millions. I mean, I think I saw a Monet in the living room. A *Monet*, like the kind you see in a museum. Can you fucking believe it? I could get lost in this place, it's so big. I guess it's really an estate. And it has a name. Casa di Rosabela."

Beckett sighed. "I've always wanted to live on an estate with a name and a Monet. Can I come and visit? I promise not to pee in the pool."

I rolled my eyes. "Beckett, I'm seriously a little freaked out right now. I knew William was wealthy, but I didn't *know*, you know?"

"No."

I laughed.

"Cat," Beckett said, his tone turning serious. "So what if the guy has two private jets—"

"Five."

"Okay, five—*five*? Seriously?"

"Yes! And a villa—I mean, a mansion."

"I thought we were calling it an estate."

"Whatever. I haven't even told you about the vintage Porsche or the closet stocked with designer clothes and shoes all for me."

"And I want to hear all about them, but first you need to calm down. So what if the guy has more money than I don't know, Oprah or somebody. You're into him, not his stuff. Right?"

"Right." I knew that much absolutely. "But how do I separate the two?" I really didn't know how much of *William the Man* was intertwined with *William the Wealthy Magnate*, and I hadn't really thought about it until right this instant. I could feel my chest tightening—all my old insecurities were lurking just under the surface. "Beckett, honestly, what do I have to offer William? He can have anything and anyone he wants. I don't know if I'm ready for all this. I told you weeks ago, I'm not ready." What little I had to offer seemed pretty inconsequential compared to the spoils of William's empire.

"Cat, you know what I'm going to say, right?"

I sighed. "Stop thinking so much?"

"Exactly. You're smart, beautiful, successful, and really, really nice. And you're more than ready. You *know* that. Hold on a sec."

Someone said his name, and I narrowed my eyes. Once again, I heard music in the background and the sound of voices. "Where are you right now?"

"Just checking on your condo."

"Are you having a party?"

There was a pause. "A little one."

"Are you celebrating or something?"

Another pause. "Sort of. I've got a lead on a work thing, but I don't want to say anything yet. I might jinx it. And this is just a teeny, tiny dinner party. I couldn't pass up the opportunity to use the AGA."

I sighed, happy for Beckett but not thrilled about my condo being used for his 'teeny, tiny' party. But I knew I could trust Beckett and besides, as a pastry chef, he got more out of my giant cast-iron gourmet cooker than I ever would, given that my culinary tool of choice was my microwave. "Just clean up after, okay?"

"Absolutely. And you stop worrying so much. Have fun at your billionaire boyfriend's estate with a name, Cat. Why don't you take a bubble bath and have a glass of wine? He makes it there, right?"

The idea actually sounded pretty good. I had to stop turning everything over in my mind because it was only freaking me out. I might wish things could be simple with William, but they weren't.

Nothing was or would ever be simple with him. He needed me here and I couldn't be his rock if I was preoccupied with my own issues. Beckett and I hung up and I got off the huge bed and headed to the bathroom, intent upon taking his advice though I'd skip the wine for now. I needed a clear head.

The bathroom was an amazing study in white marble and was wonderfully inviting. The huge sunken tub, in particular, beckoned. I ran the water and, while I waited for the bath to fill, I opened drawers and cabinets. The vanity was stocked with most of my favorite toiletries and even some of the make-up I usually used. I was flattered that William knew what I liked and had made sure it was available for me, but it was also a little off-putting. How did he know so much about me? I spotted an unmarked vial of amber liquid, opened the stopper, and sniffed. It was the same perfume William had sent me before our first date at the Art Institute. At least he was consistent.

When the tub was almost full, I added some bubbles and climbed in. Leaning back, I closed my eyes and let the warm water soothe me. One thing I knew for certain: I loved William Maddox Lambourne and I wasn't going to let what he owned get in the way of who he was in my heart. If he had nothing, I'd feel exactly the same way about him.

I tried to relax and clear my mind, but that rarely worked for me. Instead, I ran my hands across my breasts and pinched my nipples, which were still sensitive after William's oral ministrations on the plane. I could feel a pull between my legs as I rolled my nipple between my fingers and I thought for a split second about checking out the water pressure of the gleaming, silver handheld shower sprayer, but I didn't. I wanted to save my pleasure for William.

Only William.

FOUR

I found William in the kitchen. He greeted me with a long, hungry look and a lingering kiss. His mouth was warm and tasted of cilantro and lime, and the citrus spiciness tingled on my lips. When we broke apart, I saw Fernanda smiling at us. "It smells delicious," I told them, savoring the feel of William's body still touching mine.

"We're having Mexican tonight." William smiled. "My favorite. Did you rest and relax?"

I nodded. "You?"

"I had a quick workout then showered and started cooking." He gestured to the kitchen. "This is the best form of relaxation." He gave me a wicked smile. "Well, the second best. You look breathtaking tonight, Catherine."

I looked down and blushed as my belly did a slow roll, like it always did when he looked at me that way. I almost wished we could skip dinner. But I was hungry now that I was surrounded by the smell of the food. And I knew William well enough to know he believed in savoring a meal and building anticipation for what was to come.

The work out explained why his hair was still a little damp and curling about the nape of his neck. I loved it when it looked like that. He wore a pair of faded jeans that were slung low on his hips and a dark blue shirt that made his eyes look more blue than grey. He moved confidently between the prep area and the stove.

"What are you chopping?" I asked.

"Tomatillos for the salsa. We have a big farm garden so most of the vegetables we'll eat tonight were picked right here. Everything else is local and organic."

"Can I help?"

"Well, I've already chopped the onions, so I've think I've got everything covered." William gave me a bemused smile, but there was no mistaking the hungry gleam in his eyes. I could feel myself heating up as he looked at me. The last time we had cooked together, his instructing me on how to properly chop onions had led to one of the most sexually decadent nights of my life. He could tell I was thinking about it.

"Great!" I replied a little too cheerfully, trying to regain my focus. "So what's on the menu?"

"Well, the ceviche is in the refrigerator, and Fernanda and I are just finishing up the rest." On his way back to the stove, he handed me a bottle of rosé. "This is one of mine," he said in my ear. A zing of pleasure raced through me at his soft voice.

Back at the stove, he put some ingredients into a pan, and a few seconds later my mouth was watering from the smells that filled the kitchen. William turned and said, "The table is set under the pergola. Why don't you go check it out?"

Carrying the bottle of rosé with me, I wandered outside, feeling the soft breeze ruffle my hair. There were a million stars in the sky and a crescent moon looking down on me. Lights in the trees twinkled and reflected in the pool, and outdoor heaters ensured I wouldn't get cold. Beyoncé played on hidden speakers, and a fire crackled in the outdoor fireplace, filling the air with the smell of burning wood. A moment later Fernanda brought a bowl of warm homemade tortilla chips and the salsa William had made and beckoned me to sit at the table.

I realized belatedly I'd forgotten to bring out any wine glasses, but William showed up a minute later with two. He poured the wine and held his glass for a toast. I followed, smiling. This was all so unlike him.

"To dining *al fresco*," he said, "with the most beautiful woman I know."

I grinned. I was loving romantic William tonight and I felt again like I was the luckiest girl in the world. My nervousness at the airport, at William's wealth on display, was slowly fading into the background of this perfect evening.

We clinked glasses and moments later Fernanda brought out a tray heaped with the most beautiful Mexican food I'd ever seen. Tacos and burritos were staples of the surfer diet and I'd eaten Mexican food for most of my life, even in Mexico, as I'd spent time on just about every major beach in Baja. But this was Mexican *haute cuisine*, and on a whole different level. There were small glasses of ceviche bursting with big, pink shrimp and a platter piled high with crispy fish, cabbage, and a white sauce that looked a bit like sour cream. There was a bowl of steaming rice and I detected the heady aroma of cilantro. There were beans and fresh tortillas, fresh guacamole, and a dark mole sauce that William said was made with chocolate. It was casual food but beautifully presented, and it smelled incredible.

"This looks absolutely delicious. I can't believe you made all of this. You're amazing. And there's no way I can eat all of it," I protested, but I was practically salivating.

"Fernanda is my secret weapon. I give her all the credit. I just helped." He was trying to be modest, which was so cute, but he was obviously pleased by my compliments. "Dig in."

When I tasted the first taco, I smiled, closed my eyes, and nodded approval. The dish looked simple, but the flavors exploded in my mouth. "Oh my God. William, this is *so* good." I tried not to giggle. I was having what Beckett would call a "total M.O." or mouth orgasm. He was always equating food with sex in ways that cracked me up. But that was very different from food and sex with Mr. Lambourne. I loved that William continued to dazzle me with his culinary talent. His skillful cooking and his deep appreciation of food and wine, of eating and enjoying it, were some of the most surprising things about him and I loved them. I loved *him*.

"It's an old recipe," William told me, still pleased with my response. "The secret is the batter. It's made with beer."

"It's wonderful." I took a sip of my wine. "I love this wine too," I said.

"That I'm especially glad to hear. This is from our first bottling of rosé," he held up his glass and swirled the deep pink liquid in it. "Rosés are tricky. This is *rosato*, which is what it's called in Italy. It's a very old kind of wine—ancient actually. We follow the traditional method, which means we press the red grapes early and allow only about a day for skin-contact. That limited maceration is what imparts the color and most of the flavor. It's not a wine meant to be aged. The flavors are too delicate. So far, I've been very pleased with our results. But like I said, this is our first bottling. Who knows how next year will go."

My head was reeling, I was so impressed. "But you said you mostly make whites?"

He nodded. "We do. Sparkling mostly, with the Chardonnay and Pinot Meunier grapes. But I've been trying a few reds too. Small bottlings. And of course the rosé. I'll arrange for a tasting tomorrow and you'll be able to sample all of it. It's a small operation, but I'm really proud of our bottles."

I listened as he continued to talk about the vineyard and its operations. He was animated and so obviously passionate about making wine. I wondered if he was as passionate about his other business ventures.

The combination of the spicy food, the outdoor heaters, and the wine made me feel warm and cozy, but the real warmth I wanted was from the man sitting across the table from me. I wanted more than talk. We'd been in bed at The Peninsula, making love, just over twelve hours ago and that's exactly where I wanted to be again: in bed, with William, with his heavy muscled body pressing on top of mine and his hard cock pressing between my legs. Our petting session on the plane had been fun, but it hadn't come close to quelling the deep ache for him I felt in my core.

William reached across the table and took my hand, and I realized I hadn't been paying attention or speaking for several moments. His warm hand drew my attention back to him, and he gave me a tentative smile. "I know you must be wondering about why we're here—about my brother."

My attention snapped to his face. I knew him well enough now to see the fine lines of strain about his eyes and mouth. My lust would have to wait. This was difficult for him, and I loved him for telling me anyway. This was what I had been waiting for too: him finally opening up to me. "I have been wondering," I said. "I know it's hard to talk about."

"You've waited long enough," he said, his hand stroking mine. He looked down at our clasped fingers. "I died the day I lost my family. I was eleven, ready to start middle school, when my parents and Wyatt died in the plane crash."

"Oh, William." I wanted to hug him, but I knew I had to allow him to speak without interruption.

"I was at summer camp when it happened. That's why I wasn't on the plane." His eyes met mine. They were a dark grey I hadn't seen before. He looked sad and in his gaze I saw a piece of the little boy he'd been. "And being spared was its own kind of hell. Why me? Why was I the lucky one?" He gave a bitter laugh. "I wouldn't even call it luck. I can't count the number of times I wished I'd been on that plane. I wished I'd died too."

"No." I shook my head, feeling helpless to comfort him.

"I was just a little kid and I lost everything. Everything I knew and loved in my life was gone. I said goodbye when they dropped me off at camp and then I never saw them again. Ever. Of course I had my aunt and uncle. We'd always been close to them, but becoming a member of their family was a lot different than spending Christmas afternoon at their house. They tried." His gaze was far away as though remembering. "They supported me, and I know it wasn't always easy. I wasn't easy. People said I *had a hard time adjusting*, and I was pretty fucked up. My life changed completely. Our house in the city was sold and everything was sold with it or put into storage. I went to live in Lake Forest, which meant I had to start a new school and say goodbye to all of my friends.

"It sucked. I went for months without really talking. I was sullen and withdrawn, not exactly the kind of kid voted most popular. And I got into fights, a lot. That went on until I finished college."

I couldn't imagine William being violent, but he was a big guy with an impressive physique and an even more impressive presence. I had no doubt he could more than handle himself if provoked, but that wasn't something I ever wanted to see. "What about counseling?" I asked.

He nodded. "I went into therapy. Spent years dissecting and being dissected, but it didn't help. It didn't bring them back."

We just sat there for a minute, not talking, as his story began to sink in. Finally, I said softly, "My heart breaks for you, William."

And it did. I couldn't imagine the kind of loss he endured. Even Jace's death didn't compare with this.

He rose and ran a hand through his hair, staring toward the dark shape of the mountains. I missed the physical contact with him immediately.

"The first year was the worst," he said, still looking away. "But it got better." He looked at me then, and my heart twisted. I tried not to ascribe any significance to his words and that look, but it took all I had.

"My aunt and uncle tried to protect me. I started a new school in Lake Forest, where I didn't know anyone. Unfortunately, everyone knew who I was. I'm sure you know that my family's tragedy and my survival was all over the news for months."

I had Googled him and read some of the articles about the plane crash, but I nodded noncommittally. This was his story to tell.

"The media dubbed me the *poor little rich boy*. That was when I learned money could be a curse as well as a blessing." He began pacing, at first walking slowly without purpose, but picking up speed as he spoke. "Do you know where my money came from?" He didn't wait for an answer. "Originally the Lambourne family owned a coffee and tea business that my great-great-great-grandfather grew into the largest institutional food supplier in the United States. My great-grandfather sold it all to a huge conglomerate and since then, the only thing the Lambourne family has made is money." He sounded almost ashamed of this, but I couldn't see his face because he paced away from me.

"My father was particularly gifted in investment and financial management. He took his inherited wealth and grew his portfolio via his firm, which is my firm now. He was a *very* wealthy man when he died."

I wondered what constituted *very* wealthy to William Lambourne. I had a feeling it was more money than I could imagine.

"I inherited that wealth. I was the sole heir. That wasn't how it was meant to be, but that's what happened and everybody knew about it." He stopped pacing and turned to face me. "And the first extortion attempt came when I was a freshman in high school."

"Extortion?" I gasped, all but choking on my wine. "I don't understand."

He gave me a sad smile. "That's what I love about you, Catherine."

I blinked, telling myself he hadn't said he loved me, just that he loved something about me. Not the same thing. I set my wine glass down and stared at him. "What do you mean by extortion?"

"I mean a threat used to elicit payment. My Uncle Charles, who also happened to be my father's lawyer, received a series of letters from a woman who claimed to be my father's mistress. She also claimed to have had an illegitimate son with my father and she wanted her child to receive his rightful portion of the Lambourne fortune."

"Oh my God." A sick feeling of revulsion rose in my throat.

"There was an investigation," William said, crossing to me and taking his seat again. He refilled his wine glass and I noticed his hand shook slightly. "Her story was easily discredited, but that was hardly the last attempt to get my money."

I reached for his hand, wanting to comfort him. I'd never seen him so vulnerable. It scared me.

"Less than a year later, a man was caught outside my aunt and uncle's house with a taser gun, rope, handcuffs, a hood, duct tape—all sorts of goodies."

I shook my head as though I could make any of this go away.

"He also had three loaded guns on him and a ransom note. He had intended to kidnap and then ransom me for five million dollars. Security was increased, but that didn't stop the Wyatts."

I frowned at him, confused.

"At least three different men—or their, shall we say, *representatives*—have made contact through the years, all claiming to either be my brother or to know where Wyatt is. Their stories as to how Wyatt miraculously survived the plane crash have varied, but the motivation has been the same."

"Money."

He nodded, his mouth twisting into a wry smile. "Exactly. Wyatt Lambourne could be produced for the right price. All of these men were discredited and one of them was arrested after we discovered he planned to kill me if I didn't pay him. You've asked me about George before, Catherine. This is why I need him. He worked for my father and stayed on as head of my personal security detail. He has been involved in every investigation. Every single one."

His lips grazed my knuckles. "After high school, I was sick of living my life in the shadows, but that didn't mean I could disregard security. I had to agree to certain…measures to protect myself. And George is part of that protection."

I thought back to the portfolio I had found on Jenny Hill at William's penthouse. *Certain measures* meant having his dates pre-screened and investigated. It made more sense now, though the screening still went further than I was comfortable with. I wished he'd have told me this before. I wish he could have trusted me. It would have made our relationship so much easier.

"I planned to go to Northwestern, where several generations of my family went before me, but I couldn't start college until I knew more about the accident. I had to investigate it myself. I was so young when it happened and so much was kept from me. That was as it should have been at the time, but I wasn't a kid any longer. I wanted to know, for myself. I wanted to find the wreckage…or them. I wanted closure, I guess."

I nodded. I understood that. I remember needing the closure of saying goodbye to Jace at the funeral. Seeing his body, devoid of any life, made his death real to me, but William never had that. There would always be a small kernel of hope and disbelief in his mind.

"Initially, my Uncle Charles was against another investigation, but eventually he consented." William's eyes, stormy grey now rather than steely, met mine. "As you know, Catherine, when I want something, I won't give up until I get my way." He gave me a knowing smile that caused heat to rush between my legs. I shifted, and his brow arched as though he knew.

"So you went to Alaska," I said, trying to keep my focus on the conversation, rather than all the sinfully wicked things I was aching for William to do to me.

"I spent over a year there when I was eighteen, right after I graduated from high school. I reopened the investigation and went over everything—the model of the plane, the pilots, everyone who saw or touched the plane that day. I wanted to be certain sabotage hadn't been overlooked. Everything, down to the smallest, most minute detail, was scrutinized. I hired experts to analyze the weather and flight patterns. We re-traced the search efforts and I learned everything I could, down to the types and sizes of the nuts and bolts, about the plane my family had been on.

"For nothing." His shoulders slumped. All of these years later, he was still disheartened. "It didn't change a God-damned thing. It's still unbelievable to me in this day and age, when the world seems so much smaller and instantly navigable, that an entire plane full of people could just disappear without a trace and never be found." He sat back and ran his hand through his hair. He stared at the sky and said, almost to himself, "But Alaska is a very big place and, believe it or not, planes disappear there all the time." His words sounded rehearsed, as though he'd heard them uttered a thousand times. Perhaps he had. I'd read similar statements when I'd scanned the articles on the Internet about the crash.

"I'm pretty sure that's what happened," he added.

I leaned forward. "Pretty sure?"

He lowered his gaze to focus on me, as though he'd forgotten, for a moment, I was there. "I believe in logic and reason. But as much as logic and reason say that weather or equipment failure or some combination thereof caused the plane to go down—as much as logic and reason tell me no one survived the crash—there's a minuscule possibility something else happened." He ran a hand over his face, looking sad and weary. "I know it's not probable. But it's...something, you know?" His gaze met mine. "I don't hope they're still alive, but I hope someday I'll know exactly what happened. No matter what, a part of me can't stop wanting that."

I reached out and took his hand again, stroking it because there really wasn't any other comfort I could give. I understood what he wasn't saying. What William really wanted was absolution—to know there was nothing he could have done to change the course of events. To know he was not responsible.

It made no rational sense. Of course an eleven-year-old boy, thousands of miles away at summer camp, couldn't have been responsible for a plane crash in Alaska, but I knew all too well that rational sense had nothing to do with it. There was nothing rational about a broken heart. I knew because my own heart had been broken once too.

I rose from the table, walked to William, and sat in his lap. I put my arms around him, this big strong man who harbored a lost little boy somewhere inside. I kissed him tenderly, held him, and whispered, "I understand. I understand all about hope." I held him for a long moment, feeling some of the tension leave his muscles, feeling his body melt into mine. "So this latest Wyatt is just another scam, right? And George is on it." I hoped I sounded confident, as William clearly needed my reassurance that he had everything under control. After all, this was why we were in Napa. This was why I'd dropped everything to be here with him.

The silence between us lasted so long I was half afraid he hadn't heard. But he had heard perfectly. I felt his shoulders stiffen, and he drew out of my embrace. "It's a little more complicated this time. And I'd rather keep you out of it. You don't need to know."

I recoiled as though slapped. "What? What do you mean I don't need to know? I don't understand."

"You don't need to know, Catherine," he said in that deep, dominant tone that clearly indicated his mind was made up and he wasn't to be questioned. "Just trust me. It's being taken care of and it will all be over soon enough. Don't worry about it."

He pushed me gently off his lap. Left with no other choice, I stood beside him. He rose as well and stretched. He really wasn't going to say any more, and I stared in stunned disbelief, reeling from the emotional whiplash.

William had just opened up to me more than he ever had before and for those few moments, I felt so emotionally connected to him, so in love with him. And now, he was shutting me out. Just like that. Just because he wanted to. What the fuck?

I wanted to call him on it. Bad. I wanted to have a knockdown, drag-out fight, right here, right now, and scream that he couldn't just ice me out because he felt like it. But I knew that wouldn't get me what I wanted. I couldn't make him open his heart to me no matter how loudly I demanded it. Still, a part of me rebelled against giving him a pass. He was acting as though nothing had changed between us and that everything was perfectly normal. It was frustrating and maddening and confusing as hell.

I was still trying to process what had just happened when William put his arm around me and pulled me close. I was torn between punching him and burying my head against his chest and sobbing.

"I'm so glad you're here." His breath was soft and warm against my neck and a delicious shiver of yearning raced through my body. No matter how angry he made me, his touch still had the effect of bringing every part of me immediately into awareness. His lips grazed my ear teasingly. "I want to share Casa di Rosabela with you. Why don't we have dessert upstairs? I have a special treat in mind."

Heat flared in me at his words, and I sighed in anticipation of what was to come. A pass it was. There'd be no more talk about William's secrets tonight.

FIVE

Someone had already prepared the master suite, as the lights were dimmed, romantic jazz played softly in the background, and a dozen or so candles flickered throughout. I hadn't noticed the terrace earlier, but now the doors were open, and the soft fragrant breeze gave me the chills. A small pitcher of honey and a plate of *sopapillas* sprinkled with powdered sugar and cinnamon sat beside a bottle of champagne and two flutes on a side table.

William came up behind me, his hands trailing from my waist to my shoulders. "You're tense," he said. "How about I give you a massage?"

If I was tense, it was his fault, but I refrained from mentioning that. "I should be the one massaging you," I said, turning to him. "I know you have a lot on your mind."

"You're the only thing on my mind right now. Let me take care of you, Catherine. I like taking care of you." His hands kneaded my shoulders.

How could I argue? I was tense and tired, and a massage sounded wonderful. "Alright," I agreed. I felt his hand slide down the zipper of my dress and I stepped out of it and stood facing him in just my kitten heels and my pretty pink lace and silk bra and thong, which I had found in my closet of couture delights.

William's eyes went immediately dark with desire, that molten grey color I loved. I wanted to see more of that look, so I slowly brought my hand to the front clasp of my bra and unsnapped it. I'd done a sexy fantasy striptease for him last night at the hotel and he'd just about come undone. I wanted that reaction again. I let my bra tumble to the floor, feeling my nipples harden and pucker as they were freed. William watched me as I touched myself.

"I love your breasts, Catherine," he said, voice husky. I could see the outline of his thick erection straining against his jeans.

"Show me," I said. His look said he was humoring me and my demands. He stepped closer, putting his hands on my shoulders and sliding them tantalizingly down my flesh. He cupped my breasts, his thumbs rubbing across my sensitive nipples, making them harden until it was almost painful not to be touched. His thumbs plucked and teased until I was breathless, and then he bent and replaced his fingers with his hot, wet mouth. He stroked my swollen point with his tongue and then took it in his mouth, drew it out, and sucked. Wantonly, I pushed myself against him as I ran my hand down his tight abdomen and across his hardness. I felt him twitch and pulse in response. Then his lips released and he pulled his head up and moved back, leaving me incredibly turned on.

"Lie down on the bed," he ordered me. My thong was damp and I knew I was already slick and slippery with arousal. I wasn't sure how much of a massage I could take, but I was willing to try. I complied and got on the bed, leaving my shoes on. William shook his head. "On your stomach. I'm giving you a massage, remember?"

I turned over, angling my head so I could see him behind me. He withdrew a bottle of oil from the bedside table and warmed some in his hands. Then he straddled me and began slow, deep strokes across my shoulders and back. I groaned in appreciation and in pleasure too. William had me pinned, but I couldn't stop my hips from rocking ever so slightly back and forth, and I knew he could feel my telltale movements. I tried to focus on the massage and then I noticed the scent was familiar.

"Is that oil the same as the perfume you gave me?"

"It is," he murmured in affirmation, his fingers like magic on my tired muscles. "I have a friend who's a perfumer. I had it made for you. You're the only one in the world who smells like this."

"I like it," I groaned again as he started to work on a knot beneath one of my shoulder blades. I closed my eyes and allowed the sweet scents of vanilla and ginger lily to wash over me. Then I felt his strong hot hands stray downward to my ass and thighs. His fingers moved slowly, caressing me, kneading me. I felt heat rising, and I tingled everywhere in response. This was not relaxing—his touch was making me more and more tense. His thick fingers brushed closer and closer to my sex, and I held my breath. Just when he was right there and I should have felt him on the most intimate part of me, his hand slid away. I sighed into the pillow and tried to keep still.

"Turn over," he told me.

I obeyed. Once I was face up and settled, he continued to massage me, though his strokes were less therapeutic and much more teasing. His hands slid up my legs, over my belly, until he lightly kneaded my breasts. His fingers brushed lightly over my nipples then skirted away. I couldn't help the little grunts of pleasure that escaped from my lips every so often. Oh God, I wanted more. I wanted his mouth on me, his body pressing me into the bed, his touch urging me to pleasure. His caresses turned more erotic as his hands skimmed my warm flesh, pausing on my belly, then my hips, dipping lower and then moving away.

"I know how turned on you are right now," he said. "You're already wet, aren't you?"

"Yes." I reached for him, wanting to pull him to me, wanting to feel the pleasant weight of his body on top of mine.

"Stay still," he said, though his hands roved maddeningly over my sensitive flesh. "Keep your arms at your sides."

"William—"

"Just relax. I want to awaken your senses. And I want to explore you in a new way. I want to know every facet of you."

That sounded promising. I wanted William to know every facet of me too, especially the parts that were already wet and swollen and waiting to be conquered.

"Remember the night I returned from London?"

"How could I forget?" I still flushed when I saw a grape and felt the icy chill on my hot clit as he pressed first the grape to my skin, then his hot, wet mouth.

"Remember our dinner and champagne?"

My body remembered even better than my mind. I writhed in anticipation of a repeat performance. The way William had fed me, had played on my senses—smell, taste, touch—aroused me like never before.

"Remember I blindfolded you? And then I tied your hands?"

I remembered how he'd used his grey and black striped tie that night, though it wasn't the first thing that came to mind. Still, there was a part of me that had loved him restraining me. With my wrists tied above my head, not being able to touch him had been maddening at first, but then I'd come so hard the second his mouth was on me. That part of me ached for him now.

I didn't know how much more of this massage I could take. Need rushed through me, making my breath come short, and my body moved to make his hands go where I wanted them.

"Would you like to do that again?"

A flutter of nervousness raced up my spine, but it was nothing compared to the heat flooding my core, to the steady pulse of need I felt between my legs. "What did you have in mind?" I asked.

"Something a bit different, but nothing you can't handle." His hands continued to stroke me, keeping me in a highly aroused state. "We can stop at any point. Anytime it's too much."

I swallowed nervously. Part of me wanted to say no. I wanted more emotional commitment from William before we went further sexually—we'd already gone farther than I ever had before. But another part of me wanted to be a sexual adventurer and see what pleasures lay ahead. William would be my guide.

"Okay," I breathed. "But do we need to have a safe word?" I knew enough about sex games to know about safe words and I wanted to be able to stop this if I didn't like it.

He laughed. "Would you feel better if we had a safe word?"

"I guess," I said. "I'm not into pain or anything, William."

"Neither am I, Catherine. This is something else entirely. And I promise, you'll like it and I'll never hurt you. But if you'd feel better with a safe word, why don't you pick one?" He looked at me, waiting for my answer.

I thought for a second. "Rosé. That's my safe word. Rosé."

William chuckled again. "Rosé it is. If you say rosé, everything will immediately come to a stop. Agreed?"

"Agreed," I said breathlessly. "Thank you." I smiled up at him. I was still incredibly turned on and more than ready for him to pleasure me however he wanted.

"Let's get started then." He smiled and reached for the nightstand. He withdrew a long red silk scarf and, very slowly, he tied it about my eyes. Everything went dark, and I became hyper aware of the sound of my harsh breathing and the warmth of William's body beside mine. I heard another sound, and then he gently stretched my arms above my head and guided my fingers until they grasped the ornately carved wood headboard. Something soft and furry snapped around first one wrist then the other.

"These are handcuffs," William told me. "They're fur lined, so they shouldn't pinch."

"Handcuffs?" I teased. "Now this is getting kinky."

I heard a quiet laugh. "Oh, Catherine, you have no idea." He moved away from me, slightly, and I shifted to get a sense of where he was. The handcuffs had enough give to allow me to move my arms, but just barely. I didn't know what he was doing or what would come next.

From the moment I'd met him, I knew he had a dark sexual side. It alternately thrilled and unsettled me. Jace and I had been completely vanilla. I'd never thought of myself as someone who wanted to be tied up, who wanted to be dominated—let's face it, that's what this was. William made no secret he liked to be in control and I was submitting to him. More than willingly. That was something to think about later.

The silence continued, and in my nervousness, I reached to fill it. "So what is this? Handcuffs in the nightstand? Do you chain women to your bed often?"

He laughed, but it sounded more devilish than reassuring. "No, I bought these specifically for us. I've thought about having you like this since the day I licked chocolate off you in your kitchen. Do you remember that?"

I nodded. My thighs tensed as I recalled the feel of his tongue on that sensitive skin.

"Since that day, I've fantasized about this over and over."

The bed sagged, and I felt his warmth beside me again. The bare flesh of his thigh rubbed against my torso. He'd obviously gotten undressed. He didn't touch me but just his nearness was enough to make my hips arch involuntarily again.

"We can stop at any time you don't like it, but you look so fucking hot, cuffed to my bed, so turned on and at my mercy. What's your safe word, Catherine?"

My breath hitched in and I felt a gush of dampness between my thighs. I was more turned on than I could ever remember being, and he hadn't even touched my sex yet. "Rosé," I managed to say. My heart was hammering in my chest as I waited in anticipation. I felt him shift and then his mouth pressed gentle kisses on my belly, and I gasped and moaned. "Oh fuck. William. Don't stop."

He laughed quietly as his tongue, wet and warm, swirled over my flesh. He nudged my knees apart, probably sensing how close I was to coming. I was soaked and pulsing and could have made myself come so easily if I pressed my legs together.

"Please don't stop," I begged. I wanted to push his head to my sex but my raised arms strained against the handcuffs instead. "Please, please, please…"

"I'm just getting started." But then his hands left my body and he got up off the bed. I whimpered. And then for a long moment I felt and heard nothing.

"William?"

Then the bed shifted and he was back again. "Relax and try to open yourself to every sensation, Catherine. Don't anticipate or second-guess. Just feel. Do the cuffs caress your wrists? Is the fur silky? Is the wood on the headboard warm under your fingertips?"

I hadn't noticed all the tiny sensations. When I concentrated on them, I felt my body come more alive. I was aware of the cool breeze from the open terrace door skating over my flesh, of the way it flicked over my nipples and teased the end of my hair. My shoes pinched my toes slightly, my knee itched, and I could just make out a sliver of light where the blindfold covered my nose. But mostly I felt the heavy warmth in my belly. My thong was soaked with my need, my sex swollen in anticipation.

Something light and soft touched my shoulder, and I jumped.

"Relax. I won't hurt you. I'll never hurt you. This will always be about pleasure, never about pain."

I felt the sensation again, and this time it tickled up my arm to my wrist and over to the other side. It disappeared and then I felt that light flutter on the slope of my breast and over my nipple. I moaned again, my buds hardening.

"I can see you like that."

The fluttering dipped lower, tickling my belly, and if I hadn't been so aroused, I would have giggled. "What is it?" I asked.

"What do you think?"

I concentrated on the airy sensation as it glided over my thong and skated across my thighs. I couldn't help but part them. "A feather," I said suddenly. "A long feather." I could picture it in my mind, see its weightless fronds teasing my skin.

"That's right. Let's try another."

My body was already aching for him, and I still felt pouty and petulant from being shut out after dinner. I wasn't sure how much I liked surrendering control right now. "Can't you just fuck me?" I asked.

"I like it when you talk like that," William growled hoarsely. I knew I was getting to him. "Say it again." His hands slid down my belly, and his fingers slid under my thong.

"I want you to fuck me."

I lifted my buttocks as he slid my thong down and I felt every single sensation involved in removing it. Then I felt him between my legs, his knee nudging me to open even wider. "I'm looking at you, Catherine, all pink and swollen and glistening wet. You're ready for me, aren't you?"

"Yes." I was writhing now, knowing his gaze was devouring me. I felt his knee press against my sex, and then the feather fluttered over my clit. I groaned, my muscles clenching, begging for release.

"Say it again."

"Fuck me."

His finger slid inside me, penetrating me and then sliding up to circle my clit. My breathing came shallowly and my hips rose off the bed. I was close, so close.

And then his touch was gone. "No," he said, moving away. "Not until I say."

I cried out in protest. My body wanted to jump over the cliff. I jerked my hands, my instincts telling me to touch myself, but I was cuffed to the bed. "William!"

"I'm right here." Then I felt fur, much like that on the cuffs, slide over my belly. It was warm and velvet soft. "What is this?" he asked.

I didn't answer. I didn't want to play his games, especially when they mirrored our relationship. He gave me a taste of who he was and then pulled it away. Was this some sort of punishment or was he on a power trip? Either way, I didn't like it.

I was about to say *rosé* and stop his exquisite torture when the fur slid up my body, circling my breast and brushing over my nipples, causing me to shiver from head to toe. Instead of speaking, I groaned, low and guttural. I just wanted to come. I needed to come.

"Tell me what you feel," he ordered.

I tried to concentrate. "It's fur…a fur glove, I think."

"Good." The fur slid down my body, slowly, so my every nerve could revel in the sensation. "How does it feel?"

The fur slid lower, over my belly, and my sex pulsed with need. I struggled to form a coherent thought. "Soft."

The fur brushed over my thighs, teasing their inner sides. "What else?"

"Silky, like velvet."

The glove moved slowly over my center, and I clenched in anticipation. But William moved it away, brushing it over my belly. I dug my fingernails into the wood headboard, resisting the urge to scream at him to make me come already. The fur was like the feather—soft and ticklish. My sensitive flesh couldn't take much more. As though reading my mind, the fur was gone, replaced by something rough and scratchy.

I flinched at the sudden contrast until I realized it was William's cheek. He rubbed his stubble across my belly, the warmth of his skin making mine heat in reaction. He kissed my belly, his cheek moving down toward my hip. His stubble punished my sensitive skin, rubbing it raw until his soft lips soothed the hurt.

When I felt the prickle on my thigh near my apex, my breath caught in my throat. Without William even asking, I spread my legs even wider. His rough stubble scratched against my tender flesh, moving higher and higher until I felt it on my sex. His tongue parted me, and his prickly stubble brushed against my clit. I cried out, wanting his mouth on me more than I'd ever wanted anything in my life. I knew his harsh beard could be replaced by a soothing lick. I felt the tip of his tongue tease me, and I pushed against him, wanting him to suck and lave until I begged for mercy.

"Catherine."

I shook my head. I didn't want to talk. My whole body was shaking with need. I was trembling, my legs tense, my hands white-knuckled on the bed post.

"Not yet."

He was crazy. He was some sort of sadist. "I can't stop," I said, my voice breathless with arousal.

"You can. And you'll come only when I give you permission."

"Fuck you!" I cried because as soon as he said the words, my orgasm receded, leaving me uncomfortably on the edge and in desperate need of relief. "Why are you doing this to me? Are you punishing me?" I was pissed off now, and throbbing with desire.

"This isn't punishment. But you have to learn to trust me. To do what I tell you, even when you don't like it."

"I don't have to learn anything. Take these handcuffs off." I was angry and frustrated, but the warmth of his lips on my neck made me still.

"Are you sure you want me to do that? If you want me to stop, use your safe word." His mouth moved up my neck, making me shiver all over again. His lips closed on my earlobe, his warm breath sending shoots of pleasure straight to my core.

I didn't want him to stop. "Please," I said, too aroused to be embarrassed at the pleading in my voice. "Oh, William, please. Just fuck me. Please just fuck me."

"You have to get me ready, Catherine. If I'm going to fuck you properly, I need you to get me hard."

The man was rock hard at the word *sex*. I seriously doubted he needed any assistance now, but I felt him move away and then return. "Open for me, Catherine."

I turned my head away from him. I was handcuffed to the bed, my legs spread—what else did he want?

"Open your mouth."

I knew better than to ask what he would feed me. Obediently, I turned back and opened my mouth. Something warm and sticky slid inside. His finger was coated with honey. I'd noticed the bowl of honey sitting over a small tea light. Now I understood he had other plans for the honey besides as a topping for *sopapillas*. He swirled his finger around my lips, and then I took it inside and sucked hard until I swallowed the sweet coating.

I could hear his ragged breathing, and I knew he couldn't keep this up much longer. "More," I said, hoping to push him over the edge.

"I love your mouth, Catherine. I love those wet, pink lips sucking me off."

William slid down the bed again and between my legs, and this time I felt his finger on my clit. It was sticky and slightly warm from the honey, and he licked it off, swirling his tongue on my swollen bud until I was straining hard against the cuffs. His finger stroked and probed, teasing my skin until one slid lower and pressed gently against my anus.

I jumped. "William." The sensation was new and I wasn't used to being touched there. I'd never had anal sex but William had made it clear it was only a matter of time before we would try it. I knew it would be amazing, but that didn't make me any more comfortable right now.

"Relax," he said, mouth still on my clit. "It's just a finger. You can enjoy it." He pressed his finger, moist with my own wetness and a swipe of honey, slowly against my tight rosette. "Open yourself to it." I tried to relax and felt his thick finger press more firmly now, going in and then out and a bit deeper with each slow stroke. "Feel the sensation."

The unfamiliar fullness of his thick finger slowly sliding in and out of me brought me to a place of pleasure I'd never been to before, and a dark and almost primal moan escaped from my lips in response. I moved with him now, urging him to thrust his finger deeper in my ass, to lick my clit harder. I could feel my toes curling and my back arching as my orgasm built and built until I was just about to tumble over the edge, and then suddenly William was gone.

I cried out in pain as much as frustration. I moaned, and William actually chuckled. "I'm in control, Catherine," he murmured. "Don't forget that. I decide when you come—how hard and how fast. You'll come when I say, not before." He leaned over me, and I could smell the sweet scent of honey.

I took in a ragged breath, my body vibrating with tension and deferred need.

"Open your mouth."

I must not have obeyed quickly enough because he said it again. "Open those pink lips for me."

I did, and I felt something smooth and sweet and hard…oh my God. He'd coated his cock in honey. He slid it into my mouth, the honey sliding over my tongue as I felt his tip hit the back of my throat.

"Lick."

He pulled back and my tongue danced over him, rolling over his thick, hot member, swallowing the honey. It was warm and slick as it slid down. He withdrew and I could imagine him coating himself with the honey again.

"Open," he ordered as he pushed his cock into my mouth again. I let my throat relax as he thrust in and out, his hard member swelling as I pressed my lips tightly around him.

"Catherine." His voice was ragged and harsh, and I felt his honey-slicked hand pluck at my breast. I thought he would come in my mouth, and it turned me on—the taste of him mixed with the taste of honey. But he pulled out suddenly and I felt his hot mouth on my nipple, licking the honey off.

"Yes," I moaned, and then I bucked when warm honey trickled on my belly. His mouth was there to lap it up, and then his sticky warm tongue dipped lower and slid over my swollen clit.

I heard his rough whisper of "*Now*" and then the orgasm crashed through me, taking me so hard I couldn't even make a sound. My body came off the bed, and I dug my heels in to keep my balance. Every sensation imploded as my orgasm went on and on. And just when I began to come down, William's mouth left me and his hard cock slammed into me.

I came again, this time pulling hard against the cuffs, hard enough that the fur provided no cushioning against the unforgiving cold metal that held me back. My wrists screamed with pain, but I didn't care. I wanted more of him inside me. I wanted to be closer to him, even though he was thrusting deep and hard, his flesh swelling until I knew he was close. I was just aware enough, the pleasure and the pain together just bearable enough, that when he swelled and spilled into me, I was coming again or still, I couldn't tell which. I felt wetness on my thighs and William groaned and buried his face in my neck as my swollen pussy gripped him over and over again.

Wrapped in the whirlwind of sensation, I couldn't hold onto a coherent thought. And I was still blindfolded, so I couldn't see. But I could feel. I desperately wanted to hold him but I couldn't. I wanted to wrap my arms around him, to pull Willam close to me so he could feel my heart racing, hear my ragged breathing. He'd laid me bare and

I wanted him to feel *me*. But my arms were chained above my head. Even in the midst of this most intimate act, he kept me at arm's length.

I loved him, but in that moment I hated him too. And I didn't know which emotion I felt more.

SIX

I awoke with a start and bolted upright. William's hand on my shoulder was the only reason I didn't scream. "What's wrong?" I gasped.

"Nothing. I'm sorry I startled you," he said. He was standing next to the bed, fully dressed and looking down at me. I hadn't even realized he'd gotten up.

It was still dark outside, but through squinted eyes I thought I could make out some grey on the horizon. "What time is it?" I cut my gaze to him and took in his blue pinstripe suit and a blue and grey abstract tie. He smelled of soap and shaving cream.

"Early. I have some meetings today, but I didn't want to leave without saying goodbye." He smiled, one of those earnest, genuine smiles of his that made my heart swell. He was an early riser and I wasn't, but we agreed that he'd always wake me up to say goodbye. That smile indicated he remembered our promise and I loved that. But even in my sleepy state, the fact that he was leaving me stung. An early morning workout I'd expected, but not him ditching me for work, especially after last night. I wondered, too, what kind of meetings required a suit and tie on a Sunday morning. Very important ones, I guessed.

William must have read my mind because he took my face in his hands and kissed me tenderly, his tongue swirling ever so gently in my mouth to make contact with mine. My lips still felt bruised and swollen and a delicious shiver ran through me.

"I'd rather spend the whole day right here, with you. You know that, right?" His voice was low and soft.

"I know," I answered with a sigh.

"Thank you for last night."

"*I* should be thanking *you*."

"Thank you for trusting me. I need you to keep trusting me, Catherine."

"Okay." That was cryptic. He straightened up, and I realized again that he was leaving. I didn't want him to go. "When will you be back?"

"I don't know exactly, but not soon enough. Go back to sleep, beautiful girl. And then just relax and enjoy the estate. It's going to be really nice today. I'll see you later."

He bent down again and kissed me while stroking my hair, then he turned and left, his footsteps echoing across the wood floor. I watched him go, then stared at the doorway. The cavernous room felt instantly emptier without him in it and I felt emptier too. But the bed was still soft and warm where I had burrowed in on one side. For once, I was too tired to dissect William Lambourne and what he was doing to my heart, so I closed my eyes and went back to sleep.

*****

I woke several hours later, sat, and groaned. I didn't know what happened to me during my second sleep, but I was sore all over—my legs, my abs, my arms. Every single muscle in my body felt both sated and spent. Last night I'd clenched over and over as William brought me to the brink of orgasm, only to rip what I wanted away. I closed my eyes again, and flashes of fur-lined handcuffs, honey-slicked lips, and silk scarves battered my mind. I touched my wrists gingerly, noting they were tender. I looked at them closely but didn't see any bruises. Still, when I stretched up to wind my fingers around the carved headboard, I couldn't stop a small rush of anticipation flooding through me as I felt a familiar muscle strain ripple through my shoulders. I wanted more of the dark pleasure William could give me. I thought I didn't, but I had liked last night. More than liked it, actually, and I tingled all over just remembering the way he had ordered me to lick, to suck, and to come. I'd never come like that before and though maybe I could do without the handcuffs, letting him call the shots had been intense. And amazing.

The sun was high in the sky by the time I ventured out of the master suite and crept—yes, crept—downstairs. Last night we had taken a long hot shower together after our sexcapades. William had been very attentive, gently washing me to remove all the sticky honey. But I'd been more than a little freaked out when we came out of the bathroom and found the bed remade with fresh sheets and the handcuffs placed neatly on the nightstand. How the hell did his staff know we needed clean sheets, and who had been in the bedroom while we were in the shower together? William had been completely unfazed, as if having hired help tidy things up after he'd chained me to his bed and fucked me senseless was as natural as could be, but it had weirded me out.

Someone in his household knew what we'd been up to, and I wasn't exactly looking forward to running into whoever that was this morning. But my stomach was rumbling and I had to eat.

I found Fernanda in the kitchen and she gave me a warm smile and asked if I would like breakfast. She looked me right in the eyes without the tiniest bit of judgment in her gaze, so I guessed she wasn't the midnight cleaning crew. I decided on a latte and a fruit and yogurt plate, and she brought it out to me by the pool.

The morning was cool, so I'd slipped on a pair of skinny jeans in royal blue and an oversized grey sweater, both unearthed in the massive closet William had filled for me. The pool came equipped with a decorative fountain, and I planted myself on one of the plush lounge chairs, leaned my head back, and listened to the running water. I closed my eyes. I missed William already and wondered where he was now. Doing something he didn't need me for, I guessed.

Business? He didn't need me for that. Dealing with the latest Wyatt to appear? I thought he'd needed me to cope with that situation, but apparently not. Sex? Maybe *that* was the real reason he needed me on this trip. I actually hadn't thought of that until this instant. Maybe the whole reason he brought me here was so I could be available to fuck him, at his convenience, after his important *meetings*. Maybe his plan was to tie me to his bed every night and make me come so many times that I lost all will to fight and became his sex slave.

Ok, as good as some of that sounded, it was also total crap. I knew I was more to him than just a sex toy and what was between us was way more than just sex. I loved William, and I knew he cared about me too. Of course I still hadn't told him how I felt. I'd felt so close to him when he told me about his family after dinner, but then he clammed up, and before I knew it, I was chained up, blindfolded, and at his mercy. *That* hadn't been the perfect time to declare my love. I knew that and I hated that his absence was stirring up all of my insecurities.

"Give it a rest, Cat," I muttered under my breath. Annoyed with myself, I paced around the pool in an effort to clear my head. Finally, I gave up and texted Beckett.

How was the party?

A few minutes later my phone pinged. *Fabulous. How was the sex?*

I sputtered a laugh. *What sex?*

Ha-ha. Spill.

I thought for a minute about how to describe last night's activities with William. I decided on *Amazing and a little bit kinky.*

Really? I could hear Beckett's voice go up a half an octave. *Kinky???*

I bit my lip. *Handcuffs and honey.*

There was a long pause, and I watched the little dots on my screen blink. *OMFG. Major. Am insanely jealous!!!!*

No kinky sex with Alec? Alec was an assistant art director with Fresh Market and was a great guy—fun and funky and so cute—and I was thrilled he and Beckett were dating.

Not yet. Beckett texted back. *Some heavy petting last night.*

At the party?

That was *the party!*

I shook my head and laughed again. I'd heard more than just Alec's voice in the background when I called last night. I didn't care. Beckett was so fastidious; I knew he'd leave my condo cleaner than when he'd arrived. But I got the feeling there was something he wasn't telling me. *Who else was there?*

He listed a few of his friends, and I felt a pang of sadness that I'd missed out. I didn't go to an office every day, which meant it was hard for me to meet new people. I didn't have a lot of friends in Chicago, and now several prospective friends had partied at my house last night without me.

So what was the occasion? I texted. *New opportunity? With who? Fresh Market? Someone else?*

Another long pause. All of William's secrecy was clearly making me paranoid—now I felt like Beckett was keeping secrets. Beckett and I didn't keep secrets. Or we never used to.

Finally, he texted back. *Don't want to jinx it. Just cross your fingers and toes for me.*

You got it. Legs crossed too.

That won't last long.

Beckett could always make me laugh.

Enjoy the sun. Cold and dreary here. Laters!

Ciao for now! XOXO, I texted back.

I glanced at the clock on my phone. Barely noon. "Shit," I muttered aloud again. Okay, that was no problem. I had work to do. I could keep myself busy for a few hours. William would probably be back in time for dinner.

I retrieved my laptop and brought it outside to work. I definitely couldn't have done this in Chicago, but in Napa, the pool, the pergola, the weather were all perfect. I felt like I was vacationing at a luxury spa. Sure, it was a little weird to be at William's home without him, but I tried to focus on work and I succeeded for a little while. By the time I closed my laptop and stretched, rolling my neck to work out the kinks, the shadows were growing long. I checked my watch and heaved a loud sigh. It was almost four and still no word from William. I tried to snooze on the chaise by the pool but that lasted about thirty seconds. I wandered around the outdoor area a little bit, but I didn't feel comfortable exploring the vineyard on my own and truthfully, I didn't want to. I definitely didn't want to run in to any of more of William's staff, but really it was because I wanted William to show me how he made his wine. He was so proud of what he did here and it seemed only fair to wait for him to show me everything like he promised he would.

If he knew me better, he would have realized that leaving me to hang around by myself all day was probably the worst possible thing. I wasn't good at just sitting around, and I never had been. It was one of those things that I realized about myself after Jace died. It's why I liked to take Laird for long walks, why I liked to run along the lakeshore. And it was why I built my darkroom. I needed to be busy, to be occupied. Me alone with my thoughts was not always a good thing, and sometimes, I needed *not* to think. I could lose myself for hours developing film and experimenting with different print techniques, but my eyes were crossed by now. I needed a break from work. And sometimes just an empty hour with nothing to fill it was too much. I guess that's what happens when you become a twenty-two-year-old widow after six months of marriage. Yes, I had turned a corner since I met William. But old habits died hard.

I may still have been behind on my sleep after the late night at The Peninsula, then the long trip here and William's early morning wake up, but the last thing I needed was time to laze around and think. Kind of like last night's massage, which had not relaxed me. At all. But at least that had ended well. I thought again about the handcuffs, the honey, and how I felt with that red silk scarf tied across my eyes. I felt a chill race through me even though it was toasty warm in the sun. That feeling of surrender and of letting William control my pleasure had been incredible, like nothing I'd ever felt with him or with anyone else before. I rubbed at my sore wrists, which were still bruise-free. I couldn't wait to feel it again.

By dinnertime, I was bored, antsy, and lonely. The house with the grounds and the vineyard was an enormous estate, but I still felt trapped. And a little pissed. My cell had been by my side all afternoon and though I had picked it up a zillion times, I hadn't gotten so much as a text from William. I couldn't wait any longer, so I finally gave in and punched in a text of my own.

Where are you???

I waited and waited. Nothing. This was what I feared.

Fine. I decided to call him. It rang and went straight to voicemail. Which pissed me off even more.

I stayed on my chaise. The sun had already set, but the outdoor heaters were lit and the well-placed landscape lighting created a warm halo of light over the whole pool area. Fernanda all but insisted that I eat dinner, and as she walked up carrying a tray, I was desperate enough to finally ask her if she knew anything. I'd wanted to ask her all day, but I had held my tongue. "Do you know when Mr. Lambourne will be back? It's getting late."

"No, Miss Kelly, I'm sorry. I don't." She smiled and shrugged as she set the tray down on the table next to me.

"Do you know where he is? I haven't heard from him since this morning, and I'm getting worried."

"Mr. Lambourne is a very busy man, Miss Kelly. I am sure he's fine and will be back soon." She was polite, but her look told me this sort of non-communication from William was not unusual. "Can I get you anything else, Miss Kelly?"

I quietly sighed in frustration as I looked at the beautiful meal set out for me. I wasn't very hungry, but I didn't want to offend Fernanda and maybe she really didn't know where William was or when he'd be returning. "No, I'm fine. Thank you, Fernanda. This looks delicious."

"Enjoy your dinner, Miss Kelly." Then she turned and walked back toward the house.

I ate the warm chorizo and spinach salad I'd chosen for dinner—which was super fresh and delicious—and drank the entire carafe of white wine that came with it.

And I kept waiting.

*****

I'd always loved swimming. I was on swim team when I was a kid and I surfed most of my life too. I spent hours in the water, I felt at home there and completely comfortable, which is how I started photographing surfers. I was a strong swimmer and a halfway decent surfer, but managing heavy camera equipment while out on a board in riotous surf required strength and confidence too.

I went back up to the empty master suite after dinner and sulked some more. When William walked in the door, I wanted him to know exactly how mad I was. But, surprise, surprise, I was too antsy to stay in the room. I needed to *do* something, and looking about, it dawned on me what. I found a skimpy red string bikini in my Narnia-like closet and pulled it on. I felt decadent wearing a bikini in January, so I texted Beckett a picture and typed, *How's the snow?* before heading back down to the pool for a swim.

It had been a while since I'd worked out in a pool, but after a few laps, my body relaxed and I focused on the repetition of my movements. I must have been swimming for the better part of an hour when I surfaced and spotted William sitting in a chair just a few feet from the edge of the pool. *Finally*, I thought. I was relieved, and excited too.

I wiped my eyes, half expecting him to be a mirage. My heart was already pounding from exertion, but it beat even harder from seeing him in the flesh. He was sprawled in the lounge chair, wearing the same shirt and pinstriped trousers I last saw him in. The sleeves of his pressed shirt were rolled to the elbows, the top buttons undone, and his tie loosened. He held a highball in his hand, and his dark eyes watched me intently, like a hungry lion quietly watching his prey. I was more than ready to be caught.

He looked so good I had to remind myself to continue treading water. I could see the stress of the day on his face, but somehow it only made his chiseled features more handsome. His hair blew lightly in the breeze, and he sipped from the highball, his gaze hot on mine.

I didn't know why he was keeping me at a distance or where he had been all day, but the way he looked at me, the yearning in his expression, pulled at me even more acutely than any words he might have spoken could have. He needed me.

And I needed him.

Without another thought, I swam to the side of the pool, hoisted myself up, and left a trail of water as I walked over to his chair. The air was cool, but the heaters kept the pool area warm, and I didn't even grab a towel to dry off before I straddled him. I didn't want to talk.

With a smile, he sipped from the highball. "Nice suit."

I cocked my head. "Where's yours?"

"I don't really need one, now do I?" His free hand was splayed across my bare back, steadying me on his lap. Slowly, his fingers crawled up my slick flesh to the strings holding my bikini top in place, first the tie around my back and then the tie around my neck. Slowly he pulled at each one and the scrap of fabric fell away in a wet heap on the ground beside us.

My nipples puckered from both exposure and his hot gaze. Keeping that gaze on me, he raised the glass filled with amber liquid—bourbon, I guessed—and rubbed it across my hard nipple. I sucked in a shallow breath. The cold glass was a sharp contrast to my skin, which was still warm from the heated water, and my nipple pebbled painfully tighter.

"Cold?" he asked.

"A little."

"Let me warm you up."

My eyes never left his as he dipped two fingers in his drink then swirled them around my nipple until the amber liquid dripped onto my stomach. I could smell the heady aroma of the liquor and feel the warmth of it on my skin. William set the glass on the table, leaned forward, and lapped the bourbon from my breast and belly, heat blasting through me as his thick tongue burned a trail across my wet flesh. When he'd caught every drop, he took my now aching peak in his mouth and sucked long and hard. I moaned. "Oh God, William. Please." My voice was deep and husky, and I felt a rush of heat between my legs.

"Please what, Catherine? More?" He dipped a finger in his drink again and brought it to my other nipple, then his mouth was back on me and he bit down ever so gently on my hard point. I moaned again, louder this time, and then arched my back and pushed myself toward him.

He was breathing hard and I felt his urgency as his hands went to the ties on each side of my bikini bottoms. A moment later those were also released and the swathe of fabric was on the ground. I was naked and still straddling him on the deck chair. Heat swirled and pulsed where our bodies touched. I wanted his hands on me so badly.

Then his mouth was back, kissing me gently above my breasts and up my neck. I felt the scruff of his beard scratching against my skin and his hot breath close to my ear, which gave me goose bumps all over before he pulled me hard toward him and crushed his lips against mine. His tongue invaded my mouth, hot and probing, and my entire body responded to his kiss. I was wet from the pool, but wet and swollen with arousal now too. I could hear myself making rough sounds of pleasure as our tongues danced and William's large hands gripped my ass and ground me firmly against his hard cock.

I knew where this was going, and I wanted it to go there. My body was begging to go there, begging me to open the button on his bulging trousers and take him inside me with long, hot, hard strokes. But I hadn't forgotten he had completely abandoned me today, hadn't texted or called, and hadn't even answered his phone when I called him. And now that he was back, it was all about sex again.

His hands moved from my ass and rested on my thighs, and I covered them with my hands to keep him from moving inward. His gaze met mine, and I saw the question in his eyes.

My heart was beating so hard I could barely speak, but I managed to say, "I didn't think you'd be gone so long today."

He didn't attempt to free his hands, but he did rub his fingers in small circles on the bare skin of my thighs, which seem to shoot little sparks of electricity straight to my clit. I tried not to squirm. "Neither did I. The meetings went longer than expected."

"What sort of meetings were they?" I asked, still breathless. "Work or Wyatt or something else?"

He looked away. I wasn't surprised. He was back in vintage William Lambourne mode—his version of don't ask, don't tell. "A little of this and a little of that," he finally said.

His hands were distracting me, but I wasn't going to let this go. I wanted to say *I came all the way from Chicago to be with you, and on the first day, you take off for fourteen hours. I think I deserve more than a cursory answer.* But instead I just looked at him and didn't say a thing. I let my silence do the talking.

We sat there for a minute or two, not saying anything. Then his eyes, an icy blue, met mine. "It's nothing that concerns you. If it did, I would share it. Please know that."

I blinked, stunned. I started to wriggle to move off of his lap but he clamped his hands down hard on my legs and held me in place.

"Catherine, you have to trust me. There are some things I can't discuss. You're safe here. The security team is here. Everything is fine, and there's nothing for you to worry about."

"You were with her, weren't you?" I asked. I had no idea where *that* accusation came from. I didn't even know I was going to say it, but the image of the dark-haired woman at the airport, who I hadn't thought about at all today, just popped into my head. I remembered the two of them together on the tarmac, the way she'd placed her hand possessively on his arm. The way she'd 'accidentally' brushed her breast against him when they stood beside one another.

William's eyebrows came together. "With who?"

I don't know what was wrong with me. It was like my mouth was on autopilot and I couldn't *not* keep going since I saw her so vividly in my head. "That woman you met at the airport. The one who couldn't keep her hands off you." Maybe it was my imagination, but I thought I saw a flicker of guilt in his eyes.

He took a moment to reply and when he did, his response was careful and measured, which of course I noticed. "She was with me today, but not in the way you seem to think."

"So *she* can know what's going on, but not me?"

"Catherine." His voice turned soothing, velvet and warm, and he was back to breathing normally. I was impressed that he could compose himself so quickly given that I was naked and straddling him right out in the open on his pool deck. Anyone could have walked out and seen us. "There is nothing going on between Anya and me. She's an old friend and occasional business associate. That's all."

"And her name is Anya?"

"Anya Pierce. She's not your rival. You have no rivals." His hand traveled up my thigh to cup my hip. The soft stroke of his fingers forced me to take a shaky breath. I wasn't quite sure Anya Pierce was nothing to William, but it was also true he was here with me now.

"I'm yours, Catherine," he said quietly. "I don't want anyone else."

Suddenly I felt possessive of him. Very possessive. His gorgeous eyes, now liquid and all but silver; the toned and muscled body I knew was under his clothes; the face that looked almost Photoshopped. All of that was mine. And I wanted him to know it.

I reached up and stripped off his tie. I tossed it on the ground beside my wet suit. It was probably a five hundred dollar tie, but I didn't care. Next was his shirt. I flicked the buttons open and slid my hands inside. My fingers roved over his sculpted chest and shoulders, enjoying all the hard ridges and planes he worked so hard to tone.

I glanced up at his face, and saw he watched me intently. He was exercising restraint, allowing me to have my way with him. He was letting *me* take control, but he clearly knew that at any moment he could touch me, and I'd melt and forget about everything but the pleasure. Before that could happen, I put my hands between my legs and grabbed his slim leather belt, unfastening it and then the button of his trousers. His cock was hard and waiting, and with a slight urging down of his zipper and a push of fabric, I held it in my hands.

I slid my fingers down, enjoying the length of him and the way the veins pulsed with need for me. I angled my hips and spread my legs. My folds were slick and I wanted him to see. William's hands tensed on my legs, and his hardness jumped in my hand.

"You're killing me right now," he said, his voice hoarse.

Something about the sound of his voice, the raw emotion in it, was my undoing. I was still angry at him for leaving me today and hurt about all he wouldn't share with me, but this was something he would share. He would share his body—fully and completely. In these moments, he was mine. He needed me. And I needed him.

I slid forward, guiding his cock where I wanted it, but he stopped me and motioned me to stand. I did so, slowly and with my legs trembling in anticipation. I wondered what he had in mind, but he merely motioned for me to turn around. His hands slid to my inner thighs and pushed them apart so I straddled him again. Then he pulled me down so my back was against his chest. I could feel his hardness pressing against me. "Ride me like this." His direction came out rough and raw.

Of all the ways we'd come together, this one was new. My breath caught in my throat as a wave of arousal hit me hard. His hands on my hips guided me, sliding my ass along his abs until he settled me over his cock, his tip hot and hard and pulsing at my entrance. Slowly, I took him in, enjoying the feel of every solid inch of him sliding into me. I was so achingly full that I gasped, but still there was more of him. When I was fully seated on him, I cried out with pleasure. I was ready to come from just the feel of him filling me, and my legs were twitching and trembling. I wasn't sure how long I could go like this, but William's strong hands held me by the hips and guided my movements.

"You don't know what you're doing to me," he murmured. "God, don't stop."

He helped move my hips up then down as I took him, and one of his hands moved up my abdomen to my chest. I had to lean back to keep my balance, which had the added effect of pushing my breasts into his hand. He cupped them, stroked them, and then brushed his palm over my sensitive nipples. "Deeper," he urged me as his hand circled one nipple then the other, making them harden and heat.

"I don't think I can," I breathed, concentrating on my balance and now so close to orgasm I could hardly speak.

"Deeper, Catherine," he said, nudging my legs farther apart. I rose up and then slid down again, taking him so deep I didn't think I could stretch any farther. My legs were noticeably shaking now. I could feel every ridge, every swollen inch of him inside of me. I could feel my sex tightening and gripping him so hard, but before I could come around that glorious cock, William murmured, "Not yet," in my ear.

"No, no, I can't, I can't wait," I protested. I was riding him and my body was poised and oh so ready to let go.

"Not yet," he rasped again in my ear.

The orgasm that was right there slipped just out of reach. I couldn't go over the edge. Not without his consent. I groaned and rode him faster and harder, frantic with desire.

Slowly, as though he wasn't equally as close—but I could feel exactly how close he was and I knew he couldn't hold back for much longer—his hands slid down my body until one rested on my hip and the other cupped my sex, just above where we were joined. His finger touched our hot, wet union and came away slick. Then he parted my folds and found my clit. I shuddered as he caressed me, while his cock filled me from behind. I couldn't think. I could only feel the waves of ecstasy radiating through me with every hard stroke. William's finger circled my clit until I was moaning and begging him. My words didn't even make sense. I was beyond pleasure now. The pool, the cool breeze, the sounds of the cool California night were gone. There was only William and me, and the universe of his filling me, bringing me closer and closer to a climax I knew would shatter me.

My hands went to my breasts, plucking at my nipples, and my head fell back against his shoulder as I took him viciously. He was slicked with sweat, his muscles tense with restraint. "Oh God, Catherine," he finally moaned. "Come for me." His finger pressed harder against my engorged clit, and his cock swelled even more as the first gush of semen pushed against my walls.

My body responded instantly, shaking violently as wave after shuddering wave crashed through me. I could make no sound at all— I could only feel, only take what he gave me, take more and more of him as I clutched him over and over again. And then it was over, and I was so weak I all but collapsed. William's strong arms caught me, and he turned me around, holding me against him, stroking my hair, and shushing me.

God, I loved him so much. My heart was still thundering in my ears as I clung to him, relishing in the warmth of my bare skin pressed against his. I felt complete in his arms and never wanted to leave them. Part of me wanted to tell him, right now, how I felt. But part of me didn't want to break the silence of the moment, which was somehow perfect as we held each other tightly, so many things between us unsaid but not unfelt. He needed me. And I needed him.

We stayed like that for a few more minutes and then finally, William spoke. He whispered against my ear, "Do you still doubt I'm yours? You own me, Catherine."

And then he kissed me, lifted me up, and carried me inside.

SEVEN

I opened my eyes and knew without even turning my head that William wasn't in bed with me. There was just the cold expanse of crisp 600-thread count Italian sheets on either side of me and barely an indentation of where William had been the night before. Exhausted after my swim and our poolside sex, I'd pretty much passed right out after carried me upstairs and tucked me in. The last thing I remembered was him undressing, crawling under the covers, and then spooning my naked body with his. His arms had pulled me tight against him, wrapping me in a delicious warm embrace as I drifted off into a deep, dreamless sleep.

I had no idea when he'd gotten up. I fumbled for my phone and peered at the time. A little after 8:30. Great. I was all by myself in William's giant bed. Again. What a way to start another day at the glorious Casa di Rosabela. I wanted to wake up in his arms like I did at The Peninsula and spend the morning talking and laughing and exploring each other.

I sat, but I knew William wasn't in the master suite. I could usually sense him—when he was near, all the little hairs on my arm prickled. My arms felt absolutely nothing, but I looked around for him anyway.

Empty.

William's words from the night before came back to me. He'd assured me we were safe. He'd told me the security team was here. Obviously he viewed this new Wyatt, whoever or whatever it was, as a threat he took seriously. Equally obvious, he didn't want to talk to me about said threat because he thought I'd be safer that way. Or maybe he thought the less I knew the less I'd worry. Yeah, right. Worry was practically my middle name. What he didn't seem to understand was I worried about *him*. And about us. I didn't care about safe nearly as much as I cared about him—I owned him. Just thinking about what he had whispered in my ear last night made my pulse race. I wasn't sure that a man like William could ever give himself completely to a woman, but I wanted to believe him. Desperately. God, I loved him.

I flopped back down and closed my eyes. I could almost hear my yoga instructor's soothing voice as I slowly inhaled and exhaled a few deep, cleansing breaths through my nose, trying to expel any negative thoughts. But it wasn't working.

I took another deep breath. I had to stay cool. I couldn't let Cat the Dramatic win the day, so I'd try to think positive. William probably got up for his usual before-dawn workout and was downstairs, doing something to stave off the mysterious crisis that brought us here. Or maybe he was out tending to his grapes and he didn't wake me up because he was just being considerate. I could give him a break.

With those thoughts, I took a quick shower, put my wet hair into a ponytail, pulled on a pair of jeans, a tank top with a T-shirt layered over it, and a pair of flip flops, and then headed downstairs for coffee and to find William. On my way, I glanced out the front windows and noted the Porsche was parked out front, but all but one of the big black SUVs the security team used were gone. Okay, something was up. "Oh no," I muttered as I tried not to panic.

When I walked into the kitchen, I expected to see Fernanda. I stopped and stared instead at a man and a woman I'd never seen before, both in black pants and starched white shirts and looking very professional. It jarred me, having people I didn't even know in the house with me while I'd been sleeping.

"Good morning, Miss Kelly," the man said. "I'm Sam, and this is Nancy."

"Um, good morning. Where's Fernanda?"

"She has the day off, Miss Kelly," Nancy, a woman with her dark hair pulled into a tight bun, told me a little too cheerfully.

"And William?" My cheeks burned when I said his name. Was Nancy the one who'd changed the sheets after the night with the honey? Did Sam know about the kinky stuff William and I had done? Handcuffs, sex by the pool... I wanted to turn around, run back upstairs, and bury myself under the bed covers. With William. As it was, I couldn't make eye contact with either of them.

"Mr. Lambourne is fine," Sam said. His hair was long, grey, and pulled into a ponytail. I hated ponytails on older men.

"What do you mean fine? Where is he? If he's out in the vineyard, you can just point me in the right direction and I'll walk out and meet him."

Sam kept looking at me, his face expressionless as he answered, "He had some business, but he'll be in touch soon."

For a minute I was too stunned to speak as I processed what Sam just said. William couldn't possibly have done it to me again, but it was obvious that he had. Sam and Nancy were trying to play it cool and act like it was no big deal, but William wasn't here. He left me on my own again, this time without telling me and without waking me up to say goodbye. And that was a huge fucking deal in my book. "Some business? Where is he exactly?" I sputtered at Sam. I was about to lose it and I didn't care if they knew.

"Mr. Lambourne is fine and will be in touch with you soon," Sam said again.

"Is there something I can get you?" Nancy chimed in. "Coffee?"

I ignored chipper Nancy. William had left and that fucking hurt. I thought we were so past the waking up alone, leaving without saying goodbye or even a note stage, especially after the last two nights. Then the niggling thoughts began—he was never going to let me in. He was never going to be what I needed him to be, starting with honest. How could I possibly keep trusting him like he asked when he obviously didn't trust me? I could feel the tears starting to well up in my eyes. "Great," I said. "Just great." Then I turned around and stormed out.

I ended up out by the pool again. I'd gone upstairs first and grabbed my laptop thinking I'd try to do some work to calm down. I was parked on my lounger for about five minutes before Sam appeared and set out a carafe of coffee along with a tray of cups and pitchers on the table.

"Nancy is bringing you some fruit and yogurt," he told me. "Is there anything else?"

"Nope." I glared at him. I wasn't in the mood to be polite and I hadn't even asked for coffee or breakfast. I surveyed the three little pitchers of milk marked skim, 1%, and 2%, the selection of sugar and its various substitutes, and the half dozen little cups of coffee flavorings I could add. There wasn't much else I could want for.

Except William.

And explanations.

But I wasn't going to get those, so I supposed I would have to content myself with coffee.

Yesterday work had distracted me, so I fired up my laptop again and worked for a while on the Fresh Market pictures of asparagus and cherries for the Fresh for Spring campaign. The shots were good, but they needed to be edited, retouched, and refinished. I lost myself in my work for an hour or so, but I was too distracted to really focus. I kept checking my phone, hoping for some word from William, but there was nothing.

Then my phone buzzed, indicating I had a voicemail. I couldn't push the buttons fast enough. It was from a number I didn't recognize, but maybe William had called from another number.

"Hi Catherine, this is Emmy Schmidt."

As soon as I heard the woman's voice, my heart sank. It wasn't William. And did I even know an Emmy Schmidt? I kept listening.

"I work for Hutch Morrison, executive chef at Morrison Hotel. I'd like to set up a meeting with you and Mr. Morrison at your earliest convenience."

Hutch Morrison? I didn't know him, but I remembered Beckett talking about Morrison Hotel. It was one of the hottest restaurants in Chicago right now.

Emmy Schmidt rattled off her contact information and asked me to call her. I jotted down the number, but I kind of wanted to know more about this guy before I committed to a meeting. I called Beckett, but it went straight to voicemail. "Hey, Beckett, it's Cat. I just got a call from the PR person for Hutch Morrison. She wants to set up a meeting. Do you know anything about him? Any idea what this could be about? Call or text me when you get a chance. Bye."

I couldn't sit around the pool any longer. The chair William and I had done it on last night was pushed back into place in front of a small coffee table near the outdoor fireplace. Every time I looked at it… Fuck it. I was going inside. I had a mission.

I started in the living room and worked my way through a media room and finally to William's study. I wasn't exactly looking for anything specific, but just for something, anything really, that might clue me in to what the hell was going on, William's privacy be damned.

I couldn't get over how much different this house was from William's penthouse in Chicago. Everything here was warm and inviting, textured and bursting with color. I found framed photos of William and his family all through the house, along with souvenirs he'd obviously collected on his travels. And the art, which was everywhere, was spectacular. The house, like the penthouse, could have been a museum, but whereas his penthouse *felt* like a museum, this place felt like William's home.

In his study, I found more photos as well as several framed pictures of celebrities, all signed to William. The one from Michael Jordan seemed to occupy the center spot, though Walter Payton and Dick Butkus were prominently displayed as well.

I imagined William as a kid, treasuring these mementos of his heroes. I sat at his desk and opened the drawers. I rifled through them and found a bunch of papers but nothing terribly exciting or damning as far I could tell. No dossiers on other women George might have found for him to date.

There were framed pictures on the bookshelves behind his desk: one of his family a few years before the crash and a more recent one of him and his aunt, uncle, and his three cousins. And then I spotted another one. In a corner, almost hidden behind the family photographs, was a framed shot of a group of kids, several in college sweatshirts. It didn't take me long to find William in the picture. He looked young, maybe nineteen or twenty, and little thinner, but just as handsome. Standing beside him was someone else I recognized— Anya Pierce.

She too looked younger, but still beautiful. She was probably more beautiful now because she'd attained an aura of sophistication. In the picture, there was no trace of that. She was looking at William, who looked out at the camera. She had eyes only for him. Anyone could see that.

So there *was* a history there. And there was attraction, at least on her side. I didn't want to think about the two of them together, and I wondered if William was with her right now. That would explain all the secrecy. He left me stranded at his house while he was off with his old girlfriend, conducting important "business." Business, my ass. Maybe he was the commitment-phobe I had originally thought he was after all, and I was just the idiot who fell for his little game. I didn't want to believe it, but I really didn't know what to think right now.

I felt like my throat was closing and I couldn't breathe. I needed to get out of here. Now.

I walked out of the front door and arrowed toward the nearest field of grapes; I wasn't going to wait for William's promised grand tour of his vineyard after all.

I hadn't strayed far from the house when I noticed I wasn't alone. A big, muscular guy with a shaved head and a military look was following me from a distance. Maybe I was imagining things.

I wandered a bit further, trying to clear my head and burn off some of my nervous energy. I headed toward the olive grove. I saw William's hand in the order of the trees, which were planted in perfect rows, beautifully cultivated, and pruned. I felt as though I could see William everywhere on the estate. His heart was here, I was certain of it. But where was he? I could feel the tears welling in my eyes again, but I wiped them away, irritated at my own emotional outburst.

The burly military guy was definitely still following me. I cut down a row of grapes and backtracked, flanking him.

"Hey," I said. He spun around, clearly surprised I'd outmaneuvered him. "Who are you?"

"I'm Darius, Miss Kelly," he said when he approached. His voice had a slight eastern European accent.

"Why are you following me, Darius?" I asked.

He gave me a tight smile. "Just making sure you don't get lost."

Right. I'd bet he was assigned to keep an eye on me. What the hell was William afraid of? I really had questions now. "So, Darius," I said, "Where is Mr. Lambourne?"

"He's fine," he said. "He will be in touch shortly."

How many times had I heard that already? My definition of *shortly* didn't seem to mesh with my absent boyfriend's.

I stopped near the far edge of the olive grove, which I could see was completely charming, even under my frustrated gaze. A table and chairs were set up in one area under the shade of a large tree, and I wished I had my camera. I tried again. "Will William be back for dinner?" I asked Darius casually.

"I can't say, Miss Kelly. You'll hear from him soon."

The answer didn't placate me, but clearly Darius wasn't going to tell me anything. And I couldn't help but feel William was in some sort of danger. Why else would he leave without telling me?

I spent the remainder of the afternoon back on my chaise by the pool, my stomach knotted with worry. I heard nothing from

William. No texts, no phone calls, nothing. The staff was as cheery as ever, acting as though the communication blackout was the most normal thing in the world.

Around six o'clock, I walked into the kitchen to demand some answers from Sam and Nancy. I wanted to know what the hell was going on, but I was met with tight lips and the unmistakable scent of pasta sauce. They were cooking, probably for me, but I didn't want to eat another dinner alone. Both Sam and Nancy remained pretty much unresponsive to me, but I saw them exchange a few nervous glances. Then Darius appeared and escorted me out of the kitchen, saying, "Relax and enjoy your stay, Miss Kelly. Mr. Lambourne will be in touch very soon."

Why wouldn't he stop saying that? It was a lie. I wanted to scream that I wasn't relaxed and I wasn't enjoying my stay. Food was the last thing on my mind, so I escaped to the master suite. An hour or so later, Nancy timidly knocked on my door and brought in a dish of pasta and a carafe of wine, but I didn't have much of an appetite. I picked at the food, but I drank all the wine and flipped channels on TV for a while. Finally, I fell asleep, alone, my heart breaking as my eyes fluttered closed.

So much for Napa. And so much for my boyfriend.

*****

I woke up Tuesday morning sweaty and agitated, with my throat sore and my pulse raging. My cheeks were still wet with tears. There were no telltale signs that William had ever made it to bed and I was kind of glad I was by myself: I'd had the dream. I hadn't had it in a long time, but it was a familiar one. And a bad one. William didn't need to see me like this.

In my dream, Jace and I were out on our boards beyond the break at Pleasure Point, the spot we always surfed in Santa Cruz, and we were waiting for the next set to roll in. It was early, just before sunrise, and overcast, so the cliffs had an eerie dark cast in the distance. We were silently bobbing up and down on our boards, our wetsuits black and glistening in the grey Pacific, and Jace kept turning his head over his shoulder to watch the water. "The next one's yours, Cat. Get ready."

I maneuvered my board and laid down in position. My arms started to move furiously as I propelled myself forward. I could feel the water rising beneath me as the wave started to crest. "Go, Cat! Go!" I could hear Jace yelling in the background.

Just as I popped up and got my footing, ready to ride the wave into shore, I was hit hard in the back and knocked off my board. It knocked the wind out of me and I couldn't breathe. I was pulled down, down into the frigid dark water, deeper and deeper. It was a dream, so I could still scream even though I was submerged and my throat and lungs burned as I struggled for air.

"Jace, Jace, help me! Help me! Pull me up!" But I couldn't lift my arms. No matter how hard I tried, I couldn't lift them up. I struggled, I twisted, but it was like they were tied to my side. "Jace, I can't move! Help me!" I continued to sink down, down, down. I kept twisting and turning, trying to break free of whatever was holding my arms and start swimming toward the surface. But I just kept sinking deeper into the cold darkness and all I could hear was Jace, his voice getting fainter and fainter, saying "Go, Cat! Go!" And then I woke up.

The location changed sometimes, and sometimes it was daytime and sunny. But there was always the weird grey cast to everything and the same events occurred: my catching the wave, being knocked off my board, not being able to breathe, and then sinking like a rock with my arms unable to move, and Jace in the background saying, "Go Cat! Go!" I'd talked to Beckett about the dream lots of times over the past three years. Ever since Jace died. Sigmund Freud Beckett thought it meant I was afraid of being swallowed by forces hidden in the depths of my unconscious. Like the guilt I felt about the accident. I didn't know what it meant, but I knew it scared me and stirred up too many painful and upsetting memories, that I always felt unsettled and on edge after I had it.

I took my bad dream as a sign that I need a change of scenery. I got up, showered, and dressed, then I marched into the kitchen and demanded, "Is there a car I can use? I want to go into town." St. Helena was nearby, and when William and I had driven through it Saturday night, it looked like it had some cute shops and historic charm.

At my request, Nancy and Sam exchanged a look. Sam cleared his throat. "I'll ask Darius."

"I can drive myself. My license is perfectly valid here," I called after Sam.

I ignored Nancy's offers of breakfast while we waited. A few minutes later Darius appeared, looking as big and buff as ever, but carrying car keys. "Where would you like to go, Miss Kelly? I'll drive you."

Big surprise. Darius was going to keep playing shadow.

"I want to go into St. Helena and do some shopping. And I might sit in one of the cafés and work. For the entire day." Anywhere but here, obsessing about William. I reached for the keys.

"I'll drive you, Miss Kelly."

I raised a brow. "I know how to drive, and I don't need a babysitter."

He didn't even blink. "Mr. Lambourne's orders, ma'am."

"Whatever." I knew I was being a petulant brat, but I didn't care. I grabbed my laptop, camera bags, and purse and joined Darius in the remaining big black SUV.

St. Helena was surprisingly quiet on a Tuesday morning. Darius parked outside one of the shops that lined the main street, and I climbed out, shouldering my bags. I looked in a few boutiques that showcased local artists and clothing designers and all the while, Darius stood guard outside the shop or lumbered behind me as I walked. What did he think was going to happen here?

I'd been so happy with William the night we'd gotten back together and I really thought everything was going to be perfect between us. And things had been going pretty well, but now we were right back to what broke us up in the first place. Except now I loved William—at least I thought I did. But I was starting to think maybe love wasn't enough to forgive all the secrecy and the way he had closed himself off to me. I needed more. I deserved more. I knew that, but I still felt totally miserable at the thought of breaking up with William again. I didn't want to. At all. But then there was the Anya Pierce situation to contend with, though even I had to admit that I was grasping at straws there.

Just then, my cell buzzed, and I paused in front of a boutique and pulled it out of my bag. A dozen steps behind me, Darius paused too. I guess the cell service wasn't so great because it had gone straight to voicemail. As soon as I heard my dad's voice, my stomach tightened into knots.

"Hey! How's my favorite girl? Just checking in. Call me, Cat."

I pocketed the phone and took a deep breath. Darius was watching me, so I made a point of wandering a bit more, feeling a weird sense of nostalgia and unease. It was strange to be back in Northern California again. It felt so familiar, but with Darius never far from sight, I felt like I was hiding out in the witness protection program or something. My parents had no idea I was here. I wondered what my dad would make of William and all of his bullshit. He would definitely be hurt to know I was in Napa and hadn't come to see him. There was a thought. Maybe I should steal the keys to the SUV from Darius or find a rental car agency and drive to Santa Cruz and play it off like an impromptu visit. I could say I was homesick or something.

I was caught up in my fantasy escape planning when my phone buzzed again. This time it was a text from Beckett.

Sorry I didn't reply yesterday. Super busy. Trying out new recipes. You?

I stopped walking again and Darius stopped too, so I could answer.

Sulking. William is AWOL. Again.

Tough hanging out at the mansion by yourself.

I knew I didn't make a very pity-worthy subject, but I didn't care about mansions and vineyards. I just wanted William.

More like a gilded cage and I ditched it. Now I'm shopping, I answered.

Boo hoo you, but that sucks. Maybe you should just come home.

Maybe I should.

Hutch Morrison is waiting.

I'd totally forgotten about that voicemail. *So who is he? Big shot chef?*

Biggest of the big. He's so hot right now. Seriously hot. And Morrison Hotel is the most sought after ticket in town. Literally. You have to buy a ticket to get in.

A ticket?

Check it out.

A moment later a link came through. I clicked on it, and it took me to the Morrison Hotel restaurant website. It looked like a high-concept restaurant with really elevated cuisine. From what I gathered, the entire menu and concept changed on the chef's whim, and Hutch Morrison's whims leaned toward rock albums. It was global news when he announced his next theme: *Sticky Fingers* was coming next. Interesting…

A few moments later, another text came through. *Here's the man himself.*

An image of a tattooed guy appeared on my phone. A seriously hot tattooed guy.

This is Hutch?

Oh, yeah. He's a Southern boy, lots of charm but with a hard rock-and-roll edge. He used to be in a band, so the rocker thing is legit. Ticket to the restaurant is worth it just to ogle him.

There was no doubt Hutch Morrison was a sexy bad boy type. He had the bedroom eyes, the slow, sexy smile, and the hard body— a nice canvas for the tattoos. I was intrigued at the thought of meeting him. I bet he was just as hot in person; guys like him always were.

I'll give him a call tomorrow.

Tomorrow. Don't forget. Big chance for you, don't miss it.

Right. See you soon.

I put my phone in my purse, then pulled it out again and stared at the picture of Hutch Morrison. I'd call his publicist tomorrow or later in the week. It might be interesting to do some shots of this guy's food. Or of the man himself.

My mind was going around and around in circles and I was too. After I passed the same wine bar three times, I decided to take a break. Coffee and work sounded perfect.

With Darius right on my heels, I went in a café called the Bean and Brew, dropped my bag on a couch, and went to the counter. I studied my choices and ordered my old standard—café latte. The coffee shop wasn't busy, and my drink was ready quickly. I carried it back to the couch where I'd left my laptop as the door to the café opened.

I stopped dead in my tracks, staring at the man who walked in. I heard someone—probably me—emit a small cry and then I felt hot liquid splash on my feet. The mug I'd been holding smashed on the floor. Jace was standing in front of me.

EIGHT

Seeing Jace's face again, seeing him live and in the flesh, sucked the air right out of me. I gripped the back of a chair for support and struggled to gasp in a breath. My whole body shook, and my knees felt like they were about to give out. I had to lean heavily on the chair to stay upright.

Of course, I knew it wasn't Jace. He was dead. I'd seen his lifeless body on the table at the morgue in Hawaii and then I'd buried him outside of Atherton. This wasn't my husband. Of course it wasn't. And there was only one other person who looked this much like Jace: his brother.

"Jeremy," I stuttered.

He looked as shocked to see me as I was to see him. "Cat?"

I nodded, blown away by how much his voice sounded like Jace's. I heard that voice in my dream this morning—or a version of it—but it had been so long since I'd heard it for real. So long since I'd seen Jeremy, not since…I didn't want to remember that.

I didn't know what to do. Part of me wanted to hug him and another part just wanted to run. Jace and Jeremy weren't twins. Jeremy was almost a year younger than Jace, the same age as me, but the resemblance was striking. I remembered remarking on it the first time I met him. I tried to focus on the little differences between the two brothers now. Jeremy's hair had always been darker than Jace's and his eyes were a little closer set. He didn't have the surfer tan Jace always sported, and though he and Jace shared many of the same expressions, the one on his face now wasn't one of Jace's. I thought of it as Jeremy's smug look.

"What are you doing here, Cat?" Jeremy asked, stepping closer. Clearly, he could see I was shocked, but he wasn't going to give me any room.

"I…"

"God, it's good to see you, babe." Jeremy pulled me into his chest in a warm embrace. I had two options: I could push out of his arms and make an excuse to go, or I could let it happen. I could go with it and take a step back into the world I once knew.

Yesterday I probably would have made a beeline to the exit, run right back to Casa di Rosabela, and told William everything. But William wasn't there waiting for me and I didn't know where the hell he was. I was confused and in desperate need of a friend. Right now, Jeremy felt like home.

"Do you want to sit outside and have a cup of coffee?" I asked.

"Sure." He nodded to the one I'd dropped on the floor. "Let me get you another. Latte, right?"

"Right."

He moved to the counter, and with a mumbled apology to the barista cleaning up my mess, I moved outside and sat at a table in the sun. I shouldn't be with Jeremy right now. If Beckett knew, he'd tell me to get the hell out of here.

And he'd be right.

But I couldn't stop thinking about the way William was behaving. He'd completely ditched me for basically three days in a row, and I didn't understand why. I'd felt closer to him these past few days and, sexually, we couldn't get any hotter. Whatever distance was between us now was all his doing, for reasons he refused to tell me. And it hurt. It wasn't as though he could throw stones. He was probably sipping coffee with Anya Pierce right now.

I hadn't wanted to come back to Northern California—for good reason—but I'd done it because William asked me to, because he said he needed me. But ever since we stepped foot off his plane on Sunday night, he hadn't seemed to need me at all. And now I was in the exact situation I most feared, without any backup.

I looked through the glass of the coffee house window and saw Jeremy heading my way, cups of coffee in both hands. *I can handle this*, I told myself. My relationship with Jeremy might be weighted down by a ton of baggage—by things I wasn't proud of—but if I steered us clear of difficult topics, we could both get through this. Maybe it would even be pleasant.

"Latte," Jeremy said, handing me a cup and taking the chair opposite mine. "So what are you doing back here? I thought you moved to Chicago."

I sipped the latte, giving myself time to think of an answer. "I did. I've only been here a few days. I came with a friend who was unexpectedly called away on business. I'm still living in Chicago." My gaze strayed across the street to where Darius was stationed. He was making no secret of the fact he was watching me. As I stared at him, he lifted his cell and spoke into it. So he wasn't only a babysitter, but an informant too.

I wondered what Darius was saying—and to whom. That I was having coffee with an attractive man? William probably wouldn't be happy to hear that. Good. Maybe he'd wonder what I was up to for a change.

"Good time to visit," Jeremy said. "I bet the weather in Chicago sucks right now."

"Yeah, it's pretty cold. It's taken some getting used to." I was surprised Jeremy didn't try to press me for more details, though I wouldn't have offered any if he had. I wasn't ready to make my relationship with William—whatever the state of it was—public knowledge, especially not to Jeremy. He didn't need to know what I was doing here. Hell, right now I didn't even know what I was doing here.

"How are you?" I asked.

Jeremy's whole face brightened. "I'm great! I graduated from law school last summer, and I'm engaged."

"Really? That's terrific. Congratulations. Anyone I know?"

"Nah." He shook his head and sipped his espresso. "Her name is Amy, and we met at Stanford. She's a lawyer too, but she works for the state in child advocacy."

I nodded, a little surprised by his enthusiasm. I might not want to share the details of my life, but Jeremy was happy to tell me everything.

"The wedding is at the end of June," Jeremy revealed. "We thought we might do it at the beach, but we haven't decided yet. Amy is kind of freaking out because she says it's getting late. Guess you gotta book wedding stuff way far in advance."

I didn't want to talk about weddings with the guy who had been one of the only witnesses to mine. "So where are you working?"

"With Dad's firm in San Francisco. Corporate law, which pays well, but the work weeks are brutal. I'm only out of the office today because I'm up here meeting a client. I'm talking ninety-hour weeks, and…"

I realized I was just watching Jeremy talk and not listening to his words at all. It was hard not to stare at this man who looked so much like the man I'd married, so much like the man I'd thought I would share my life with. I remembered Jace so clearly. My heart clenched when Jeremy twisted his mouth in just the way Jace used to.

But Jeremy wasn't Jace and I tried to focus on his eyes and his hair. Those were different, weren't they? Maybe I was I just manufacturing differences to keep my heart from breaking at seeing Jace's look-alike. After three years, I wasn't sure how well I really remembered the details of Jace's face. A picture was one thing, but in the flesh, he and Jeremy had been so alike.

Their voices might have been eerily similar, but Jeremy was rattling on about mergers and liquidation of assets and Jace never would have talked about something like that. He would have rolled his eyes and pretended to fall asleep. Not very mature, but—

"Hey, Cat, I want to apologize for my mom."

My eyes snapped to Jeremy's, and I stiffened. I did *not* want to talk about Jace's parents. "Jeremy—"

He held up a hand. "She was awful to you. I know that and she knows that now. She tried to reach out to you."

I pressed my lips together.

"Obviously, she didn't succeed," Jeremy said, reading my expression.

Hell, no, she didn't succeed. I would never forget how she'd stood over my hospital bed in Hawaii, pointing her bony finger at me and screaming, "You killed my son. You killed my Jace."

Mr. Ryder had to drag his distraught wife out of the room. That was just the first episode of her awfulness after the car accident that had killed Jace. There had been others, several of them in fact, and the Ryders were one of the reasons I didn't want to come back to California, with or without William. I didn't want to face them or the ghosts of my past and then wallow in all the grief and misery again. I'd been there, done that, and I'd escaped.

I caught a movement out of the corner of my eye and saw that Darius was off his phone and facing me, arms across his broad chest. I couldn't see his eyes behind his sunglasses, but everything about his stance indicated he was not happy. I felt as though I was a teenager again, doing something I shouldn't. But I wasn't doing anything wrong. I hadn't done anything wrong, and I was tired of being shut out. I wanted out of here. I wanted to go back to Chicago, where I was Catherine Kelly, where I'd made a new life for myself.

"So I just wanted to apologize for everything, Cat. I know it wasn't right," Jeremy continued. "My mother is sorry too. Hey, I have to head back to the city, but it was good catching up with you." He rose.

"Wait."

He paused, looking down at me, and I heard myself say, "I know this is asking a lot, but since you're heading back to the city, do you think you could drop me at SFO?"

"Now?" His brow wrinkled.

"Yeah. Um…" I had to think fast. This wasn't something I'd planned, but as soon as I said it, I couldn't wait to leave. "I'm booked on a flight tonight, but I thought if you drove me, we'd have more time to talk, to catch up. I was going to take a cab, but…"

"Sure. No problem, but what about your luggage?"

"I…have it right here." I gestured to my purse, computer, and camera bags. Those were all I cared about anyway. I could leave the rest.

"In that case, let's go."

I hefted my bags onto my shoulder and followed Jeremy to a blue Prius parked in front of the coffee shop. I was in and Jeremy had the car started before Darius made it across the street. I watched in the side mirror as he pulled his phone out of his jacket and angrily punched the screen with a finger. Then I leaned back, rested my head on the seat, and smiled. It had been easier than I thought to ditch him.

"So what did you want to talk about?" Jeremy asked.

Shit. It was a 90-minute drive to San Francisco. I didn't want to talk about the accident, and I didn't want to talk about William Lambourne. I needed to keep it light.

"You know what I was thinking about?" I said, forcing a smile. "You mentioned Stanford. Remember the first time I met you?"

"When you and Jace came up for the Stanford-Cal game?"

"Yeah. Jace and I had only been together for a few weeks," I said as we passed the last of St. Helena's buildings. It was a small town, quickly left behind, and then we were on our way to San Francisco. I'd really done it. I'd really just left William. I thought I'd feel relieved, but instead I felt incredibly sad.

"I remember thinking he had it bad. Every time he looked at you, he got this look in his eyes."

"Really?" I'd heard this story so many times and I knew Jeremy had too, but we were both looking for things to talk about to fill the time and Jace was our common denominator.

I didn't remember any look, but Jace and I had started dating my freshman year at UC Santa Cruz. He was a sophomore and, with his blond hair and big smile, he was irresistible.

"You weren't his usual type at all. You were this sweet, beautiful hippie girl. Really mellow."

"Sweet? Hardly. Remember the parties after the game?"

He laughed. "Well, you did match my frat brothers shot for shot of tequila."

"See? Not so sweet. I think I passed out in your dorm room. You were lucky I didn't puke." We both laughed at that.

I stared out the window at the rolling fields and hills of Napa, but in my mind I saw Jace and all the fun we'd had together that year. Jeremy and I reminisced about a few other parties and friends we'd both lost touch with, and then the conversation turned to when Jace dropped out of college at the end of his junior year.

"My parents were so pissed," Jeremy said. "I don't think they've ever gotten over it. But hey, not every surfer is offered a spot on the ASP World Tour. What was he supposed to do, say no?"

"It was his dream," I agreed. Jeremy had always supported Jace. I remembered that now. He'd been Jace's biggest advocate with his parents, and I had to give him credit for that. He'd been a good brother.

"And my dad never said it, but I know he was proud of him. For standing up to them, for doing what he wanted."

I nodded. "I think Jace knew that too." Neither of us mentioned Mrs. Ryder. Both of Jace's parents were pieces of work. Mr. Ryder had been, and still was, a successful corporate lawyer. The kind of guy who went after the jugular. She was icy cool. She'd been born into the upper echelons of San Francisco society and never let anyone forget it. She sat on charity boards and hosted events, and beneath her gracious demeanor, she was a complete and total bitch. When Jace dropped out, she threw a fit. No son of hers was going to be a college drop-out. She had plans for her eldest, and they didn't include the pro-surfing circuit or a hippy, artsy girlfriend.

She'd hated me, and our relationship didn't improve even when Jace and I got married. I was his wife, but she still thought I was just a phase Jace was going through.

I remembered when the Ryders came to San Diego for Jace's first tour outing at Trestles. I'd just been his girlfriend then, so it was pretty easy for them to be civil but basically ignore me—not that Carolyn Ryder ever treated me civilly, and she always did her best to ignore me, even after I was her daughter-in-law.

"Oh my God, remember when your dad gave Jace that shark tooth necklace at Trestles?" I hadn't thought about that necklace until just now. Jace had been so nervous and he really wanted to make his parents proud. They ignored me, but Jeremy hung out with me. We'd both been there when Mr. Ryder gave Jace the hokey necklace.

"Jace loved that necklace," Jeremy said.

"Yeah, I know. He wore it in just about every competition. He thought it brought him luck." And maybe it had. But it was too bad Jace's parents couldn't have given him more than a cheap necklace. They'd left that day before his first ride to catch a flight back to San Francisco. They didn't even say goodbye. Their departure had hurt him, but I remembered Jace fingering that jagged little piece of bone dangling from its black leather cord, his dad's small gift easing some of their rejection. They never came to another of his pro events.

I couldn't believe that after all this time, I'd never thought about that necklace, not once. I had no idea what had happened to it. Did he have it in Hawaii? Was he wearing it at that last party on the beach? Was he wearing it when that red pick-up truck had crashed into us just a few hours later? I didn't know. How could I not know?

"He was so good," Jeremy said almost wistfully, snapping me back to our conversation. His eyes were on the road, but I could see his thoughts were years in the past. Mine were too. "I knew he was good, but he amazed even me."

Once Jace realized his parents weren't going to support him unless he followed their dictates for his life, he just pushed harder for what he wanted. And part of what he'd wanted was me. We got married as soon as I graduated. I knew his parents weren't going to like it, and truthfully, mine weren't thrilled when they heard about it, either. But my mom and dad came to accept it and us. But not Jace's mother. She had been a vocal opponent of our marriage, and she was pretty nasty about it. At one point she'd even accused me of getting pregnant to snare Jace. I didn't know if Jeremy ever knew about that, and I wasn't going to bring it up to him now. I'd never forget Mrs. Ryder suggesting there were other ways to deal with a pregnancy besides marriage. But I hadn't been pregnant, just in love.

"Your parents were pretty cool about you guys getting married, right?" Jeremy asked, almost reading my thoughts.

I shrugged. Compared to the Ryders, my parents were saints. It was getting harder for me to talk about this, but I managed an answer. "They were concerned. They thought I was too young, too impulsive. But they came around."

"You and Jace impulsive? I knew the first time I saw the two of you together he'd found The One. I was surprised you waited until after you graduated."

"Jace wanted me to finish." But I thought about what Jeremy said, and now that I was older, I realized my parents might have been more supportive if I'd let them in a little. They never really knew Jace or how I felt about him—how we felt about each other. Jace and I had our own private space. It was always just the two of us. Jace and Cat against the world. We had each other, and that was all we needed and all we wanted.

Of course, it hadn't lasted.

We were almost in San Francisco when I realized we'd been quiet for quite a while. I was lost in my thoughts, trying to put the pain and grief that had bubbled to the surface back into their little compartments. I glanced at Jeremy, still struck by how much he resembled Jace, and how surreal this whole encounter had been. It was as though parts of Jace were right beside me, and it made me miss him so much more. I'd made my peace with that part of my life—well, with most of it anyway—but I wasn't certain I could stare it in the face, remembering what I'd had and lost, for much longer.

The car slowed and stopped, and I blinked and stared at the airport terminal.

"Here you go," Jeremy said. "Service from Napa to San Francisco."

"Thanks, Jeremy. I really appreciate it." I gathered my bags and reached for the door. I stepped out and turned to tell Jeremy goodbye, but he wasn't in the driver's seat. He'd gotten out and was right beside me.

"Cat." He grabbed my hand and pulled me close so I could hear him over the noise of the busy airport. "We never talked about what happened between us."

Oh no. This was I wanted to avoid. I tried to pull my hand back, but Jeremy didn't let go.

"You just left, Cat."

"I know. I'm sorry. But I had to." Did we have to have this conversation now? I was still feeling raw from William's rejection and all my memories of Jace. Why had I thought I could avoid this? Stupid, stupid, stupid. Jeremy and I had a history, separate but still entwined with my history with Jace, and it was a history I never wanted to revisit. I was so dumb to think he wouldn't bring it up.

"No explanation. No goodbye. I didn't have any idea where you'd gone. I had to call your mom to find out you moved to Chicago."

"I know. I'm sorry. I'd just…I needed some distance."

"But you're back now," Jeremy said, squeezing my hand. "And I'd really like to see you again. I'd like to give us another chance."

My throat felt as though a rock had caught in it. I couldn't breathe or speak. There had never been an *us*, not really. But there had been something, and just remembering made me feel the shame and heartache all over again. I couldn't do this. Not here, not now. Not ever.

"Jeremy—" I wanted to get away. I had the urge to tear my hand from his and run. Perhaps he sensed it because he moved closer, essentially boxing me in against the car.

"I know I'm getting married, but Amy…" He waved a hand, dismissing his fiancée. His eyes, so much like Jace's, met mine. "Amy isn't you, Cat. No one else is you."

I shook my head. "I have a different life now, Jeremy. Everything is different. Everything." I placed a hand on his chest and pushed him back. "I have to go, okay?"

"Cat!"

But I pushed past him and headed for the doors to the ticket counters. "I'll call you," I yelled over my shoulder. "I have to go."

I strode into the terminal without looking back. I didn't know if Jeremy was still standing beside his car or if he'd driven off. I didn't care. I waited in line at the ticket counter, my cell in hand. I kept waiting for a text or a call from William, but there was nothing.

Finally, I reached the counter. Lucky me, I could hop on a flight to Chicago leaving in two hours. I was ready to pay the full fare and was handing over my credit card when the smiling blond who was manning the ticket counter was flagged over to take a phone call. I watched as she picked up the receiver of the wall phone mounted just a few feet from her computer terminal. She nodded, then looked at me, then nodded again. I was just standing there, waiting, but her conversation seemed to go on forever. More nodding, more looking over at me. Did I look like a terrorist or something? Maybe it was because I was traveling one-way and didn't have any luggage to check. I waited and watched as her phone conversation continued. I didn't understand why this was taking so long. Then I overheard her say, "Yes, sir. I understand, sir. No, I think she's fine. Alright. Goodbye."

I had no idea what that was all about or if it had anything to do with me and at this point, I really didn't care. I just wanted to go home. Once she was back in front of me, I handed her my credit card and she processed my ticket. "Have a nice flight, Miss Kelly," she said as she handed me my ticket. "You're at Gate 32."

"Thanks," I said, grabbing my bags and purse and walking away.

When I got past security, I checked my phone again. Nothing. No voicemail, email, or texts from William. It had been two days since I'd spoken with him. Two whole days with absolutely no communication. I couldn't believe it. And then the whole thing with Jeremy. So typical. The man I wanted was MIA, and the man I hoped never to see again was begging me to be with him. I would go crazy if I thought about it anymore. I pulled my headphones from my bag and turned the music way up. I wanted to forget everything—Jeremy, William, Darius, California. I just wanted to get home.

Finally my flight boarded. I sat down and held my phone in my hand. I'd have to turn it off in a few moments. One more text to William? Something to explain where I was?

I had the feeling he already knew. William was a smart guy. He'd figure it out.

NINE

The flight was four-and-a-half hours and I wasn't nearly as comfortable on a commercial plane as I had been on William's private jet. I was exhausted and weepy, and when I went to the bathroom, I realized I'd gotten my period. The day didn't seem like it could get any worse.

I was so confused. I wasn't sure if I was happy to be heading home or sad to be leaving William. As pissed as I was at William, I knew I needed to cut him some slack because he had a lot going on right now. I was a complete mess, totally over emotional, and I kept needing to swipe tears away from my eyes. Fortunately, the passenger sitting beside me had his nose buried in the *Wall Street Journal* and didn't even look at me.

The flight attendant came by and gave me a sympathetic look. "Can I get you a drink, honey?"

"Just water, please."

She came back later to offer food, but I shook my head. I wasn't hungry, even though I hadn't eaten all day. I typically lost my appetite when I was upset. Regret filled me, leaving no room for anything else. I was so stupid to think I could spend any time with Jeremy without dealing with our past. It wasn't sharing all of our memories about Jace that bothered me. It was remembering our history after Jace.

We shouldn't have had a history after Jace. But I'd fucked up and made probably the biggest mistake of my life. I'd slept with Jeremy. *Slept* really wasn't the right word. More like I started *sleeping with* Jeremy, because it went on for a while after Jace died. When William and I first met and I resisted him, I told him I didn't do the fuck buddy thing. That was because I *had* done it—with Jeremy—and it had been a complete and total disaster.

I'd been so desperate to get out of Napa today I thought I could just pretend my and Jeremy's little fling never happened. But Jeremy hadn't forgotten, and now he was ready to pick up where we'd left off. Shame washed over me. Even though so much time had passed, I still felt that hot, dizzying emotion. Why didn't Jeremy feel it too? Why couldn't he see how much I loathed the person I'd been before I'd moved away?

I wasn't Cat Ryder anymore. I wished I could get away from her and her stupid mistakes as easily as I could jump on a plane and get away from Jeremy. I just wanted to go back to Chicago, back to my life as Catherine Kelly.

I couldn't help but wonder if that life would include William. I wasn't going to put all the blame on him for the failures of the past few days. I'd messed things up too, because I'd had the wrong expectations from the outset. I could see that now. Why did I ever think this was going to be a romantic getaway? The trip to Napa wasn't a vacation for William. He'd gone because he was being threatened. Again. He'd gone to protect his family and deal with whatever psycho was after his money now. It was never about me or us.

I should have known that. And I shouldn't have come in the first place. But I had come, and then I'd had my naïve expectations smashed. That was part of why I was so upset. Not just because William left me to take care of business or because he didn't stay in touch, but because my unrealistic hopes hadn't come to fruition. I'd been so swept up in the romance of our night at The Peninsula, so excited about being back together with William and the *I love you*s I thought were sure to come, that I'd somehow turned this trip into what I'd wanted, rather than seeing what it was.

And what it was did not look pretty. Yes, we'd had amazing sex. Really amazing sex. I looked down at my wrists, which were still sore from pulling against the handcuffs, and I felt myself stirring. All I had to do was think about William and I started to heat up. I couldn't help it. Sex was never going to be the problem between us.

Everything else on our little getaway had been the problem. I had turned jealous and whiny and wore my every insecurity on my sleeve, and I hated that I'd been like that. And William might have given good lip service to being more open with me, but his actions said otherwise. Why he thought it was perfectly acceptable to be secretive and controlling whenever he wanted and to disappear without explanation for days was beyond me. I needed to accept that this was the way he operated. I had seen it before. He wasn't going to change.

All the talk about Jace on the ride from Napa had made me remember how great it had been between my late husband and me. Why couldn't things be like that with William? The two of us against the world, fighting off the bad guys. Together. He'd asked me to trust him, but why wouldn't he trust me back?

I was glad I hadn't told William I loved him. Those words didn't come easily to me. They were precious, and right now, I didn't know if I still did love him. I didn't know if I ever could. And that made my heart shatter.

*****

It was after eleven o'clock by the time the plane landed. I was exhausted, and the weather in Chicago didn't help matters. It was cold and damp and raw outside, and I shivered as I headed out to the cab line. I was wearing just the lightweight dress and sweater I'd thrown on this morning; my winter coat was left at Casa di Rosabela. Oh well, guess I'd be doing some shopping this weekend. Luckily for me, a taxi pulled up right away.

The driver must have noticed my clothes, because as soon as I told him the address he said, "Where'd you fly in from?"

"California."

"Warmer there, I guess. You hear about the snowstorm?"

"No."

The driver was more than happy to rattle on about the coming Snowmageddon. One thing about Chicagoans: they loved to talk about predicted blizzards and past blizzards. By the time we arrived at my condo in Lincoln Park, I knew more than most weathermen about the coming storm. I paid the driver and headed upstairs. I'd seen my light on when we pulled up, so I knew Beckett was here. I was glad. I didn't want to be alone.

I opened the door and called, "Hello?"

Laird was the first to greet me, running full tilt, tail wagging furiously. I dropped my bags and gave him a hug, getting doggie slobber all over my face in the process.

Beckett raced to the door from the direction of the kitchen. I could smell something delicious baking. "Cat? Oh my God. You really came home."

"Sorry. I should have texted." I'd been too busy checking for texts from William. Still nothing. Tears filled my eyes, and Beckett's brows rose.

"I gather these tears aren't because you didn't text."

I shook my head.

Beckett pulled me to my feet. "Come on. I have chocolate."

He wasn't kidding. He'd obviously been on a baking rampage. I couldn't even see my counter for all the muffins, cupcakes, cookies, and tarts covering it. He heaped a plate with samples, poured me a glass of milk, and sat me down at the table. "Spill it." He nodded at the desserts. "And take your medicine."

I laughed, then I started crying again. It came in fits and starts, but I told Beckett most of what happened at Casa di Rosabela while he listened and compulsively checked on his creation currently in the oven.

"So how'd you get to the airport then, after you ditched the bald guy? Did you take a cab or rent a car? God, please tell me you didn't hitchhike. That would give both me and William heart attacks."

I took a deep breath. I knew I had to tell him. "I ran into Jeremy."

"What?" Beckett asked. He spun around and stared at me, looking shocked and horrified at the same time. "You have to be shitting me. Jeremy as in *Jeremy Ryder*? Your weasely once brother-in-law?"

"Yep, the one and the same."

Beckett took a seat at the breakfast bar. "No eff'ing way. I can't believe it. The stars really aligned for you, didn't they? I mean, what are the chances?" He was in shock and a part of me still couldn't believe it either.

"I went in to this coffee shop and he walked in a few minutes later. He's a lawyer now."

"Working for his asshole father?" Beckett interrupted.

"Exactly," I continued. "He said he was up there seeing a client. We sat and talked for little while. My security thug was never going to let me out of his sight and William was gone wherever, and I just wanted to come home. Jeremy was leaving to go back to the city, so I asked him for a ride and he said yes."

"Fucking Jeremy Ryder," Beckett said when I'd finished. "What's that line about gin joints?" He gave me his best Humphrey Bogart look. "Of all the coffee houses in all the world, he has to walk into yours."

"Beckett, stick to cooking. Your impressions suck."

"Now that's the Cat I know," he laughed. "Any other great revelations or was that it?"

"Pretty much. It was weird, but okay I guess." I'd tell Beckett about what Jeremy said at the airport tomorrow. I was too tired to talk anymore but I added, "It made me miss Jace."

Beckett got up, walked around the breakfast bar, and pulled me into a big bear hug. He kissed the top of my head as he held me. "I know how much you miss him, Cat, and it must have been hell to see Jeremy."

"Yeah, it was," I whispered as Beckett kept hugging me.

"It's really snowing out there now. Mind if I stay over again?"

"No, but I don't know where the sheets are for the guest bed."

He raised his brows seductively. "Honey, I haven't been sleeping in the guest bed and I'm not starting tonight. That room's a mess, by the way. Guess that means we'll have to share *your* bed. William had better watch out."

I laughed and left Beckett to clean up mixing bowls, muffin pans, and cookie sheets while I took a shower and threw on my warmest flannel pajamas. I checked my phone one last time; still nothing. I turned it off.

I felt a lot better when I climbed into bed with Beckett and Laird. The shower and comfortable clothes helped, but Beckett was also a salve. He always made me laugh, and he was the most loyal friend I had. I could trust him implicitly.

Beckett watched one of the late night shows while I stroked Laird's back. Pretty soon my eyes were closing, and Beckett turned off the TV, and we both dozed off. I loved my best friend, but I really missed William.

*****

I woke up to a winter wonderland. Beckett was never an early riser, so I quietly got out of bed, fed Laird, and then stared out my front window at the snow covering everything. I'd seen snow before, but this was my first big snowstorm in Chicago. I couldn't believe how the white extended as far as I could see. The snow sparkled in the early morning light, as yet untouched and pure, and I found myself completely enchanted.

Thank God I'd left when I did or I would have been stuck in California. I was glad to be home even if I felt a hollowness where William should have been.

William. I found my phone, pulled it out, and turned it on. Five texts and three voicemails from William. I read and listened, glad Beckett was still asleep so he couldn't see me crying again.

Catherine, where are you? I need you.

That was the text that broke my heart. His voicemails were brief. "Catherine, I'm worried about you. Are you okay? Darius said you left with an unidentified man. Are you okay? Just call me. Please."

Catherine, I can't believe you left without any word. Are you okay???

We needed to talk. That much was obvious, but I didn't want to talk right now. I wanted to think a bit more about my next move.

Plus, it was really early in California. Still, I knew what it was like to worry, so I texted back, *I'm home. I'm fine, and I'll call you later."*

I'd barely hit send when my phone buzzed. It was William. I wanted to roll my eyes. So now he couldn't wait to talk to me. I thought about not answering, but I was never the sort to play games. "Good morning, William."

"Catherine." I could hear concern and frustration in his voice. "You're okay?"

"I'm fine. And I'm home."

"I'm relieved to hear that." There was a long pause and I could hear him breathing into the phone. "You scared me."

"I understand. Really, I do. And I'm sorry, but you scared me too."

"Catherine—"

"No, listen. Two days, William. Two days without hearing from you—not a text, an email, a message in a bottle. Nothing. How was I supposed to tell you I was leaving? You just disappeared."

"I didn't disappear. And you were at my home, and you were safe."

"Safe from what?" I interrupted him.

He ignored me. "I knew where you were and that you were being looked after. That's what I wanted. That's what I needed."

"I was being looked after? Like some sort of dog?"

"That's not what I meant."

I stood and began to pace. "I don't need to be looked after. I need to be treated like someone you value. You completely shut me out and cut me off. I thought we talked about this. You said you'd change."

"How was I supposed to know I'd be called away from Napa? I had to go."

"Why?"

Silence.

"See, you're still doing it."

"Catherine." He sounded incredibly frustrated. I could imagine his fists clenched and his eyes icy blue. "I did what I thought was best. I didn't leave you alone. You were safe. You only needed to wait a little longer."

"No, William. No, I didn't need to wait. And you don't get it. It wasn't okay to leave me like that. It isn't okay to just drop off the face of the earth with no explanation. That's not what boyfriends do. Correction: that's not what *my* boyfriend does."

"What are you saying?" His voice was dark.

"I think…" My throat was suddenly dry. We'd just gotten back together, and all I wanted was to be with him. But I knew what I had to say. "We need some time apart."

"No."

"I'm not saying we break up. We just slow things down."

"No."

I ignored him. "This isn't easy for me to say. We just got back together, and I…I really want to be with you. But I think a break will do us good. We can both get our heads on straight."

"No. Absolutely not. I have no interest in taking a break—or whatever the hell you want to call it."

"I don't think you get to choose."

"The hell I don't. I'm on my way home and I want to see you ASAP."

"There's a blizzard, William. Even *you* can't fly in a blizzard."

"I'm on the jet now. We've been diverted to Omaha, but as soon as we get clearance, we're heading back. I'll see you tonight."

"I'm not going to hold my breath."

"This isn't over." Then he hung up.

I threw my phone down on the couch and buried my face in my hands. Half of me was so fucking pissed at him. Who was he to tell me I couldn't call things off? This was my relationship as much as his. He couldn't call all the shots. But as soon as I got really good and mad, I burst into tears. I didn't want it to be over. I didn't want to tell William goodbye.

God, I was a complete basket case. I was glad Beckett wasn't awake because if he saw me now he'd make me eat more dessert, and I didn't think my waistline could handle it.

Finally, I got it together, washed my face, and pulled my hair back into a ponytail. I'd dropped everything on the floor when I came in the night before, so I started unpacking. There wasn't much to put away, but I needed to charge my laptop. I brought my bag to my desk, plugged my laptop in, and noticed a stack of paper in the printer. I couldn't remember printing anything, and when I lifted the sheets, I realized they weren't mine.

Beckett had printed several copies of his résumé. He hadn't said anything about looking for a job. I put them back and finished unpacking, and when Beckett came out of the bedroom, hair sticking straight up, I brought him coffee and the résumés. "What's up? Are you applying for a job or something?"

He didn't answer right away—no whimsical quip, which was unusual—and I got a sick feeling in my stomach. I'd thought he was the one person I could always trust and believe in. "What are you not telling me?"

"It's nothing, Cat. Well, it *is* something, something that could be really big. The problem is I can't talk about it."

"Seems to be a common theme right now," I muttered.

"*Legally*, I can't talk about it. I had to sign a nondisclosure agreement and everything."

"And that includes me?"

"Yeah. But I'll be able to tell you soon, okay? You'll be the first one." He rose and put his hands on my arm. "I promise."

"Okay. Great." But it wasn't great. What the hell was going on? Now even Beckett was keeping secrets from me? We'd always shared everything.

"Look at this!" Beckett said, staring out the window. "You know what this is?"

I joined him. "Snow?"

"A snow *day*."

"What's a snow day?"

"A day when we don't do any work. We gotta go play in the snow."

It was as good an idea as any, especially given that I'd just kind of broken up with my boyfriend over the phone. I needed a distraction.

I dressed warmly and put Laird's leash on. Right before we went out, I grabbed my Leica and a few rolls of film. The three of us tromped around the neighborhood. I took pictures of the icy landscape while Laird made it his personal mission to pee on every buried fire hydrant, bush, and tree stump. Beckett and I built a snowman, made snow angels, and had a snowball fight with a couple of kids who lived across the street. We laughed at the lawn chairs that were already starting to line the streets as people began digging out and claiming parking spaces. I was glad I paid for a parking space for my Volvo, but I'd be shoveling it out soon enough too.

After lunch, we went back out and walked through Lincoln Park down to the lake. I took pictures of everything—the gunmetal grey sky with hints of sun peeking through, the snow on the frozen water, a fallen branch covered with intricate ice crystals, a pair of cross-country skiers *whooshing* quietly across the snowy drifts.

As I snapped photos, Beckett talked. Apparently, he'd seen Alec a few times while I was in Napa. "Are things getting serious?" I asked.

"Things are progressing."

I lowered my camera and gave him a look. "Progressing? What does that mean?"

"I really like him, Cat. I think—no, I *know* I'm falling for him."

I felt my frozen face break into a huge grin. "Really?"

"I might even be in love. I'm not sure yet. Is that weird? Not to know?"

"Not at all." I could definitely relate. "You'll know soon." I gave him an impulsive hug. "Beckett, I'm so happy for you. I really like Alec. I think you two will be good together."

"We are."

"I'm sorry I blabbed so long last night that you didn't get a chance to tell me about things with Alec. I've been a sucky best friend lately. It's all *Cat, this* and *Cat, that*."

"It's not every day I get to rub elbows with the girlfriends of the über-rich. I forgive you. Did you hear from William yet?"

"Yeah," I said, not holding back on the resignation in my voice. "He's on his way here. I told him even he couldn't fly in a blizzard."

Beckett looked at the sky. "It's not snowing now."

No, it wasn't.

We headed back to my condo, and though I told Beckett he could stay, he said he was anxious to get home. I sent as many of the desserts off with him as I could, and then I closed the door and leaned against it.

I needed to get ready. I wasn't certain what I was getting ready for, but I didn't want to be caught off guard. I checked my phone again. No more calls or texts from William. Presumably, his plane had been allowed to take off again, and he was on his way. Knowing him, he wouldn't call. He'd just show up.

I decided to take a long bubble bath. I wanted to warm up after all day outdoors, and I lingered until my fingers were prunes. Then I climbed out and dressed in skinny distressed jeans and a chunky ivory grandpa sweater. I took a little extra time with my make-up and hair. I had a smattering of freckles across my cheeks from my time in the sun, and I didn't want to cover them up. I dusted a light sheen of powder on my nose, happy to see I didn't look quite as pale and pasty as I had before the trip, and then slicked on some berry lip gloss.

I padded out of the bathroom, checked my phone again—still nothing—and headed to the kitchen to feed Laird. I'd taken all of three steps when the buzzer sounded.

TEN

William usually circumvented my buzzer, so there was a moment when I wondered if it was really him. But when I pushed the button, he said, "Buzz me in, Catherine."

My whole body warmed at the sound of his voice. Despite everything, I had to admit I'd missed him. I opened the door as he came to the top of the stairs, and I felt my mouth go dry. He looked so good. His face was slightly flushed, his hair mussed and curly from the damp weather. He wore a heavy black wool overcoat with a red scarf loose at the collar. He carried about six bags of groceries and the bag I'd left in California.

"William," I began. I didn't know what I was going to say, but it didn't matter. He stopped before me, dropped the groceries and my bag, and pulled me into his arms. His mouth was on mine, and he wasted no time teasing or coaxing me. He wanted nothing less than a complete surrender. His tongue filled my mouth, his lips demanding and possessive. Oh God, I wanted to be possessed. I couldn't help it. The heat I'd felt at just the sound of his voice ratcheted up a thousand degrees, and I melted into him. I pressed against his big muscled chest and my arms wrapped around his neck, pulling him closer. With a growl, he shrugged off his coat and scarf, and then smothered me with his warmth.

I never could resist William. My body betrayed me every time. But it felt so good to be held by him, to be safe in the circle of his embrace. He never kissed me the same way twice, but each kiss made my head spin and my muscles go weak. I was strong and independent, but something inside me needed the pleasure only William knew how to give me.

His tongue mated with mine in a fierce, passionate battle I knew he would win. And if he won, I won. I nipped at his lips, and he smiled, running his hands down my back as he pushed me against the doorframe and continued to take my mouth completely. I couldn't nip at him now. He kissed me deeply, and when we pulled apart, I was gasping for breath.

I realized we were still standing in the hallway, the bags at our feet, his coat and scarf in a pile next to them. "It's been three days since I've been inside you." His hand caressed my face, tracing the line of my jaw. "I've missed you, Catherine. Missed you terribly…" His voice trailed off and his hot breath landed on my neck as he trailed light kisses up toward my ear. I arched my neck to the side to give him better access and shivered with anticipation, imagining how good it would feel to wrap my legs around his waist while he thrust hard and fast into me. His erection bulged in his grey trousers. I felt it pressing against my belly and knew he wanted me. I wanted him too, though my emotions were in complete turmoil. As always, the physical connection between us overpowered anything else I was feeling.

He pulled his head back and glanced down at the shopping bags. "But we need to cook and then eat. And we have lots to talk about. You, beautiful girl, will have to wait."

I stepped back from his embrace. "You should come inside." I watched as he lifted the groceries and my bag and brought them inside.

He must have seen my frown at my luggage because he said, "I brought your clothes back, along with some of the things I picked out for you."

"So you did go back to the house?" I asked, following him to the kitchen, where he dropped the bags. He looked as though he'd come straight from a business meeting. He wore charcoal trousers and an ice blue button-down shirt, open at the collar. Somewhere along the way he'd lost his tie and suit jacket. He'd also rolled the sleeves to his elbows. My gaze flicked to his bronzed, corded forearms.

"Yes, but there was no reason for me to stay without you there." He smiled a tentative smile and ran his hands along my shoulders and arms then across my breasts. I winced and pulled back. His expression was instantly concerned. "What's wrong? Are you alright?"

I felt my face flush with heat, but not from arousal. Really, after everything we'd done and shared, I didn't know why a little biology should embarrass me. And maybe if he knew, he'd ease off the physical stuff and give me a little time to start thinking with my head again. "My breasts hurt. That's typical for me when I have my period."

"I see." He didn't blink, and his eyes never left mine. "Maybe I can find a way to make them—and you—feel better." Instead of shying away from me, his hand began to gently caress my left breast. His touch felt surprisingly good, and when he touched my other breast too, I let out a slow, ragged breath. He leaned close, and I could smell the scent of his shampoo and aftershave. His mouth dipped below my ear again, and I felt his breath on the tender skin there. He feathered hot kisses onto my skin and pressed that hard erection firmly against me.

"William…" I could hardly catch my breath. My cheeks felt hot, and I knew some of the flush in them was from embarrassment. I was wet for him, my body responding as always to his touch. I should have known William wouldn't be put off. For most guys that time of the month was a deterrent, but William didn't seem turned off in the least.

As though reading my thoughts, he said, "Your bleeding doesn't bother me. Are you uncomfortable with it?"

"I…" Was I? I had no idea. "I guess not."

"Good. Orgasms can help with cramps." He smiled down at me, and it was that charming, playful smile that always managed to slay me. I felt my heart clench in my chest, and tried not to think too hard about it. I had a suspicion I was still in love with William Maddox Lambourne.

I shook my head, trying to muster some defense. "I don't even want to know how you know that."

"All that matters is I know it to be true." He gave me a long, promising look then turned to the bags on the counter. "Let's get these unloaded and I'll tell you what's for dinner."

From the amount of food William had purchased, we were obviously cooking together and staying in for dinner. With the weather a mess, that made sense, but I still felt a stab of disappointment. If we went out, we'd have a public space as a buffer between us. Right now I felt like I could use that buffer—obviously I wasn't upset enough with him to be able to resist his kisses or caresses.

But I wasn't going to suggest we go out. I knew how much William loved to cook, and now that I saw him, saw how concerned he was about even a little wince I made, I felt guilty for leaving him in Napa. He must have been sick with worry. And he didn't need that on top of everything else that was going on. I never thought I was the kind of girl who bailed on her boyfriend during his time of need, the kind of girl who got all selfish and needy when she wasn't a guy's number one priority every second. Unfortunately, that was exactly the way I'd acted, and I regretted it now.

"So what are we having?" I asked when we were done unloading. I surveyed the wrapped meat, herbs, mushrooms, and a bottle of red wine. If I'd been a chef, I would have been able to put the ingredients together into a meal, but I had no clue. Fancy hamburgers?

"Beef bourguignon," William said. "Have you had it before?"

"Maybe…"

"It's a really simple French stew—good for a cold winter night—with beef braised in red Burgundy with garlic, onions, herbs, and mushrooms. It's delicious."

I nodded and watched as he unwrapped the ingredients and pulled out pots and pans. He poured two glasses of wine and handed one to me. I'd learned to stay out of his way when he was cooking. If I tried to help, I only amused him. "Why don't you chop the onions?" William said, indicating a cutting board and knife.

"Sure."

"You remember how?" he asked, his voice teasing.

"Yes." I started chopping, my thoughts returning, no doubt as William intended, to the night he had showed me how to chop onions at his penthouse. The blindfold and frozen grapes night. But tonight William didn't stand behind me, guiding my hands as I quartered and turned the onion. His muscled chest wasn't pressed against my back; his warm, sure hands weren't over mine on the knife.

I paused and glanced over my shoulder at him. He stood at the AGA over a large Dutch oven. Already a wonderful herby aroma scented the kitchen. William looked exhausted. Faint smudges darkened the skin under his eyes, and his shoulders slumped slightly. But even as I watched, he rolled those same shoulders and took a sip of wine. The act of cooking was relaxing him and helping to ease some of the tension between us, thank God.

I took another sip of wine, figuring it couldn't hurt. It hadn't escaped my notice that we still weren't discussing the really important issues. By the time I finished chopping and drank a second glass of wine, William had finished assembling his stew. I was warm and slightly buzzed and ready to talk. "So where were you on Monday?" I asked, leaning against the counter and playing with the rim of my all-but-empty wine glass. "And how about Tuesday? Why did you leave me alone?"

He didn't speak immediately. I saw his back straighten, but he continued stirring the big cast iron pot simmering away on the AGA.

"You haven't offered any explanation," I pointed out. "Why did you leave me alone?"

"You weren't alone, Catherine." He glanced over his shoulder. "You were at Casa di Rosabela with my staff at your service. I thought you'd enjoy it, actually. You were comfortable, your every need was seen to, and you were safe."

"Yes, safe as a bird in a cage."

He frowned at me and looked back down at the Dutch oven, lifting his spoon to stir again. "I hadn't planned to be gone more than a day, but plans don't always work out."

"I get that, but that doesn't excuse the fact that you didn't tell me any of this—not where you were, when you thought you'd be back, what was going on with the whole Wyatt situation." I stepped forward, anger surging through me. "You didn't contact me for three days, William. We talked about this, remember? No more secrets. You promised me no more secrets." I heard my voice rising, reaching an almost shrill pitch. I hated it. Not only was I the girl who'd left in his time of need, now I was the shrill nagging girlfriend.

William set down the spoon and turned slowly to face me. "I was in Canada. In the Yukon, just north of Whitehorse. I couldn't get any cell service, which was why I couldn't call or text. I'd planned to be back by Monday night, but there was heavy snow and we couldn't take off. My staff told you I was fine, and I was. I was just delayed."

Shock shuddered through me. I felt as if I'd been hit by a blast of arctic air. "Do you even hear yourself right now? Fucking unbelievable!" I had to move. Had to do something besides throw a plate at his thick skull. I stomped out of the kitchen, then turned and stomped right back in again. This was so not over.

"How can you think telling your housekeeper or your hired thug you're fine is the same as telling me? I don't work for you. I'm your girlfriend, not your employee. I'm entitled to hear from you directly."

"Catherine." He stepped toward me, but I held up a hand. I wasn't even close to finished.

"And how do you justify flying off to God-knows-where Canada without even a head's up? *Hey, Cat, going to fly to Canada tomorrow. Might not be back for dinner.* You just left. And you didn't even say goodbye. Why did you go there? Obviously it had something to do with the whole Wyatt situation, but that's a guess because you're keeping me in the dark about that too."

I stepped closer to him, inches from his face. "I care about you, William. I worry about you. Do you think I *wanted* to go to Napa? You said you needed me. You said you couldn't do it alone. I wanted to be there for you. Why couldn't you let me?" I swiped a hand across my cheek, wiping away tears. I didn't want to cry. I hated crying in front of other people, but my frustration and anger and worry had all coalesced into a hot ball in the pit of my stomach. The tears came unbidden. "Why won't you let me in?"

"Don't cry." William pulled me into his arms. "I don't want you to cry." I resisted but his arms tightened around me and I buried my face in his warm, muscular chest. I was still pissed as hell, but it felt so good to be held by him as I sobbed. This was where I felt safest—in his arms, surrounded by that musky scent that was uniquely *him,* and hearing the steady thump of the heartbeat in his chest.

The stubborn tears continued to fall, and gradually William pulled away and tipped my chin up. He used his thumb, large and masculine, to wipe the tears away. Why did everything have to be so complicated between us? We could be so good. I *knew* we could.

"You're killing me right now. I hate seeing you this upset. I'm trying, Catherine. I'm still new to this boyfriend thing. Listen, I didn't want to be away from you. You have to know that. But I'm here now, and we're together. That's what matters." He kissed me, his lips gentle and apologetic.

He was being sincere. I heard the regret in his voice. But sincerity, no matter how heartfelt, didn't change the fact that he'd done the very thing he'd said he wouldn't do. It didn't change that he frustrated me to no end. I pulled away, and I couldn't help myself. I couldn't stop myself from asking, "Was Anya with you? She's part of your team, right?"

He stiffened, his head jerking up and his eyes hardening slightly. "Anya was there. So were George, Anthony, and a few other security personnel."

I'd assumed the security detail had been with him, but hearing him say it made chills run down my spine. He'd needed that much security? That much protection? From what? And how was Anya protecting him? "I'm sure sexy Anya made the cold Yukon nights a little less frigid."

William tilted his head, wary. "What do you mean?"

"I saw the picture in the library. You two go way back, don't you?"

"We do. I met Anya in Alaska when I was nineteen. She's been a good friend to me."

Alaska. I'd had no idea. That must have been a particularly vulnerable time in his life. He'd reopened the investigation into his parents' plane crash, putting off a year of college to do so. "Is that all she is?"

"That's all she is now." His tone was careful.

I reeled back. She was a former lover. I knew it. But I wasn't prepared for the stab that went through my heart at that revelation.

"Do you really want to talk about this? Trust me, it doesn't matter now, Catherine. It was a long time ago." His voice was cold and unwavering.

"Well, I'd like to know."

He crossed his arms over his chest. "Fine, but be prepared to answer my questions as well." His eyes were icy blue, the color I thought of as his take-no-prisoners-business negotiation eyes. "Like who were you having coffee with in St. Helena, and who drove you to the airport?"

Shit. I'd known this was coming. But I'd started it, and I wasn't going to back down. "You got it. You first."

"Ask away." He gave me a curt nod.

I took a shaky breath. "Have you slept with her?"

"Yes." No hesitation. That knife in my chest twisted. For whatever reason, I was prepared to twist it more.

"Did you love her?"

"I thought I did at the time. It was as serious as a first real love affair can be, but I was nineteen." William raised a brow in challenge.

"Was she your college girlfriend or something?"

He let out a low chuckle, and I hated that he did that. "Not exactly. Anya's a few years older than me, and we didn't go to college together."

"How much older?" I wanted to know everything, no matter how painful it might be.

"She's twelve years older. I was nineteen, she was thirty-one."

I didn't quite know what to say. I was almost embarrassed by the disclosure. I hadn't thought she was that much older. She'd aged well. But more importantly, even if Anya wasn't William's first, I'd bet money she was definitely the woman who had tutored him sexually. "Couldn't you find someone your own age?" I had no idea where that had come from. It was a dumb thing to say. I was beginning to regret starting this conversation, and I dreaded William's answer.

"Age had nothing to do with it. I've always had exceptional taste in women. Anya was a wonderful teacher."

I swallowed the lump in my throat and told myself to breathe.

"I told you, don't read anything into it." He wasn't embarrassed at all—not about being involved with a woman twelve years his senior when he was barely even legal. Not about having her with him while I was stuck back in California. "Anya's family is a player in the Alaskan oil and gas industry. Her father was invaluable to me when I reopened the investigation, and I've invested in some of his companies in recent years. Anya works for her father. She's the executive vice president of global logistics and splits her time between Fairbanks and Vancouver. She travels all over the world for work and I rarely see her. And she's married and has three kids. We're friends. Nothing more."

If I had thought this conversation would make me feel better, I was way off base. I felt shittier than ever now. William, not surprisingly, had outplayed me. He'd revealed something he clearly didn't mind discussing, and now I would have to do the same. Except I did mind discussing Jeremy. I was cornered.

And I was jealous and feeling insecure. Which pissed me off. I didn't want to feel insecure, but how could I not? Anya was successful and stunning. She probably knew more about sex and seduction than I ever would. I understood what William saw in her. What man wouldn't want her? How could I possibly compare? The short answer was that I couldn't.

But cornered as I was, William wasn't about to let me slink away. "You had coffee with a man in St. Helena. Who was he?"

"So Darius *was* babysitting me! I knew it. I wouldn't even have gone into town if you hadn't left me alone for two days without any explanation." I was evading. This sort of ploy had always worked with Jace, but I had a feeling William wouldn't be so easily outmaneuvered. "Why could Darius get through to you, but I couldn't?" I challenged him. "I thought we weren't going to play games with each other."

"There was no game," he said, sweeping my smokescreen away effortlessly. "I'm trying to be honest. I didn't speak with Darius. He was able to reach my pilot via the satellite phone on the plane and leave an update with him. I wanted to know you were okay, Catherine."

I jumped in, a last ditch effort to derail him. "So that gives you the right to keep me in the dark?"

"The situation is complicated."

I snorted at that. *Complicated* was one of those catch-all words that seemed to say something but really said nothing at all.

Undeterred, William went on. "I don't want to pull you into it. The less you know, the better. Now, who was that guy?"

I sighed. There was no getting out of it. "It was Jeremy Ryder. He's my former brother-in-law."

William stared at me, not speaking. His eyes were wide, and he actually looked a little stunned.

"Don't tell me you didn't know. Darius didn't allow me out of his sight, and I know George is an expert at finding information for you." We both knew what I was referring to. We were back to those dossiers I'd found at William's penthouse. Dossiers about women William might date.

But instead of looking angry, he looked utterly deflated. "Catherine." His voice was flat, my name more a whisper than a word. "Was your meeting planned? Was it about…your husband?"

"It wasn't planned," I said, notching my chin up. "I haven't spoken to Jeremy in months, not since before I moved to Chicago. It was nice to catch up, actually. And yes, we talked about Jace." From the corner of my eye, I saw William's color pale. This wasn't what I had been expecting from him at all.

"Did he hurt you in any way?"

"No, it wasn't like that. We talked a lot about Jace, that's all. And then he gave me a ride. Why?"

William started running his hands through his hair. He looked up at me, frustration clearly evident in his eyes. "I hated that you left with him, but once I knew you were coming home, that it was what you needed, I had to let you go."

I stiffened and stopped sniveling. "What you do you mean you *knew* I was coming home and you let me go?"

"You skipped out on Darius a little too easily—and that will be handled—but my security trailed you. Once you got to the airport and they saw you run away from the man you were with, I wanted them to stop you. They ran a trace on the car and it came back registered to an Amy Mason, a lawyer in Pacific Heights. She was clean but that didn't explain the guy. She's an only child, no brothers. And no roommates. They were still trying to find some link, but by then the gate agent assured me that you looked fine—a little upset, but fine—so your ticket was issued."

I was speechless. I had forgotten who I was dealing with. William was one of the richest men in America and, apparently, that meant there were few things his money, power, and influence couldn't touch—including my apparently feeble attempt at a clean getaway. I was so out of my league here and I started to feel a little sick to my stomach.

It seemed like an eternity passed before he spoke again. "You miss him, don't you?" he asked quietly.

I didn't miss Jeremy; in fact, I hoped I'd never see Jeremy again. Then it hit me. He was asking if I missed *Jace*. He thought I was with Jeremy because of *Jace*. William thought he left me alone and I had run back to the memory of my dead husband. That he could never compete with that. Oh my God, I had made such a bigger mess of things than I even realized.

I looked up at William and he was watching me closely. My eyes locked with his, silently pleading that we just end this conversation so it would go no further. I was more ashamed than ever of my history with Jeremy and I never wanted William to know about it. He'd never forgive me for it, not now. *My* baggage was what could ruin us, just like I feared it could from the very start.

Then he started talking, softly but so earnestly it leveled me. "Catherine, I understand why you're upset, but the fact remains that you can't keep thinking the worst and running away. You shut down before you even give me a chance to explain. I know you've been through so much, and it kills me that you've gone through all that you have. But you need to trust me and to let me take care of you. I need to do that and you need that too. And I'm not going anywhere. I promise, I'll always come back. Always. I won't leave you."

Holy shit.

Neither of us spoke, the hiss of the burners the only sound in the kitchen. We were at an impasse. My body was rigid with tension and anguish, with grief and guilt, and I kept my hands wrapped around my upper arms as I stared at the floor.

"The stew has to simmer for a while," William said. "And I need to clear my head. I'm going out."

I raised my eyes and must have looked shocked because he immediately added, "I'll take Laird for a walk." Laird, who'd been lying on the floor keeping an eye on the two of us, jumped up at the sound of his name. "I enjoy the quiet after a big snow," he said, whistling for the dog. Laird followed. Even he couldn't resist William Lambourne.

I stood in the kitchen without moving. I knew William was upset. The only other time he had walked away from a discussion was when I told him I was a widow and that I knew about his family's deaths. William Lambourne was a man who didn't like surprises and that had been a huge one. He hadn't been prepared to handle it that night. But he had handled it eventually, and he was doing a much better job of handling it now than I ever could have imagined. *Holy, holy shit.* I hated fighting, and I hated that I'd, again, made him so upset he needed a break. And I hated that I had the power to really hurt him and I was already doing it without even trying.

I poured another glass of wine and sipped it, moving to the couch. Between the aromas of the food making my stomach rumble and all the thoughts swirling around in my head, I couldn't concentrate on anything and didn't try. I just sat.

A while later—it was probably an hour, but it felt like three times that—William and Laird returned. Laird greeted me with a cold nose and a furiously wagging tail. William nodded and headed into the kitchen. I followed, watching while he checked on the stew. He stirred and tasted it. "Should be ready soon."

"I'll set the table," I said. Anything to get away from the tension. The air seemed pregnant with it. I carried two plates into the dining room and stopped cold at the sight of Beckett's baking bonanza. I'd eaten my way through quite a bit last night and Beckett had taken as much as he could carry, but there was still a lot left, and it was spread out on the dining table. I consolidated the smaller treats—the cupcakes, tarts, cream puffs, and éclairs—onto one plate and set it aside. But that still left a small but untouched chocolate cake. Neither Beckett nor I had wanted to cut it last night. He'd frosted it in pink vanilla buttercream and styled it to look as though it was covered with rose petals. It was so pretty that I almost wanted to photograph it, but now I had to move it. I didn't have any more room out here, so the cake would have to go to the kitchen.

Cake in hand, I walked around the breakfast bar and spotted an empty square of counter near where William was cooking on the AGA. We'd said no more than ten words to one another since he'd returned, and I wasn't expecting him to speak. But just as I moved past him, he abruptly turned. I couldn't stop in time and smashed the cake into his expensive tailored shirt.

I gasped, and William muttered, "What the hell?"

Pink frosting and crumbled cake plopped from his shirt onto the floor, and we both burst out laughing. We couldn't have planned it if we'd tried. We'd both been in exactly the wrong place at the wrong time. "I am so sorry," I said between giggles.

"I didn't see you."

I set what was left of the cake on the counter and stared at the damage. William's hands had frosting on them, as did mine, and I grabbed two towels and handed him one, using the other to wipe my hands. He licked a finger. "This is good. Beckett's work?"

"He goes overboard when left unsupervised with the AGA," I said. I crouched down and wiped cake and frosting from the floor. Above me, William unbuttoned his shirt and tossed it on the counter. I rose, intending to throw the ruined cake into the trash, but William, now shirtless, stood in my way. My breath caught, and I stood there with cake in my hands, staring at his sculpted torso. Those four AM workouts might annoy me, but the results were evident. Every muscle of his naked chest and abs was clearly defined. His trousers were loose and hung on his hips without the shirt tucked in. I could imagine slipping my hand into the waistband and teasing him into arousal.

Instead, not really knowing what I was doing, I reached over and smeared pink frosting onto his nipple. He was cold, his nipple was hard, and I leaned forward and put my hot mouth on him, licking the pink frosting off with a swipe of my tongue. He didn't move. He didn't even seem to breathe. He stood completely still. I was too afraid to look at him, to see his reaction, but he hadn't stopped me, so I swiped frosting on his other nipple and licked that off too.

I could feel his arousal in the heat radiating off him. I saw it in his tight stance, and the way he fisted his hands at his sides. I looked up at his face and saw his eyes had turned molten grey. The color of arousal. My favorite color these days.

With my gaze locked on his, I wrote a C on the center of his chest in bright pink. It was my version of branding him. Then, licking my lips, I bent and marked him with my tongue. I lifted my hand to write the A—I could have done this all evening—but William moved first. His hands closed on my waist and he lifted me to the counter, his mouth coming down hard on mine as he sat me down. My legs wrapped around his waist, pulling him closer, pulling his hard heat against my core.

"You're so sweet," he murmured as our mouths came together again and again. I knew he was tasting the frosting, and I rubbed my tongue along his to give him the full flavor. He groaned, and his hands on my hips tightened. His mouth turned fierce, his kisses mirroring his need for me. Slowly, deliberately, his hands moved up my body, exploring, tracing, teasing, until I was breathless and pressing my hips against his hard erection. He cupped my face, slanting his mouth over mine again and again until I was dizzy with desire.

"Damn." William pulled back, and I grasped his shoulder to keep from falling sideways. From somewhere far away I heard a buzz.

"Timer," William said.

"I knew that."

He gave me a knowing smile, and pulled me to the edge of the counter. I slid down his body until my feet landed on the floor. We stood like that for a long moment, pressed together, our gazes lasered on each other. And then he pulled away, silenced the timer, and announced that the beef bourguignon was ready.

We cleaned up then sat at the table and ate the delicious meal. It was rich and hearty—perfect, as William had said, for the cold night. We drank wine and kept our conversation casual. Clearly, the tension had passed. For the most part. I knew our disagreements were waiting just under our comfortable truce, but neither of us wanted to raise them to the surface again tonight.

I presented the plate of Beckett's creations for dessert, and William chose a chocolate éclair and a cheesecake pop. I nibbled a deep pink raspberry macaron that reminded me of the color of William's rosé in Napa, and resisted the urge to eat a cupcake.

"These are better than expected," William said, licking his fingers. "They'll be perfect."

I frowned. "Perfect for what?"

"Just perfect," he said with a shrug. By the time we'd finished cleaning up the kitchen, William was yawning. He tried to hide it, but I caught him once or twice. He must have been exhausted. Not only had he gone on a long walk and cooked a gourmet dinner, he'd just flown through a snowstorm to get here. If his plane had been diverted to Omaha, he'd probably spent the night there.

I also knew how much he hated flying, and he'd certainly had to do a lot of it the past few days. His nerves must be frayed and his body on the verge of collapse. Once again I'd been selfish. How could I not have realized how exhausted he must be? And yet, he'd come to see me. He'd cooked me dinner. He'd put me first.

I took his hand and led him to the bedroom, crawling into bed after him. He spooned me and nuzzled my neck. He was clearly willing to make the effort, and I was tempted to let him, but I knew he needed sleep more than sex. A moment later, his breathing grew deep and regular. I lay awake for some time, safe in his arms, and trying not to read too much into the fact that this was the first time we'd slept together and not had sex.

ELEVEN

William stirred beside me, and I opened my eyes, expecting complete darkness. It was dark, but grey light filtered through the slats in the blinds. A quick glance at my phone told me it was almost six-thirty. "What happened to your four AM wake-up call?" I said with a yawn.

"You proved too great a temptation this morning," he said, nuzzling my neck.

"Good."

"Good?" His lips moved to my jaw and his hand caressed my breast.

"I love waking up with you. I keep telling you that." It was a rare occurrence and made this morning all the more special. I turned to face him, intending to kiss him lightly good morning, but he pulled me against his chest and kissed me deeply. His hand on my breast felt good as it kneaded and massaged my tender flesh.

"William," I said with regret. "I'm still on my period."

"And?" His body covered mine, and he lowered his mouth to the breast he'd been working. Gently, he drew my nipple between his lips, applying the perfect amount of pressure to leave me breathless and somewhere between pleasure and achy need.

"And..." I couldn't think with him touching me. His hands roamed over my body, and before I knew what happened, my T-shirt was gone and his hands and mouth were on my other breast. My heart slammed in my chest and the blood roared in my ears as my body responded to his efforts. I could feel my hips rising to cup his erection, could feel my sex growing swollen and wet.

Summoning my last bastion of strength, I gave him a playful push. "Stop. I have to shower and get to work." I sat and pulled my shirt back on. William lay back, watching me lazily.

"I'm heading over to Beckett's to finish up work on the Fresh for Spring campaign. We have to submit the shots we did today. Remember, crisp green asparagus stalks and snow-flocked cherries?"

"Duty calls." His eyes were a dark, unreadable grey, and I watched him warily as I rose and headed for the shower. While I waited for the water to heat up, I reflected how the tables seemed to have turned. Usually William was the one jumping out of bed and heading to the gym or some high-powered meeting. Today, he was lounging under my covers looking perfectly content. I wasn't quite sure what to make of that. I tested the water, stepped inside, and closed the curtain. The warm water cascaded over me, and then I heard the curtain open. Naked, William stepped inside.

Unlike the shower at his penthouse, mine was small and crowded. I only had one shower head, and there wasn't enough room for both of us to stand side by side. The benefit of the cramped space was that our bodies touched almost immediately. His skin was slick and hot, and I couldn't stop my hand from running along the sleek muscles of his back. He kissed me as I touched him, then reached for the body wash and squeezed some into his hands, rubbing them together until a citrus-smelling lather formed. He started with my shoulders, his hands moving in small circles, kneading my muscles and spreading slippery soap onto my skin. His fingers slid down my arms and back up. My nipples hardened in anticipation of his slippery fingers, and he didn't disappoint. His hands slid over my skin with just enough pressure to leave me wanting more.

I was warm, wet, and soapy, but he wasn't finished. William was nothing if not thorough. He filled his hands with more soap and worked on my legs, moving higher and higher until I was all but panting. His fingers caressed my inner thighs, the backs of his knuckles brushing against my sex, but he didn't give me the pressure I wanted.

"William," I begged.

"Turn around."

I turned, and he began the same thorough, mechanical washing of my back, his hands gliding over my buttocks and sliding between them until I thought I might have to force him to touch my throbbing clit.

"Shampoo," he said. I handed it to him, and he lathered my hair, his fingers working through my scalp, massaging it until I was tingling with pleasure. He turned me to face him again and angled my head back. I rinsed the shampoo out of my hair, and when I glanced back at him, his gaze was on my up-thrust breasts. "Very nice," he said. "Now, turn around again."

"The water is going to start getting cold," I told him.

"Then I'll have to make this fast."

He spun me around, and I caught my balance with one hand on the tiled wall. His hand on my lower back guided me down until I was bending at the waist, the spray of water on my back and legs keeping me warm—along with the ministrations of William's hands. They were soapy again as he stroked my ass, cupping it then reaching between my legs to massage. One finger brushed my clit, and I bucked against him. His erection was already pressed against my ass, and he guided his cock to my center as he swirled a finger over my clit. I moaned and pushed back on the hard head of his cock, feeling him enter me as his finger slid mercilessly over my swollen clit. My legs trembled, and my body shook as I felt my release build, and then I couldn't stop it. Like a tidal wave, it washed over me, crashing into me as he entered me at the peak. I slammed a fist against the wall, gasping and struggling to stay on my feet. But William's arm wrapped around my waist kept me up as he sank his cock into me and thrust fast and hard.

I braced myself against the tile, my moans and the slap of our bodies echoing in the small space. He kicked my legs farther apart and bent me lower, filling me completely. One hand remained anchored at my waist, while the other stroked my breasts. He teased an aching nipple with his fingers, circling it faster and faster as his thrusts quickened. I could feel another orgasm building, and I tried to stave it off. My legs were already shaking uncontrollably.

"Let it happen," he ordered, his voice harsh and husky. The sound of him, raw with passion, sent me over the edge. Pleasure slammed through me as the heat of his cum filled me. His hands grabbed my hips, pulling me flush with him as my body clenched and released and writhed with pleasure.

When he pulled out, my knees buckled, but William caught me. Tenderly, he cleaned me and himself, then shut off the water and dried me. I sat on the bed for several minutes, wrapped in a towel and waiting for my legs to regain their strength and my heart to stop racing. William, seemingly unaffected, dressed slowly, and I admired his body as he went through the mundane chore. Why had I ever doubted I was in love with him? I felt safe with him, complete with him, and I knew I would never get enough. I couldn't even stand, and still I wanted more of him.

I wanted to tell him how I felt. I wanted to share that with him too, whisper my love, press my heart to his, hold him. But I couldn't. Not yet.

Finally, I got up and got dressed. We left at the same time, and he gave me a toe-curling goodbye kiss at the door to my building. "Come over for dinner tonight," he said.

"Tonight?"

He put a finger on my lips. "You haven't been to the penthouse for a while and I have something I want to show you. So yes, tonight."

"Ok."

He kissed me again and was gone. I closed my eyes and sighed, the secret I carried feeling heavier than ever.

*****

I headed over to Beckett's, taking the L to Lakeview so I didn't have to dig my car out of a snowdrift and then drive on the slippery roads.

Normally I checked email on the train, but today I couldn't concentrate. I couldn't stop thinking about Jeremy and my morning with William. I almost missed my stop. At Beckett's apartment, he and I worked for most of the morning on the shots for Fresh Market. Finally, we were satisfied—and I reminded Beckett again that his "cherries in the snow" idea was positively brilliant—and we decided to take a break before going over the images one last time and hitting send. Beckett called Alec to make plans for the evening, and when he was through, he sat beside me on his couch. "Everything doesn't have to be so complicated, Cat." He set a bottle of water beside me and sipped from his own.

"Jeremy makes it complicated," I answered, clutching one of Beckett's pillows to my chest and staring out the bay window. He lived in a cute courtyard building. His one bedroom was small but he'd made great use of all the vintage features, playing them up so the style was classic but still modern and comfortable. On the wall across from me was a framed black and white of Beckett and me at high school graduation. We looked so young and fresh-faced. That was before Jace and Jeremy.

"Jeremy is a minor complication. Can't you just forget him?"

"I wish I could. But…I didn't tell you everything the other night. There's more." I then proceeded to confess all, about Jeremy and his lame apology for his mother, and then about his saying that he wanted me back. And I filled him in on my fight with William, about Anya, about William's security people secretly trailing me to the airport, and how he said I shut down and ran before I ever gave him a chance to explain himself. "And the topper was that he thinks I was intentionally with Jeremy, talking to him about Jace, because I still can't let Jace go. Like leaving me at his house for a few days upset me so much that it drove me back to being a grieving widow who couldn't get over her dead husband. And then he promised me he'd always come back and that he'd never leave me. How about that?"

Beckett just looked at me for a minute. "Seriously? He really said all of that?"

"Yeah, he did." I waited for Beckett's response, which wasn't instantaneous.

"He's totally got you pegged. I'm impressed."

"What?" I couldn't believe Beckett said that. "Shut up! He does not! It wasn't like that at all. And that's not what I am. I care about William, and I want to be with him."

"But, Cat, you told me on the phone less than an hour after you got to Napa that you weren't ready. His fabulous manse wigged you out so badly that you were about to throw in the towel then and there. And you *were* upset that he left you. That's all you've been talking about for days. How William abandoned you at his luxurious Napa Valley estate and left you all by yourself and didn't call you. Maybe you didn't seek out Jeremy to console you about Jace, but come on. You had the dream. That means something. And you were obviously scared to be alone. Not haunted house scared, but definitely not comfortable on your own. You freaked out, right? So maybe he has a point. Maybe you aren't all in."

I was speechless and didn't even know how to respond.

"Remind me again how Jeremy makes this *more* complicated?" Beckett added.

I took a deep breath. "Because I need to tell William the truth about Jeremy. I don't think it's fair to keep it from him. I can't lie to him, Beckett. Not after that, not after what he said. Besides, I don't think it would take his team much digging to figure it out, so it's just a matter of time anyway. He deserves to hear it from me."

"I don't buy that. William never had his guy investigate you, so why would he start now? Plus, you haven't played the let's-tell-each-other-our-number game—which, by the way, is *always* a game without a winner—so you're just omitting one tiny detail about Jeremy. Do you want William Lambourne telling you about all the women he's slept with? Do not start that conversation."

"Jeremy wasn't just a number. He was my brother-in-law. I should tell William." I buried my face in my hands. "And I don't know how I'm going to. It's so awful."

"Cat, it's not that awful. You were twenty-two and grief-stricken. You made a bad decision and it was just sex. Give yourself a break. People make bad decisions in crisis times. It happens. Get over it."

I sipped the water and turned the bottle in my hands, considering. "It was more than just a bad decision."

"Ok, so it was a bad decision that lasted a few months or so."

I turned the water bottle to and fro, sick at the memories assaulting me. The first time Jeremy and I hooked up was after Jace's memorial service. What kind of wife sleeps with another man on the day of her husband's funeral? Me, that's who. I'd been drunk, but that wasn't an excuse. I knew it was wrong. And not just wrong because my husband had died only days before and I had just buried him. It was wrong because Jeremy was Jace's *brother*. That was wrong on a whole other level.

It didn't take a psychoanalyst to figure out why I did it. I was out of my mind with grief and in serious denial. Jeremy looked so much like Jace, and he had so many of the same expressions and mannerisms. He was my friend, too, and the closest thing I had to my dead husband.

That first time I think I was genuinely a little confused. Jeremy had driven me home from the horrible memorial service, made all the more horrible by that fucking Mrs. Ryder, and I'd turned to him. He should have rejected me, but he didn't. We ended up in bed—in Jace's and my bed at our place by the beach—and the next day I just felt numb. Those days right after the accident were a total blur and I was exhausted and overwhelmed and so very lonely. Jeremy helped me forget, for just a little while, the horrible turn my life had taken. But that didn't last very long.

Jeremy wasn't a bad guy. I didn't think he planned to seduce me, and it hadn't been like that. He'd been hurting too, and I'd wanted to believe we were using each other for comfort. That was my justification, though even then I'd known it was weak. And I'd known it was a lie. Jeremy wasn't using me. I was using him

Alcohol was usually involved, I was often the pursuer, and the sex between us was never very good. But to me, it was better than being alone. I'd missed Jace so badly my bones hurt and the pain was made even worse by my guilt. I'd been driving the car, I'd been drinking at the beach before I got behind the wheel, I hadn't seen the pick-up truck barreling toward us until it was too late. I was the one Jace's parents and most of our friends blamed for his death. I was lucky the police didn't blame me too, but the driver of the pick-up truck, a chronic alcoholic with a long list of previous DUIs, had been drunk off his ass and the accident was deemed his fault. He too had died at the scene, which left me the only one who walked away.

Jeremy seemed pretty oblivious to just how messed up I was, and very quickly he made it clear he wanted more than sex. I think I'd always known he was interested in me. He'd always looked at me with something more than brotherly affection. It was his chance, and I couldn't blame him for taking it. I wasn't in love with Jeremy, but even that didn't stop me from sleeping with him. When I finally came to my senses and tried to break it off, it didn't go well. And then I realized I'd fucked up my relationship with the one person who truly could have given me comfort. I couldn't share my memories of Jace with my *friend with benefits*, and he was the closest person to Jace besides me. Which meant I was back to square one: totally alone in my grief.

I was so distraught and emotionally drained that I didn't have the strength to even offer Jeremy an explanation; I just stopped talking to him. I cut him out of my life like a cancer. I stayed away from him, kept my head down, and focused on trying to get myself back together. After about a year, I left Santa Cruz and moved to Chicago. Jeremy wasn't the only reason, but he was a big motivator. And, as fate would have it, Jeremy was the person I ran into in Napa. It was like the universe was having the last laugh or punishing me for the horrible way I'd acted. And even after I was such an asshole to him, Jeremy still wasn't over me. He was engaged, and he was willing to throw that away to be with me. That was its own unique torture.

"You can beat yourself up about it all over again," Beckett said, "or you can leave it in the past, where it belongs."

"Once William knows—"

"Why does William need to know? It doesn't matter anymore. I know you feel some sort of responsibility to come clean about this with William, but no good can come of that. Trust Papa Beckett on this one."

I smiled briefly. "So…what? I keep Jeremy a secret?"

"You keep one tiny aspect of your relationship with him a secret, and you move on with your life. You enjoy your rich boyfriend and his mansions and vineyards and private jets—I still cannot believe he has five. That's ridiculous."

"You're just jealous because you haven't been on one."

"Yet." Beckett raised a finger. "I have faith you'll wrangle an invitation for me. Maybe a little jaunt to…oh, I don't know…Paris?"

"Oh, sure." Beckett was right. I needed to let the whole Jeremy affair go. It was over and it didn't matter, and I should stop worrying about it.

Beckett was waxing poetic about spring in Paris when I heard my phone. I dug in my purse, pulled it out, and frowned at the number.

"No idea who this is," I murmured but answered anyway. "Hello, this is Catherine Kelly."

"Catherine Kelly," a man repeated in a sexy Southern twang. "You're exactly the woman I was trying to reach."

Beckett was looking at me expectantly, and I gave him a bewildered look. "Do I know you?" I asked.

"Not yet, but we can rectify that quick enough. This is Hutch Morrison," he drawled. "I believe my assistant called a few days ago."

"Oh my God. Yes. I am so sorry I haven't called back." I pointed to the phone and mouthed *Hutch Morrison.*

Beckett gave me a look filled with horror. "You didn't call back?" he hissed. Then he practically sat on my lap to press his ear to the phone.

"Don't worry about that now. I like a woman who plays hard to get, and I also like a woman with the kind of talent you have. I've seen your work."

"Oh, great." It was lame, but I never knew how to respond to compliments.

"Those cock kabobs for Fresh Market were inspired."

"I—" How did one respond to that sort of compliment? I looked to Beckett for help, but he was doubled over laughing.

"And your work in *Chicago Now* impressed me as well. I think you're perfect, Miss Catherine Kelly."

"Um, perfect for what?"

"That's what I'd like to meet with you about. I'm working on a little e-book project. It's what I'd call *cutting edge*. I need someone who can pull off cutting edge. I think you're the girl I want to get in bed with on this. Say you'll meet with me."

"I…um…"

"Don't turn me down and break my heart before you've even met me in person. I don't bite. Well, I don't bite very hard."

"I wouldn't dream of turning you down, Mr. Morrison."

"Mr. Morrison is my daddy. Call me Hutch."

"I'd love to meet with you, Hutch."

"Wonderful. How about next week at Morrison Hotel?"

"Great." I frowned at Beckett who had my laptop open and was furiously typing something into the browser.

"I'll have my people get with your people to arrange schedules."

"I am my people."

"See, I knew I'd like you. I'm half in love with you already. I'll see you soon, Miss Catherine."

I set the phone down and shook my head. What the hell had that been? On the computer, Beckett had pulled up an image of Hutch Morrison. It was similar to the one he'd texted me—a tattooed, muscled guy who was sexy as hell. Beckett grabbed my hand. "Tell me everything."

"He's working on a cutting edge e-book project, and he thinks I'm perfect for it."

"Of course you're perfect for it!"

"He's seen my work—the Fresh Market billboards and the spread in *Chicago Now*."

Beckett fell back on the couch. "I cannot believe this is happening. I'm so lucky!"

"You?"

"Yes! If you meet Hutch Morrison and work with him, it's just a matter of time until *I* meet Hutch Morrison, and look at the guy. He's fucking *hot*."

"What about Alec?"

"Alec will have to find his own celebrity chef crush. Hutch is all mine." Beckett gave me a serious look. "Besides it's just a crush." His fingers were flying over the keyboard again. "You have to get this job, Cat. You have to. Hutch Morrison is the shit. Look at this." He'd pulled up some sort of curriculum vitae and read the highlights. "Hutch Morrison is thirty-three, an internationally known culinary genius. Look at this." He jabbed a finger at a list of awards.

"That's impressive." I didn't know a lot about cooking, but I recognized some of the awards. James Beard, *Food & Wine*, Michelin...

Beckett was going on and on, but I couldn't help wondering if William had anything to do with Hutch Morrison's interest in me. Did WML Capital Management have a stake in Morrison Hotel? The meeting next week would definitely be interesting, and not only because Hutch Morrison was charming and sexy. I was already intrigued by the project he'd alluded to.

"Don't worry, Beckett, if I'm brought on board and they need a food stylist, I'll recommend you."

"Oh my God. I could come just thinking about it." He fell back in mock orgasm, and I shook my head. Beckett was playing around, but I knew when he was genuinely excited. If Hutch Morrison got Beckett this worked up, he was someone I wanted to collaborate with.

"Wait until I tell Alec," Beckett said, grabbing his phone.

"You'd better tone it down a little. Alec will be jealous."

"Ha! Alec will want an introduction to Hutch too. He has excellent taste."

"Obviously." I gestured to Beckett.

"And if I piss him off, I know how to win him back."

"How?"

"He has a weakness for my flourless chocolate cake."

"What's that?" I'd never had Beckett's flourless chocolate cake, and usually he tried out his new desserts on me.

"It's something new I'm working on. I use espresso in it and I infuse it with orange peel, bergamot, and just a hint of cinnamon. It's to die for."

"Why flourless? Does Alec have a gluten allergy?"

Beckett shifted and looked back at my laptop. "No, but it's good to diversify. A lot of people have allergies."

I got the feeling Beckett was evading my questions again. He was so mysterious lately. "But you don't have to cook for a lot of people."

"You're right." He waved a hand. "Let's take a last look at these photos and email them. I'm starving."

"Okay." We looked over the shots for Fresh Market one last time. They looked great, which was good, because I was still puzzling over Beckett's secretiveness. It really wasn't like him. He usually over shared.

We sent the email, and Beckett stood. "Kuma's for lunch?"

"Sure," I said. "I could go for a burger." Now that William was back in town, my appetite had returned.

TWELVE

I was standing in front of my closet trying to figure out what to wear when William texted me to remind me to bring my camera. I'd actually forgotten he'd even said I'd need it in the first place. That was the effect shower sex—and just about any other kind of sex—with William had on me. I couldn't think straight, and it made it so easy to forget everything else. Flashes of our morning ran through my head. His growling, "Let it happen" in my ear, his voice dark and choked with need as he pounded me hard from behind, had tipped me over into an orgasm that radiated all the way to my fingertips. I had been powerless to do anything but surrender to the pleasure, to his raw desire for me, and I had loved it. *That* was the feeling that was starting to become addictive and dangerous. If letting him call the shots was what it took to make me feel like that, I wanted more.

I looked down at my watch. Shit, I was going to be late. I picked an outfit, threw on some lip gloss and a spray of perfume, then packed up my best digital camera and headed outside to where Anthony waited to drive me to William's penthouse. I could have driven myself, but the roads were still icy and tonight I appreciated his thoughtfulness in providing me with his driver.

The drive down Lake Shore Drive to the Gold Coast was quick and before I knew it, I was zooming up the private elevator to

William's penthouse on the fifty-sixth floor of one of Chicago's most impressive buildings. I stepped off the elevator into his foyer, and William was waiting for me, wearing a wide smile. "There's my beautiful girl."

"Hey," I replied, feeling the edges of my mouth turn up. The heaviness from the Jeremy secret that had clung to me all day was immediately replaced by the giddy excitement of being with William. I couldn't resist him, especially when he was being charming and sweet.

He still wore his suit from work, though he'd shed the tie, and his hair was perfectly styled. I itched to run my fingers through it and mess it up just a little. As I pulled off my coat and handed it to him, I said, "I didn't know what the surprise was. I hope this is okay." I gestured to my outfit. I was back to my favorite color—I'd changed into black, cropped riding pants, a bateau-neck, black sweater with beaded sleeves and the Louboutin black stilettos William had sent me weeks ago. Underneath, I was wearing a really sexy black Bordelle pushup bra with little red bows on it and its matching thong. I found the set in the bag of clothes William had brought back from Napa, so I knew he'd picked it out.

He strode toward me and pulled me flush against him. I tingled all over as I made contact with his big, hard body. "You look perfect, Catherine," his voice vibrated through me as his hot, warm breath tickled at my throat. "You smell good too." He took my hand, then frowned at it. "Except you're cold. Didn't you wear your gloves?"

"I…"

"Never mind. I already know you forgot them." He rubbed my hands in his, stepped back from our embrace, and led me into the penthouse. "We're in for a special treat tonight. A friend from Japan is in town and he just happens to be a renowned sushi master. He's made dinner for us."

I looked up at him. His eyes were shining and he still wore that unapologetic grin. I could tell he was really excited about this and sushi *was* one of my favorite foods. "Really? That's fabulous! Is that the surprise?"

"Part of it." He paused in the living room and gestured to the wall above the fireplace. I couldn't remember what had been there before, but what I saw now made me inhale sharply. "This is another part. Look what I found."

I stared in stunned silence at the large black and white print hanging on the wall. It was of a lone surfer executing a cutback on a massive wave, a maneuver that meant he was actually riding up the wave. It was one of mine.

"Wow," I said quietly. "This *is* a surprise."

I hadn't seen the print in years, and I thanked God it wasn't a shot I'd taken of Jace. That would have been beyond awkward. The surfer in the picture was a guy named Ian who had just been an acquaintance. The day I'd shot it, I'd taken a break from classes and headed out on the water with my board and equipment for some practice, as I'd still been getting used to balancing the heavy rigging that held my camera. Ian had happened to be the only other surfer out there and had become my subject by coincidence. He wasn't a great surfer, but every surfer has a day when each wave breaks perfectly, and that had been Ian's day. I'd been fortunate to capture it.

I tried to stay cool, but the collision of my past and present was so jarring, especially with the whole Jeremy issue so fresh in my mind. "This was one of the pieces in my final portfolio my senior year," I told William. "Then it was in the first show of my work and it sold for twice what I thought it would."

"I'm sure I paid several times that," he answered, smiling with his gaze still on the photo.

I looked back at the image. Right after I'd graduated, a real gallery in Santa Cruz had picked me up and sold all my prints. Jace and I had used the money to help with travel expenses after our wedding, when I'd joined him on tour. I wondered what William would think if he knew those details.

A moment later William held out a glass of white wine to me. I hadn't even realized he'd stepped away to pour it. "Thank you," I said as I took the glass.

"With Japanese food, I like the wine to be a background note so the ingredients take center stage."

I'd almost forgotten about the dinner to come, and I nodded and sipped. The wine was very good, cool and sweet with hints of pear. I wanted to slam the whole glass and then about three more just to steady my nerves, but I sipped instead.

"The idea is to cleanse your palate so you can better focus on the complex tastes."

I sipped again, focused on palate cleansing, and kept a tight smile on my face. "What is this? Is it one of yours?"

William was watching me closely, like he was trying to gauge if showing me the print had been a good idea or not. "No, it's French. A Chenin Blanc. It's crisp and lean, and I thought it would be a great match for Junzo's dishes."

"Yes," I answered absently. I couldn't stop looking at the image on the wall. I shuddered a little when I remembered that I'd shot it at Pleasure Point, the spot in Santa Cruz Jace and I had surfed all the time. It was also the locale of the bad dream that had woke me up in a cold sweat in Napa. I hadn't told William about the dream yet.

"You have an amazing eye, Catherine," he said, bringing me back to the present. "I wanted the print because it was yours, but I also wanted it because it's really good. Exceptional. You know that, don't you? You're very talented."

That snapped me back to the moment. I felt my cheeks heat as a blush bloomed in them. I really did need to learn to take a compliment. And I did know I was a good photographer. I would have known it even if two extremely hot men hadn't told me so today. First Hutch Morrison and now William Lambourne.

"Where did you find it?" I asked, trying to draw his attention away from my pink cheeks.

"My art consultant found it actually, in a gallery in Santa Rosa. I've been looking to build my contemporary photography holdings, and she's helping with that." He took another drink of his wine.

"When I saw it, I asked about it, and when I realized you were the photographer, I had to have it."

I was flattered. How could I not be when my work was taking center stage on the living-room wall of a billionaire who had pieces from his personal collection on loan to The Art Institute? But I was still uneasy seeing it here. No matter how firmly I put my life in Santa Cruz in the past, it continued to creep into my present. I was in my new boyfriend's penthouse, and here was a photograph connected directly to the life I'd left behind. Was I supposed to thank William for buying it? Should I tell him how weird it made me feel? I didn't want to hurt his feelings, but I really wasn't sure how to respond.

"Oh, I almost forgot," he said. "My aunt has invited us to dinner on Sunday. Would you like to go?"

"Yes!" I said with honest enthusiasm. I forgot the print for a moment and smiled. "I'd love to."

"Good. I was hoping you'd say yes."

Why wouldn't I? I'd been waiting for an opportunity to see William with his family, in a setting where he was more than just the business mogul. I'd met his aunt and uncle and two of his cousins briefly that night at The Peninsula, but I really wanted the opportunity to get to know them a little better. This was also one way I could get to know William better. I wanted to see how he was around the family who'd taken him in, loved him, and raised him to adulthood.

Just then a small Japanese woman entered the living room and bowed formally. She wore a dark red, embroidered kimono and her long black hair pulled into a bun. Despite her traditional dress and slow, deliberate movements, she was young, maybe just a few years older than me. "Dinner is served," she said in heavily accented English. I guessed she was part of the chef's entourage.

"Thank you, Midori." William gestured for me to follow Midori down the hallway to the dining room. No more talk about the print, thank God. Before I could move, he said, "Did you bring your camera?"

"Yes." I pointed to my bag sitting on a chair.

"Good. Grab it. You'll need it."

I had never been in William's dining room before, and it was very much in the style of the rest of the penthouse—stark, modern, minimalist, and imposing. It almost made me miss the accessible warm luxury of Casa di Rosabela. The ceilings soared, and several large and amazing pieces of art hung on the tall walls. The lights were low, keeping the room from resembling a gallery, and I might have moved closer to study the paintings and the large black sculpture that sat on a pedestal in a corner if I hadn't been riveted by the dining room table.

The enormous stone table could have easily sat twelve, but only two chairs, placed next to each other, were present. On the table were two women. Initially I thought the food had been arranged so as to give the impression of a woman's body, but as my eyes adjusted to the light, I realized two live women lay side-by-side, head to foot. One lay on her back and the other on her stomach. Both were totally nude except for the sushi, sashimi, and other delicacies that decorated their bodies.

In all the time I'd been photographing food, I'd never seen anything like this, a display that paired the beauty of food so unabashedly with the raw carnality of sex. The women were stunningly beautiful and the symmetry of their perfect bodies was adroitly complemented by the placement of the colorful food. There was so much to take in—the rolls, the fat salmon- and tuna-draped fingers of rice drizzled and adorned with pops of brightness from avocado and shaved ginger and fish eggs—the whole scene was both visually stunning and beautifully balanced. And sensual. The food had not been displayed to hide the beauty of the women's bodies. Everything—*everything*—was on full display.

I couldn't look at William. I stood stock still, took a deep breath, and kept my eyes glued to the table. After the handcuffs and the blindfolding and the dominance he was showing of late, I didn't quite know what to expect here. I detected the lure of a darker sexuality and my heart quickened in response, but I prayed he didn't have some kind of kinky group thing in mind. I wasn't ready to go *there*. And why had he asked me to bring my camera?

He must have sensed my uncertainty because I felt his large strong hand on the small of my back. Gently, he guided me forward, leaning down and whispering, "It's incredible, isn't it?"

I nodded, and my head felt as though it was attached to marionette strings. He kept his warm hand on my back and moved it in small circles. "It's an art form, Catherine." His breath was hot on my ear, his lips almost brushing my skin. "It's called *nyotaimori*."

I repeated the word in my mind, liking the sound of it. As I was propelled into the room, I noticed an older Japanese man in a black chef uniform standing at the far end of the table. Midori was standing by his side, and William stepped away from me and approached the couple. The chef bowed and William bowed back. They exchanged a few words I didn't quite understand and then both men broke into wide smiles. I realized William had spoken to the chef in Japanese—I could add that to the growing list of his accomplishments.

William beckoned me to come closer and then he wrapped his arm around my shoulder and pulled me to him. It felt so weird to be standing here normally, as if two naked women weren't lying on the table right in front of us, but his touch was reassuring. I needed to follow his lead.

The chef, whose name was Junzo, and Midori bowed and smiled, and I bowed in return. Then Junzo began to speak. He gestured to Midori to translate, and she started to speak in a soft voice.

"Chef Junzo says that *nyotaimori* is about beauty. The beauty of woman and the beauty of food, together in perfect harmony."

I kept my gaze on her as she gestured and spoke of the women as though they weren't there.

"In traditional *nyotaimori*, the model trains many hours. She learns how to remain absolutely still and to tolerate the coldness of the food. Before performing, her body is specially prepared so she may serve as a plate for this feast."

I turned to study the table again. The women had not moved since we entered the room. Both were lean and small breasted and completely shaved. Their eyes were open, but their faces were expressionless. The closer I looked, the more my artist's eye saw the careful artistry in the presentation. The woman on her back had a line of alternating orange and green rolls from her navel to her smooth mound. The woman on her stomach had several pieces of nigiri-sushi nestled in the small of her back and then trailing up the curve of her buttocks. "*Nyotaimori* is meant to be the highest compliment to woman. Only nature's most beautiful creature can breathe life into the dishes created to honor her. The warmth of her body perfectly warms the cold fish, allowing its ideal taste and texture to be revealed. This state cannot exist without woman. Woman makes perfection."

I began to understand and, as I kept looking at the beauty of the women with the colorful sushi, the eroticism of William's surprise dinner started to affect me. My fingers ached to grab my camera and capture the way the exquisitely prepared food caressed the curve of the woman's hip, the slope of her breast, and the taut point of her nipple, but I ached to grab William too. I was starting to get turned on. Very turned on.

I realized no one had spoken for several minutes, and I glanced at William. His gaze was on me, his eyes twinkling. Obviously, he was enjoying watching me appreciate his surprise and seeing what it was doing to me. He knew. By some unspoken signal, Midori and Junzo exited. I felt William's arm come around my waist, and he pulled me close into the warmth of his body. "Isn't it gorgeous? I knew you would appreciate the visual presentation, which is why I asked you to bring your camera." He bent down and kissed me softly, urging my lips apart with his tongue while his hand began to gently knead my breast. I moaned quietly into his mouth as I kissed him back, arching into his hand.

"It's stunning," I said as I pulled back from his lips. I was excited now for so many reasons. "Do you mind if take some—"

"That's exactly what I'd like you to do," he answered before I could finish.

I set my bag down and withdrew my camera. I needed to photograph this. William continued to talk as I prepped my digital to accommodate the dim light.

"Junzo is a *shokunin*, a traditional master sushi chef, and perhaps the most famous one in Japan. He's in his seventies now, and Midori is his daughter."

I glanced up at him. I hadn't realized Midori was the chef's daughter. Was this a tradition he was passing on to her?

"Sushi chefs are heirs to the samurai tradition."

Maybe I should have read *Shogun* before coming. I didn't know much about samurai other than they were warriors. William continued to talk, his voice warm and velvety.

"They value scholarship and have unshakable self-discipline. A sushi chef's knives are as important to him as a sword was to a samurai. Junzo's knives are legendary. I've heard it said that they're sharp enough to literally split a hair."

I glanced at the table again, wondering at the skill of a man who could wield such a dangerous knife to create such beauty. A warrior who carved art from shrimp and yellowtail and soft shelled crab, and then draped it so sensually over women's privates.

"I wanted you to experience this, Catherine. As an artist and food photographer, you'd appreciate it, I knew. Plus, it's undeniably sexy and that's something we can both appreciate." His eyes were a hot and hungry grey as he looked at me, the unmistakable color of arousal that I'd come to know so well. The heady sensuality of this private dinner was getting to him too. I gave him a knowing smile.

I took a few test photos to gauge the light, and then I began to shoot. I wanted to focus on the curves and angles—the way a long, lean thigh was accented by Junzo's culinary mastery; the way a feminine back dipped into a valley before rising to a plump buttocks, four perfect sushi rolls nestled neatly in that arc. For some time I was completely absorbed. It may have been minutes or even a quarter of an hour. Then I became aware of William watching me, studying me like I was studying the models and the food. His eyes were dark and stormy, his lips slightly parted.

He rose and stood by my side, his hand on my hip. He was warm in the cool room, and I welcomed his heat. "You can get closer," he murmured. "No need to stand apart like an observer. You can touch." His hand slid up my back. "And taste."

I shivered at the promise in his tone. He lifted a pair of chopsticks from the table and, with perfect form, picked up a sushi roll from the small of the woman's back. "I think this is crab with daikon radish." I watched as he opened his mouth wide and slid the round roll inside, closing his lips and his eyes, obviously savoring the taste. He swallowed. "I've ruined your symmetry now," he said, his mouth back at my ear. And he had, as he'd taken the roll from the center, which left a gap in what had been a perfect line. "But I want you to notice something else."

I lifted my camera and angled it on the woman's back.

"She hasn't moved, but she can't control every response. Do you see how her skin pebbles where the cold roll has been removed?" His hand caressed my arm, encouraging me to move closer. "Warmth floods her skin and makes the chill of the other rolls that much more noticeable."

I shivered from the caress of his breath on my neck. I snapped several shots, pausing when I felt his hand, light and teasing, on the small of my back—on the same spot where he had removed the sushi roll on the model.

"I don't enjoy eating alone," he said, approaching the table again. I watched, almost breathless, to see which of the delectable choices he would pick for me. His hand hovered over the thigh of the model who lay on her back and then he moved up and up to her taut abdomen, adorned with perfectly round rolls of bright orange surrounding a bed of white flecked with green. He didn't touch her and his hand wasn't even close to her skin, but through the lens of my camera, I saw the way she tensed almost imperceptibly. My own body tensed as well. I knew what it would feel like if William touched me there. I could imagine it, and I felt heat flooding between my legs in anticipation.

Finally, he lifted a roll from her belly, and I snapped a shot that captured the subtle surge of pink that flooded her skin as the roll was removed.

"It's a salmon roll, with *unagi* and *tamago*. Taste," William said, his hand cupping the nape of my neck. I lowered my camera, opened my mouth, and allowed him to feed me. It all but fell apart in my mouth as the sweet flavors of the salmon and eel, balanced by the tang of the rice, exploded across my tongue.

When I opened my eyes, William was watching me. He arched a brow. "Delicious," I said. "Much better than the California rolls I get at Whole Foods."

He gave me a chastising look. "Sushi is much better if you don't buy it from the grocery store."

I smiled. "I bet they'd sell more if they displayed it this way."

He laughed. "Undoubtedly, but then someone might get arrested." He handed me my glass of wine, and we both drank. "Here, let's try the sashimi next."

Paper thin slices of fish had been arranged into a delicate rose that covered one breast on the model lying face up. Using chopsticks this time, William lifted one petal, revealing a sliver of skin beneath. He dipped the tuna in a wasabi sauce and brought it to my mouth. I opened for him, tasting the smooth, silky flavor of the tuna along with the heat of the wasabi. The tuna was slightly warm from the model's body, but still cold enough that I could imagine how it must have felt against her delicate skin. I felt a drip of the wasabi on my lip, but before I could lick it away, William's thumb brushed against it. He licked his thumb, taking the bead of sauce into his mouth. "My turn," he said. He turned and lifted another petal of fish from the model's breast, this time revealing her nipple.

I lifted my camera, intrigued by the image of the nipple within the rose. "Watch how her nipple hardens and tightens," William whispered from behind me. His arms came around me, and his hands held me lightly at the waist. I felt the heat of his body and the hardness of his chest pressing against my back. "It reminds me of someone else I know, right before she's going to come," he whispered in my ear.

I felt my own nipples tighten and harden, pushing against the silk of my bra.

"I imagine it would be extremely sensitive to touch right now," he continued, speaking so low only I could hear. "If I put my warm mouth on that cold, hard nipple, how do you think it would feel?"

"Incredible," I murmured. I took shot after shot with my camera, but I really had no idea what I was shooting. I was dizzy with arousal.

"Are you still hungry?" he asked, his fingers on my waist spreading. He didn't touch my breasts, but I knew his fingers were close, inches below my aching flesh. I wanted him to touch me, and I watched breathlessly as he moved away, lifted the wine glasses, and held mine to my lips. I was drunk, but not on the wine. I was drunk on him, on the way he teased me into desire, on the pleasure I knew he could give me if I would only surrender to it again. My eyes strayed to the women on the table. They seemed like a symbol of the surrender William wanted, but theirs was a cold, emotionless surrender; mine would be hot and explosive.

William set the glasses aside, lifted the chopsticks, and removed a piece of maki with a plump piece of tempura shrimp bursting from it. He dipped it gently in soy sauce before tilting my chin up and feeding it to me. The fish eggs popped in my mouth and the shrimp was crunchy and salty and delicious. His hand slid from my chin to the nape of my neck. "Still hungry?"

"Yes," I murmured, my voice low and husky. "But not for sushi."

"What do you want?"

"You."

His hand on my neck tightened, and he pulled me against him. My hard nipples met the wall of his muscled chest, and I let out a moan before his mouth claimed mine. It was hot and spicy from the wasabi. I wrapped my hands around his back, pressing into him, feeling him meld into me. "Let's go," I murmured, breaking the kiss. "I want to see you. I want to feel you under my fingers."

I thought he would sweep me up and carry me to his bedroom. Instead, he lowered his mouth to my throat and teased my flesh with his tongue. "I'm still hungry, Catherine. And I think you are too."

I couldn't want him more than I did, and I fought a wave of longing when he pulled away. I needed his touch. I wanted his hands on me, stroking me, caressing me, sliding into my wet sex. I was so wet for him already.

He lifted his chopsticks again and they hovered over the curved ass of the model on her stomach. I could imagine his hands on my ass as he lifted my hips and guided his hard length into me. And then he shook his head and moved to the woman on her back. I realized I was holding my breath. Would he take a piece from her collarbone, her abdomen, her breast? The chopsticks moved lower, to the line of sushi that ended in her shaved pussy. "This is called 'The Hot Geisha,'" he said. "Junzo makes it with spiced crab and salmon, and a hot caviar sauce. It's very spicy." He looked at it, then me, considering. "I don't think I need these," he said, setting his chopsticks aside. Slowly, deliberately, he lowered his mouth to the roll closest to the juncture of her thighs. He paused, his eyes meeting mine, as his mouth hovered a fraction above her bare skin. Still she didn't move. His tongue darted out and licked just a dab of the spicy sauce from the top of the roll.

Arousal slammed through me, and I had to stifle a moan. The model was not unaffected either. Her gaze remained on the ceiling, her face expressionless, but I saw the rise and fall of her rapid breaths, the way her nipples puckered, the way her hips tilted slightly upward.

William opened his mouth and closed his teeth on the roll, lifting it away from her skin without ever having touched her. He closed his eyes as he savored his bite, and when he opened them, they were impossibly dark.

"Catherine," His voice was low and commanding and I felt the heat simmering between my legs. The promise of the pleasure I craved was right there. He motioned for me. I didn't think—my feet just acted—and then I was beside him and his mouth was on mine, taking me with his demanding lips and his conquering tongue. I could feel his hardness as he ground his hips against mine slowly and pushed me back. I thought he might press me against a wall and take me there and then. God help me, I wouldn't have protested. Instead, we pushed through the dining room door. I wrapped my legs around his waist, feeling his straining erection right up against my heat as we tumbled out into the hallway. "Time for the next course," William growled and carried me toward the master suite.

THIRTEEN

The next morning, William told me he had to fly to Atlanta for the weekend. After he'd carried me from the dining room to his bed last night, our dessert activities had gone on for several hours. I now stretched wantonly in his modern platform bed and felt delicious twinges and aches ripple through my body as I stared at the lake and part of Chicago's skyline through the bedroom's massive windows. There hadn't been any handcuffs or honey, but William had put the sash from his bathrobe to good use after we'd spent a long time making waves in a bubble bath. I still felt exceptionally well pleasured.

He'd kept his eyes locked with mine as he gave me the details about his trip, like he was looking for some sign that I was going to give him a hard time. Or worse. It was a last minute thing, he explained, something about a company he was thinking about investing in and the owner's availability, and he had to go. He wouldn't see me again until Sunday.

"Okay," I said. I'd miss him, but I understood. Then I gave him a long, tongue-filled kiss and dragged him into his massive multi-jet shower, where I pushed him against the wall, sank to my knees, and went down on him. I loved getting him off with my mouth and I thought it was the perfect send-off. He seemed to think so too.

Truth be told, I was relieved William would be away for a few days. We needed a break. I'd wanted to slow things down after Napa so I could get my head together, but he'd refused. Maybe he'd finally realized that giving us a little breather wasn't such a bad thing. Or maybe Atlanta *was* just business and last minute weekend trips were par for the course for Mr. Business Tycoon. Who knew? What I was sure of was that things were moving at lightning speed between us and we'd only met about a second ago. The intensity was exhausting and my emotions were scattered all over the place. I needed to inhabit my boring regular life for a little while and feel like me again.

The sky was grey and the lake reflected its gloominess, but I didn't mind. I spent all of Friday hanging out at home, catching up on mundane stuff like paying bills and cleaning my condo, which was actually pretty spotless thanks to Beckett. I hand-washed all of my lingerie and scattered colorful lacy bits and silky-sheer stockings around my bathroom and living room to dry. I did some work and read a few articles online about Hutch Morrison in preparation for our upcoming meeting. The guy got a ton of press, so there was more than enough information available to check out. Later, when most of the snow had melted, Laird and I went for a long walk by the lake.

I tried to call Beckett a few times but he didn't answer or text or call me back. That wasn't like him, but I figured now that he had a new man in his life, he was making the most of their time together on the weekends. I'd done the same thing with William, so I couldn't hold it against him. Still, I wondered if maybe there wasn't more to his silence. There was that thing he said he couldn't tell me because of the NDA. What the hell was that all about? Beckett had never kept secrets from me before and it was weird.

I ordered Chinese take-out for dinner and ended up going to bed before nine o'clock. I slept for nearly fourteen hours straight.

By Saturday afternoon, I felt rested and ready to get out so I called my friend Allison McIntyre to see if it was a good day to take portraits of her kids. She'd taken care of Laird so many times that I'd offered my photography services to her as a thank you. Besides, we hadn't seen each other for a couple of weeks, and it would be fun to catch up. Allison sounded excited about getting together, so I packed my gear, put Laird in my Volvo, and headed over to her house in Ravenswood Manor.

After I'd taken some cute shots of her son, Michael, and her daughter, Brooke, Allison and I hung out in her cozy kitchen while the kids romped with the dog. We chatted about her job and the kids' school stuff.

"So," she said, handing me a cup of coffee and sitting across from me at the kitchen table. She had assorted roosters and other farm animals on the walls and decorating the counters. "Tom's parents invited me to their anniversary party. It's their fiftieth."

From what she'd said in the grief support group where we'd met, I knew Allison had had a much better relationship with her in-laws than I'd had with mine. They'd been supportive all through her late husband's battle with cancer. Even so, I also knew Allison's mother-in-law occasionally drove her nuts. "Really? Are you going to go?"

She shrugged. "I feel like I should. I know they want Michael and Brooke to be there. But I haven't seen the whole family since Tom's funeral. It will be a little weird."

I reached across the table and took her hand. "Come on, you can handle it, and they're family to Michael and Brooke. Grandma and Grandpa, aunts, uncles, cousins. It'll be great."

"We've lost so much. I don't want to take anything else away from the kids. But it's so different without Tom, you know? They're *his* family. It's always so awkward." She sighed. "But enough depressing stuff about me." She sipped her coffee. "What's up with you? Are you still seeing that new guy?"

"William, yes." I'd never mentioned his last name. I didn't think Allison would know who he was, but I didn't want to get into his billionaire status and all the complications that went along with it, like last weekend's Napa excursion.

"And…?" she prodded. "How are things going?"

"Really good. He's a fabulous cook. He's charming, smart, and has excellent taste in art. We can talk about it for hours. He's great."

"While the kids are still in the other room, tell me the good stuff. How's the…you know? Still fabulous?"

I felt the blush creeping into my cheeks as I rolled my eyes. "Yes."

"Hurry!" she whispered. "Details!"

"It's off the charts, Dana. He's really good in bed. I'm not even in his league."

"Look at you glowing," she said with a smile. "Has he told you he loves you yet? Have you told him?"

"No, but it's that obvious, huh?" I sipped my coffee to hide my face, which now felt hot and red.

"I just haven't ever seen you look so happy."

The kids and Laird picked that moment to tear into the kitchen and beg to give Laird a treat. Allison had some doggy snacks in the pantry, and I said it was okay. I was glad for the interruption. I didn't want to talk about why I hadn't told William I loved him yet. Or why he hadn't told me. Our sex life was amazing, but the rest of our relationship felt so uncertain.

A burst of laughter brought me back to the present, and I watched as the kids placed a doggie treat on Laird's nose. They'd obviously taught him to wait because he didn't snatch it up. Instead, he whined and thumped his tail impatiently. "Get it, Laird!" Michael, Allison's seven-year-old, said. Laird flicked his nose, and the treat soared into the air. He caught it with a *woof.* Four-year-old Brooke broke into peals of laughter, and the sound of her unadulterated joy made me laugh.

Allison was so fortunate to have these two reminders of what she and Tom had shared. I watched her hug them and saw the way the whole family seemed to love one another so completely. They'd seen hard times, and they'd gotten through them. It was them against the world, and that was what I wanted with William. I just didn't know if we'd ever make it that far.

*****

When William got back on Sunday afternoon, I was dressed in a white blouse under a pretty white sweater with a ruffled neckline and cuffs and a black wool boucle mini with tights and black suede booties. My hair was back in a high ponytail and I was wearing a little dark eyeliner and mascara and a touch of red lip gloss. I kept my jewelry simple and had on just my diamond stud earrings and my Patek Philippe. I hoped I looked chic but not like I was trying too hard to impress his aunt and uncle.

I buzzed William up and when I opened my door, he was just topping the stairs. He was in dark tweed trousers, a button-down shirt, and a grey-blue sweater that matched his eyes and made them look even more gorgeous than usual. He looked good enough to eat, and I almost wished we were staying home.

"You're a sight for sore eyes," he said as he pulled me into his arms and kissed me. I melted into his embrace and let the essence of him overtake all of my senses. He was such a big and powerful man and it felt so good to be nestled against his muscled, hard chest as his lips pressed against mine. With my heart racing, I kissed him back, our tongues dancing and dueling as my body roared to life. He pulled away first, leaving me breathless and a little dizzy and glad his strong arms were holding me up.

He reached his hand to gently caress my jaw before he tipped my head back so I was looking up at him. "I missed you and I couldn't get back here fast enough. Georgia was a bust." His eyes were a radiant grey and I shivered, knowing we were both reeling in the powerful chemistry between us. "You look beautiful, by the way. I love you in white. It makes your skin glow and your eyes look even greener. Very pretty, my beautiful girl."

I blushed as he smiled down at me. There was that word again, *love*, but I'd take it any way he offered it. "Thank you," I replied. "I wasn't sure how dressy dinner was going to be, but I'm glad you like it. And I missed you too." I had and I wanted him to know. I leaned up and lightly pressed my lips to his. He groaned in response and we stood in my doorway for a few more minutes, softly kissing and gently becoming reacquainted with each other. I felt beautiful, desired, and cherished and I tried to make him feel the same way.

William was the first to pull away again and he looked at his watch then back at me with a mock chastising expression on his face. "Catherine, we need to leave or we're going to be late. Come on, grab your coat *and your gloves* and let's go. I'm double-parked out front. I totally forgot. That's what your bewitching lips do to me." He was grinning now and I watched as he subtly adjusted himself, obviously coping with the effects of our yummy make-out session.

"Me and my bewitching lips are ready. Give me just a sec," I laughed. I grabbed my stuff and we were off.

I was really excited to see where William had lived for the latter part of his childhood and to get to know his family better. He drove us himself in the black Range Rover and, even in the middle of winter, it was a lovely trip up Sheridan Road. The frozen lake was a dark expanse off to the right and the houses got grander and grander as we went north. William pointed out different places of interest, but mostly he held my hand and we enjoyed companionable silence.

It wasn't quite five and already dusk when we arrived at the Smith residence in Lake Forest. We turned into a gated drive that was walled on either side. William rolled down his window and punched a code into a keypad, and then the gate slowly rolled open. I looked out and spotted a security camera high in a tree next to the drive. Given all that William had been through, I guessed the Smiths had to take precautions.

William continued along the private road through the heavily wooded grounds until we reached a stone drive that led us to the front of a very large red-brick Georgian house surrounded by an expansive snow-covered lawn. I could see the lake off in the distance. His aunt and uncle were on the front steps to meet us, one black lab and two goldens trailing behind them.

"Catherine!" William's aunt said, embracing me warmly when I stepped out of the car. "I'm so glad you're here."

"Thank you for having me, Mrs. Smith."

"Call me Abigail, please. And you remember Charles?" She led me to William's uncle who had been shaking William's hand and slapping him on the shoulder.

Charles shook my hand. "Good to see you again, Catherine. This is Atlas," he said with his hand rubbing the ears of the black lab. "And that's Blanche and Ophelia. They're a hopeless lot of lunatics, but we adore them." I stroked one of the golden retrievers on the head and she wagged her big tail in response. "Please come in and get warmed up and have a cocktail. Annabelle will have dinner ready shortly."

"Annabelle's the cook and housekeeper," William said, following me into the house after Abigail and Charles and the dogs. "She's been with them for years. I can't remember a time without her."

We stepped into a large, elegantly decorated foyer and an older African-American woman came quickly down the hall and hugged William hard. "You don't come home enough, Willie," she scolded him.

"Annabelle, it's good to see you too."

She pulled away and studied me. She wore a grey dress with a white apron. "You must be Catherine," she said with a nod. "About time William brought a girl home to meet us. About time."

"It's nice to meet you, Annabelle." I held out my hand, but to my surprise, she engulfed me in a hug. She smelled like cinnamon and vanilla and freshly baked dough.

"I better get back to dinner before I burn it," she said, hurrying back to the kitchen.

"She's never burned a meal in her life," Abigail said, and I realized everyone had been watching Annabelle's reaction to me. I hoped I'd passed the test.

We had cocktails in the immense living room which felt intimate despite its size thanks to the careful groupings of furniture. The Smiths were clearly serious appreciators of very expensive antiques. Their taste in art rivaled William's too, and I wondered if Abigail and Charles had been early influencers on his collecting.

I was a little nervous about saying and doing the right things, but the Smiths were charming, easy going, and relaxed. They were interested in my work and how I'd grown up in California, but they didn't pry into my past or barrage me with questions. William sat next to me on the couch with his arm resting behind me along its back. Every so often he'd touch my hair or knead my shoulder, but for the most part he just smiled and observed as the three of us talked. The half hour seemed like no more than minutes, and then Annabelle called us into dinner.

After a delicious meal of rib-eye steak, garlic mashed potatoes, green beans, and buttery dinner rolls, Abigail offered to give me a tour of the house before dessert and coffee. I looked over at William who subtly nodded and I eagerly accepted her offer, not just to see the house but to spend a little time alone with her too.

The house was larger than I realized—eight bedrooms and who knew how many bathrooms—and lovely on every floor. When we reached the room that had been William's, I had to pause and look inside.

"William took most of his things with him to college or put them in storage," Abigail said as I gazed around the room, which was painted white and styled in a nautical theme with lots of navy blue. It looked like a boy's room, not stark or minimalist at all. "But he never liked much clutter," she said.

"I can believe it," I laughed. I moved toward a wall with several pictures hanging on it. They showed a younger William in cap and gown. "Graduation?" I asked.

"Yes. Top of his class, of course."

I peered closer. His face was more youthful, but the eyes were the same—haunted and shrouded.

"Catherine," Abigail said. "I want to say again how very good it is to see you. I can't tell you the last time I've seen William this happy."

I turned and smiled. "He makes me happy too."

"I'm so glad he found you. Every time I talk to him, he can't say enough about how talented you are, how smart, how caring. He goes on and on. I feel as though I know you already."

I opened my mouth but wasn't quite certain how to respond. William had said all of that about me? He went on and on about me? I could hardly imagine the man I knew doing that. Finally, I said, "I care a great deal about William."

Abigail nodded. "I can see that. Be careful with him, Catherine. He has a tender heart and he's been hurt so many times."

Again, her words stunned me. A tender heart? And how could *I* hurt William?

"He carries a heavier burden than most people realize," she continued. "Wealth like his comes not only with tremendous responsibility, but also with tremendous risk. He's so driven and strong and accomplished, but he's had to deny whole parts of himself to make it this far and sometimes it's been very difficult for him."

This was not at all what I'd been expecting to hear and my gaze remained riveted on Abigail as she continued to tell me more about William.

"It's been ugly for all of us at times, but that's never been his fault. I've often worried about the toll it's taken on him. Mary Alice used to call him her little Romeo. He was this sweet-natured, fearless little boy who'd take on the world just to bring her a pretty flower and make her smile."

I watched as a faraway look crept into Abigail's eye after mentioning her sister's name. She'd lost someone too, and my heart broke for her in the same way it had shattered for William. Then she looked at me and smiled warmly.

"Please excuse me, Catherine. I don't often speak like this. It's just been a long time since I've seen William let his guard down and it's wonderful to witness." She gave me a reassuring squeeze on the shoulder and I smiled in return. "Let's see how Annabelle is faring, shall we?" she asked, and we turned to head downstairs and check on dessert.

Holy shit.

*****

Still reeling from our talk, I wandered the house and found William and his uncle in the library. As I stepped inside, I heard Charles say, "I don't understand why you haven't let George handle it."

I stopped cold just inside the room. "I'm sorry. Am I intruding?"

William came toward me and slid his arm around my waist. "Not at all."

"I could help your aunt in the kitchen."

"Stay," he said, looking down at me. "You should hear this."

My heart began to pound. Finally I was going to know exactly what had been going on. The tension in the room was thick. I could feel it as William drew me farther in and seated me next to him on a dark leather couch. The entire library was paneled in dark wood and furnished with heavy pieces. A fire roared in the large fireplace, where Charles leaned against the mantel. William sat beside me, elbows resting on his knees.

"This is simply another hoax and another attempt at extortion," Charles went on. He had a highball glass in his hand and swirled the amber liquid inside. "Nothing I've seen suggests Wyatt is really alive. We've been through this, William. Why are you giving it so much credibility?"

I glanced at William and watched as he squared his shoulders and sat up a little straighter. "I was in Whitehorse last week."

"For God's sake, why?" Charles sputtered, looking genuinely shocked. "It's brutal up there this time of year. Why on earth did you go?"

"About three weeks ago, a timber company crew working about thirty miles north of Dawson City found pieces from a plane."

I froze and saw that Charles had done the same. "Go on," he finally said.

"The Canadian Transportation Safety Board was notified and a team was deployed. The scene was analyzed, but I was told there wasn't much *to* analyze given the amount of deforestation in the area and the harsh conditions. The pieces were transported to Whitehorse for further analysis and that's when I was called. Our flight pattern data could have been off— if you take the wind currents into consideration, it's possible they drifted off course and went down there. This could be their plane. The CTSB allowed me to send samples to the manufacturer in France for authentication. Now we're just waiting for the results."

We stared at William in stunned silence. His shoulders had slumped and he seemed impossibly weary. I wanted to reach out and stroke his back, but I wasn't sure if he'd allow it.

"They're gone, William," Charles said. His voice was low and sympathetic. "Even if the pieces are from the plane, it doesn't matter. I know it's hard to accept, even now, but they're never coming back. Wyatt is never coming back."

A heavy silence hung in the air and William ran his hands through his hair, a sure sign he was frustrated. Charles spoke again.

"Do you think this latest extortion attempt and the discovery of this wreckage are somehow connected? It seems a little implausible, don't you think?"

William sighed. "I can't ignore the timing. My gut says it's not just coincidence." He looked up, and I took a sharp breath at the anguish I saw in his eyes. There was heartbreak and a pain even I, who had lost someone I loved deeply, couldn't fathom. But William was far from broken. He'd been beaten, but he was not conceding defeat, not if the hard, determined set of his jaw meant anything. "I don't think that Wyatt's alive, Charles. But I do think it's possible that whoever is behind the threats might know something more about the wreckage. That's what I need to find out and that's why I haven't let

George take care of this. Yet. I'm sorry for any inconvenience the extra security may be causing. I can't let anything happen to you. To any of you." William squeezed my hand then. "But I have to see this through."

I understood now. I understood everything and I felt like the worst kind of asshole for leaving him in Napa and for doubting him ever since. Why hadn't I just trusted him like he'd asked? Why hadn't I seen his vulnerability? He had needed me to be there. He'd needed someone to take care of him. Instead, I'd made him rush back to Chicago to take care of me.

"William," his uncle said. "Abigail and I are here for you. We'll always be here. Do what you need to do. Just be careful."

William nodded and, with a pat on William's back, Charles quietly left us alone.

"I'm here too," I said. I would take care of William, the man and the hurt little boy with the tender heart. I loved him more than ever now.

Abruptly, he stood. "We have to go. Grab your coat."

"We're leaving?"

"No. I need to find something. Come with me." He held out his hand, and I took it. We donned coats and gloves and headed outside. It was dark now, but he led me down a shoveled winding path behind the house. His steps were sure and confident, as though he'd traveled this way many, many times before. Finally, a large coach house came into view.

William reached into his pocket and pulled out a set of keys. He seemed to know the key without even looking, and he opened the door and flicked on the lights. It was chilly inside but not freezing, and he led me upstairs to a room stacked high with boxes. Some of them were labeled *Christmas* and others looked old and battered. William headed for those. "These boxes are from my parents' home in the city," he said. "Abigail has kept them here for me. There's something...here it is." He reached for one of the cartons and pulled it off of a short stack of cardboard boxes.

He flipped the top flap open, and I spied a half dozen or so leather-bound photo albums. My mom had some just like them, filled with our family pictures. William removed an album and turned toward a couch covered with a drop cloth. He yanked it off and pulled me down with him onto the old couch. He drew me close, wrapping his arm about my waist and laying the book half on his knee and half on mine. Opening the album, he said, "Catherine, I'd like you to meet my family."

I'd seen a picture of his parents in his huge walk-in closet at his penthouse, so I had an idea of what they would look like, but it was still a shock to see the carefree snapshots of his mother and father as a young couple. William looked a great deal like his father, though there was some of his mother in him—he had her eyes. He flipped the pages slowly, years passing with a flick of his wrist. There was a baby and then a toddler who must have been Wyatt. His parents were beaming with pride at the little boy. His mother had a quiet beauty, while his father had much of the same charm and charisma William possessed. They were a beautiful family. I didn't remember any of my own family photos looking so warm.

And then William paused and pointed to the picture of a prune-faced newborn. "That's me."

"So you are mortal," I said. "And you don't look very happy about it."

He grinned at me. "My mother said she thought second babies were supposed to be easier, but apparently she was in labor with me for twenty-three hours. I don't think either of us was very happy by the time this picture was taken."

He flipped the page and there were pictures of him receiving his first bath, sleeping in that two-handed surrender position babies were so fond of, Wyatt kissing him, his father asleep on the couch with a dozing William in his arms.

A few pages later, there were photos of William and Wyatt playing with trucks. William looked as though he could barely walk, while Wyatt was a confident preschooler. "Do you see that truck?" William pointed to the red one Wyatt was pushing. "That was the one we always fought over. I don't know what it was about that truck, but we both wanted it."

He flipped the page again to pictures of Christmas. There were his aunt and uncle and his three blond-haired cousins. In one photo, preschool-aged William was seated on the couch, happily squished between his mom and dad. There was so much joy in that picture. No wonder he wanted closure. He wanted it for them, for their memory, as much as he needed it for himself.

There were more pictures and more albums—family vacations, birthday parties, one of William in about second grade with a skinny mongrel. William pointed to that one. "That was Joe. He followed me home from school one day. My father said we couldn't keep him. He was covered with fleas and half his fur had fallen off from mange. I cried and begged, and my mom convinced my dad to give in. I could keep him if I fed him and walked him." He stared at the photo a long time. "That dog slept with me every night, and when my parents died, he was the one who never left my side." His voice was low, and I didn't want to stare at him too hard. "He's buried in the backyard here. He was a good dog."

I leaned in to him, and I'd never felt closer. I'd never loved him so much. He turned the page again and it was filled with images of skinny boys with scabby knees and uncombed hair, beautiful parents with their arms securely around their sons. When we reached the last album, I saw immediately it wasn't filled. Its final pages were blank, but William opened it and diligently flipped through the last days of his normal life. There was his fifth-grade school picture, Christmas, a family ski vacation where everyone had rosy cheeks from the cold. William looked at one of the photos of the four of them against a backdrop of a snow-covered mountain. "That was the best vacation I ever had. Wyatt and I raced down the slopes, and I beat him twice. We ice skated and played hockey. I must have drank a gallon of hot chocolate a day."

He was pointing to one of the pictures, but I wasn't looking. I was watching him. He didn't need to say it was the last vacation he'd ever had with his family. I knew it, and I knew he would cherish those memories forever.

The album ended abruptly, and when he closed it, I covered his hand with mine. "I can see why you had to go to Canada, why you had to investigate the situation yourself."

"My uncle is right," he said, leaning back, and looking at me directly. "He didn't say it, but he thinks it's a longshot. I have to accept that I might never find any answers."

"You will," I whispered and kissed him gently. "I'll be here for you."

"Catherine." He cupped my cheek and kissed me tenderly on the lips. We pressed against one another, kissing delicately and slowly, holding each other. Finally, it was too cold in the coach house to ignore. Even William's body heat didn't warm me.

He pulled away. "We'd better head back. It's getting late."

"Your aunt and uncle will wonder what happened to us." We stood and wrapped up again, and then William lifted the box of albums and led me down the stairs. He turned off the lights and locked the door, and I followed him back to the house. Its windows glowed a cheery yellow, and when we stepped inside it smelled like freshly baked apples.

"Is that you, William?" Abigail peeked around a corner and ushered us back inside. I saw her gaze flick to the box William carried, but she didn't remark on it.

"We need to head back to the city," he said.

She nodded. "Annabelle wrapped up two slices of apple pie for you." She turned to me. "Catherine, I hope we see you again soon."

"Thank you for dinner. It was lovely."

Once we were on our way, William and I didn't speak much, and I didn't feel the need. We held hands, and I felt more connected to William than I ever had. Music played in the softly lit vehicle, and he and I were content just to be together. Tonight was the night I was ready to tell him how I felt. I couldn't hold it in anymore and I needed him to know that I loved him.

We reached my apartment, and William circled, looking for a parking place. There was a cab idling in front of my building, and I frowned at it when it was still there after William's second circle. He found a place, parked, and came around to open my door. The cab was still there as we walked down the block toward my condo.

I felt a shiver of apprehension, though there was no reason. Anyone could have called for a taxi. We crossed the street and passed the cab, and just as we reached the steps to my condo, the cab's door opened.

"Cat!"

I stiffened and turned. A guy slammed the car door behind him and started for me. Oh fuck.

It was Jeremy Ryder.

FOURTEEN

A sound very much like that of a freight train thundered in my ears and the ground seemed to rush up at me. I closed my eyes, took a deep breath, and tried not to panic. Panicking would be bad. I had to breathe. I had to stay calm.

Jeremy. Here in Chicago. And William here too.

Oh my God. This couldn't be happening. I forced myself to breathe again.

I glanced at William, and he was looking at me expectantly. Shit. He must have asked me something. I had to get it together even though I was majorly freaking out. And now Jeremy was waving and coming closer. *Shit, shit, shit!*

"I'm sorry. What?" I asked William

"I asked if you know that man, but I can see that you do."

Was it that obvious? Oh, wait. Maybe he knew because Jeremy was waving at me. *Calm down, Cat.*

Jeremy was close enough to hear us now, close enough to require an introduction, though I would have given anything to run the other way. I let out a breath I hadn't known I'd been holding. "William Lambourne, this is Jeremy Ryder, my brother-in-law." I probably should have said *ex-brother-in-law*, but it was too late now.

In any case, Jeremy completely ignored William and pulled me into his chest for a hug. I stumbled against him then jumped back as though burned as soon as he released me. I could feel the heat of William's stare against my back. Jeremy stuck out his hand. "Hey, nice to meet you. William, is it?"

William took his hand, but he didn't smile or offer a return greeting. The two of them stood like that for a long moment, my past and my present linked together. And then they broke apart and Jeremy looked at me again. William looked at me too, his face carefully neutral and his eyes a hard clear blue. I wished a hole would open up in the sidewalk and suck me down into a cold, quiet darkness. Anything would be better than the nightmare that was unfolding right in front of me.

"Jeremy, what are you doing here?" I asked. My voice sounded forced and weird, like I was speaking from one end of a long, metallic tunnel.

"Legal conference," he said. "The associate who was supposed to come came down with the flu this morning, so they sent me instead. I didn't have time to make a hotel reservation. I was hoping I could crash at your place. I would have called first, but I didn't have your cell number. I had your address, though." He grinned at me. "Come on, it'll be just like old times."

I hesitated. I had no doubt Jeremy could have found a hotel room downtown, if he'd wanted one. After what he'd said at the airport in San Francisco about wanting us to get back together—not that we had ever really been *together* together—I should tell him he couldn't stay. But I was still wrestling with my secret, and wouldn't me telling my former brother-in-law to go seem sort of suspicious to William? Jeremy was family. "Of course," I said, feeling more trapped than ever. "Come on in."

I led the way up the stairs to my condo, my thoughts racing. It had been such a fantastic afternoon and evening and now it was turning into a complete clusterfuck. My heart sank. William and I had been so connected, but now there was a weird tension again, and all because of Jeremy, who kept turning up like a bad penny. I could already tell William didn't like him. Maybe it was some male sixth sense that kicked in when a rival was near, but William was cool and aloof and watching him with a predatory acuteness.

I unlocked the door and greeted Laird, then turned on lights while William and Jeremy stood in the small entry that opened into my living room. Jeremy said, "This is great, Cat."

As soon as Laird heard Jeremy's voice, his ears pricked and he let out a frantic *woof* and practically attacked Jeremy with doggie kisses.

"Laird, down!"

Jeremy just laughed. "Hey, Laird. I missed you too, boy."

My commands had no effect on Laird, but smelling Jeremy must have. Slowly, he dropped back to all fours. I realized what had happened, and Jeremy said it before I could. "He thought I was Jace." Jeremy crouched down. "Sorry, boy. I know you miss him."

I swallowed the lump in my throat. "Come on in and get comfortable. I'll go make up the guest room." Reluctantly, I headed to the spare bedroom to pile boxes in the corner and put sheets on the bed. I had thought my dad would be my first real houseguest, but apparently it was going to be Jeremy.

I didn't like leaving Jeremy and William alone, but I didn't have much choice. I could hear them speaking but couldn't make out what they were saying. The conversation was stilted with long pauses and short bursts of sound. It was awful, truly awful. I couldn't have imagined a worse scenario and I hoped and prayed that Jeremy would keep his fucking mouth shut and not let anything slip. The worst part wasn't even the awkwardness or the fact that I was so nervous I couldn't stop my hands from trembling; it was the incredible disappointment. Tonight had been so amazing—the conversations with William I'd wished for so many times had finally happened. It was like this giant weight on my shoulders had just vanished. After Abigail's surprising revelations and then being with William in the coach house, I was done with holding back. I was ready and I was absolutely all in. I'd wanted to make love with William tonight, slowly and tenderly, and show him with my body everything I was feeling.

I halfheartedly stuffed a pillow into a case and threw it on the bed. I'd never made a bed so quickly in my entire life, and it was obvious Martha Stewart didn't live here.

"Okay, all done!" I said, rushing out of the guest room and finding them both seated in my living room. Jeremy was sprawled on the couch, Laird sitting at his knee, as though he belonged there. William sat stiffly in the armchair. Neither was speaking, and William looked up at me, his face stoic and impassive. Laird was the only one thrilled Jeremy had stopped by, and I couldn't help but feel bad for William, since Laird had never showed him much favor.

"Thanks, Cat," Jeremy said. "I thought I'd be crashing on the couch."

"We're too old for that now." I moved to stand beside William, not certain what to say or do. "Um, do you want to watch some TV? Unless you're tired. You have an early day tomorrow probably."

"Nah. I'm on California time. It's early."

"Can I get you a drink? Something to eat?"

"That would be great."

I looked at William. I assumed he'd be going home, leaving me to handle my unexpected guest on my own. Now would be the time for him to say goodbye, but instead he settled back in the chair, resting his ankle on top of one knee. "Would you like a glass of wine, William?" I asked.

"Thank you."

I headed to the kitchen, glad for something to do to get me out of that room. I could have choked on the testosterone. I pulled out some crackers and cheese, laid them on a platter, and poured three glasses of red wine. I drank half of mine, then filled it again. "Okay, Cat, you can do this." I felt as though I needed a pep talk and maybe a shot of vodka. The pep talk would have to suffice for now.

William was staying. Jeremy was staying. We'd all be together under one roof tonight. It was a disaster, but it was only one night. I could get through one night. I carried the wine and snacks to the living room, then settled on the arm of William's chair. There wasn't really room for me, but I couldn't stand or choose to sit with Jeremy over William. I was desperate to make some connection with him, but he didn't touch me.

"Great wine," Jeremy said.

"Thank you," William answered.

Jeremy cocked his head, looking at me. I filled him in. "It's from William's vineyard in Napa."

"Oh, so that's why you were in California. When you said you were seeing a friend, I didn't realize it was your boyfriend."

This was getting worse and worse. "I thought I mentioned William."

"Nope. Hey, why don't you come sit on the couch? There's plenty of room."

Seriously? Why couldn't I wake up and realize this was nothing but a bad dream?

"Okay." I stood and crossed to Jeremy. The atmosphere was tense enough without me making it worse by refusing to sit beside my guest.

"So you own a vineyard?" Jeremy asked William.

"Among other things," he answered.

"Yeah? Like what?"

William shrugged. "This and that."

This was going to be a long night if I allowed them to carry the conversation. "So, Jeremy, you're getting married soon, right? How are the wedding plans coming along?"

Jeremy had always liked to talk, just like Jace, and he launched into some of the details. Then I turned the conversation to Chicago's best attractions. Jeremy tried to talk about the past, but I brought us back to the present by mentioning Beckett and segueing into our work together for Fresh Market. I saw Jeremy looking at the photos I'd used to decorate the condo, but he didn't say anything about the lack of surfing pictures or the absence of pictures of Jace. Finally, it was late enough to go to bed. After a few awkward "Goodnights" and a strained hug, William and I went to my room. Jeremy went to the guest room.

I closed the door behind me and slumped against it. I had made it. Jeremy hadn't said anything too revealing, and William had been polite enough, though he obviously wasn't very happy about the situation. My shoulders felt like a wire was stretched taut between them. I was completely exhausted and just wanted to collapse on the bed. Something slinked along my waist, and I jumped.

"Did I scare you?" William asked. He'd wrapped his arms around me. After his lack of affection in the living room, I hadn't been prepared for him to touch me.

"No. I mean, yes. A little." I moved away, so on edge I knew I was hardly making sense. I tried to think what I needed to do and ended up pulling my clothes off and tugging on an old T-shirt and sweats. William stood across the room, one eyebrow raised.

"Interesting choice, but you won't be needing that get-up tonight."

Oh my God. He could not possibly want to *do it*—I was reverting back to my college mindset—with Jeremy in the guestroom. My condo wasn't *that* big.

"William…" He crossed to me and took me in his arms, leaning down to kiss my neck. "I don't think this is a good idea."

"Give me a minute. You'll change your mind." His hands skimmed down my sides, then under my T-shirt to cup my breasts. I jumped back.

"William, we can't do this," I hissed.

He crossed his arms. "Why not?"

"He might hear."

William reached for me again. "I'll be very, very quiet." He brushed a hand over my nipples. "I'll keep my mouth occupied and yours too." He took my hand and placed it on the front of his trousers. He was definitely hard and ready. I pulled my hand away and stepped back.

"You know I won't be quiet enough."

He shrugged. "So he hears. I don't care."

"I do."

"Why? What difference does it make if he knows I fuck you, if he knows you like it when I fuck you? Maybe it will turn him on. We can all get off tonight."

The idea of Jeremy hearing William and me having sex made my chest tighten. I just couldn't do it. I'd never said no to him before, but I had to say it tonight. I had to have some sense of decency. He reached for me again, and I skipped back. "I don't feel comfortable with Jeremy here."

The tightness in William's face seemed to relax slightly. "Then just let me hold you. Tonight…at my aunt and uncle's house…showing you those pictures. I want to hold you."

How could I resist that request? I wanted to hold him too. I wanted to keep the feeling of closeness we'd shared. "Alright." I moved toward the bed, but he shook his head.

"You're not wearing that."

I rolled my eyes. "What does it matter what I wear? Nothing more than cuddling is going to happen."

I watched as William began to remove his clothes, his powerful well-muscled body moving with an easy grace as he stripped. "Fine, but at least give me some little thrill. Take that off and let me feel you against me."

I gave him a wary look. I wasn't sure if I trusted him—or myself—if we were nude in bed together. But as he dropped his boxer briefs, I found myself pulling my T-shirt over my head. I wanted to feel his big hard body against mine. My breasts were achy and heavy in anticipation of rubbing against his chest, but I tamped that feeling down. Nothing was going to happen. I turned off the light, dropped my old sweats, and climbed naked into bed. A moment later, the mattress dipped, and William was beside me.

He gathered me in his arms and pulled me flush against him, my soft curves folding perfectly into his hard contours. His breath was soft and warm in my ear. "You feel so good." I dropped my chin to his chest and sighed with pleasure. His hand brushed along my back, making me shiver slightly. But he didn't attempt to touch me any more than that. There was just the hypnotic feel of his hand circling the sensitive flesh on my back.

"I'm sorry he showed up," I whispered. "I wanted tonight to be special."

"It was," he murmured. "I'm sure it was the first of many times we'll visit with my aunt and uncle. It felt right having you there, Catherine."

"I liked being there," I said. "I liked seeing that side of you."

"I wanted you to see it." His voice was a deep rumble against my ear. "I want you to know every side of me." He kissed me lightly, his mouth seeking but not demanding. I wrapped my arms around his neck and kissed him back. There was such a dreamy intimacy when we kissed like this, caressing each other's mouths and exploring with our tongues. It felt so good to linger on his lips, to press against his body, and I savored every moment.

I felt the evidence of his arousal hot against my belly and I realized my nipples were sensitive and hard. "William," I said, breathless. "We can't."

"I can't help the way I react to you," he said. "It just happens. You're beautiful." His hand skimmed down my back again. "And your soft breasts are pushed right up against me, and the points of your nipples are driving me crazy."

"I'm not trying to tease you."

He moved his hips, emphasizing his hard cock. "I'm not either. But it's always been this way when we're together. I always want you. I can't get enough."

Heat flooded through me at his words. God, he knew exactly how to turn me on. I didn't even think he was trying. "I want you too," I murmured. "But we can't do anything more than kiss."

"Fine. Then let me kiss you." He was being far too accommodating. I was used to the William Lambourne who demanded and ordered. This William was actually conceding to my demands.

Or so I thought.

His mouth brushed against my neck in the darkness and trailed down to my shoulder. "William! I said only kissing."

"Are my hands touching you?" he asked. "I'm only kissing you."

I couldn't argue, but he had to know his mouth turned me on as much as his hands. His wet tongue slid between my breasts and then moved over to one nipple. I moaned as he took it into his mouth.

"Shh," he said, lifting up on his elbows and blowing cool air on my wet flesh. "Quiet."

"William…"

"I'll stop whenever you say. Tell me to stop. Or say rosé. Use your safe word if you have to." He chuckled softly. I loved that he thought my safe word was funny.

Then his mouth closed on my nipple again, and I couldn't keep from arching my back, from offering my body to him for more. He licked the other nipple, bringing it to an almost painful peak of pleasure. I panted, biting my lip to keep quiet. I should tell him to stop. I should move out of his arms, go to sleep. I knew where this was going, and I could already feel myself getting wet.

But I couldn't resist his mouth. He trailed it down my belly, licking a path with his skilled tongue. I parted my legs, but he paused before moving between them. "Can I kiss you here, Catherine?"

He knew I couldn't resist him, that I didn't have the willpower to make him stop.

"Yes," I whispered.

"I didn't hear you. What do you want me to do?"

I wanted to strangle him. But I wanted his mouth on me even more. Somewhere in the back of my mind I was aware Jeremy was just in the other room. I would have to be quiet. "Kiss me," I said softly.

"Where?"

"You know where," I whispered as he slid between my legs and moved to lift my thighs over his shoulders.

"Say it. Tell me where you want me to kiss you." He blew gently on my sex and I squirmed.

"Please, William, kiss my clit. Make me come."

I heard his swift intake of breath and then his warm mouth descended on my swollen folds. He parted me, bared me, and touched his tongue to me. I bucked and gasped in sweet agony.

"Shh. Quiet, remember?" He continued to lave me, moving his tongue from my throbbing clit to my entrance and back again. Over and over and then I was coming, my hips rising and pressing my sex hard against him as I surrendered to his magical lips and skillful tongue.

"Oh, much too loud," William chided me as he slid up my body. I was barely aware of anything except the explosive currents that were still raging through me. I hadn't even realized I'd made a sound.

"Turn over," he demanded.

"But I thought—"

"Turn over." He rolled me over and lifted my hips until they cradled his erection. "That's better," he said, rubbing his hard length against me. I moaned, turning my head into the pillow. "Smart girl," he praised. His hand pressed between my legs, cupping me and stroking me. I buried my face in the pillow as his fingers slid in and out, wet and slippery, and then against the most sensitive swollen parts of me. Finally, I couldn't take it anymore. I pressed back against his hand, and another orgasm uncoiled within me, fast and hard. I managed to contain my moans and gasps in the pillow, but then William was inside me.

His hands gripped my ass cheeks as he drove into me. My breasts brushed against my sheets with each thrust, my sensitive nipples causing delicious friction. I could feel the bed shaking beneath us as William thrust harder, his thick cock stretching me and filling me completely. Finally, he stiffened, and I felt his hand come between us and his thumb circle hard against my clit. I came again just as the rush of his semen exploded against my walls in great, hot bursts. He gave a muffled grunt, but I had forgotten to bury my head in the pillow. I cried out his name, clamping my teeth on my lip too late, as my core spasmed around him

He pulled out and gathered me in his arms. I lay there for a moment, trying to catch my breath, trying to enjoy the afterglow. Maybe Jeremy had fallen asleep. Maybe I hadn't been as loud as I thought. Maybe he hadn't heard. I could feel heat creeping in my cheeks because I was relatively certain he *had* heard. I don't know how anyone in the condo—or on my block—wouldn't have.

"What's wrong?" William asked a moment later, his voice almost disembodied in the darkness.

"So much for not making any noise."

He sat and moved away from me. "Why do you care? Are you embarrassed that you're seeing me?"

"What?" I sat too. "No!"

"Then what is it? What is he to you?"

"He's my former brother-in-law, and I don't know why but it feels uncomfortable to be with another guy around him. It just does." That was partly true anyway.

He gave a low bitter chuckle. "It was sex, not a crime. We can't resist each other. I don't know why you're embarrassed about that." He rose, went to my bathroom, and returned a few minutes later. I could tell he was still exasperated with me.

"I don't like that you're upset. But you're mine, Catherine and I don't give a fuck who knows it." Then without another word, he got into bed and turned onto his side so he was facing away from me.

I stared at his back. "You don't have to stay if you don't want to."

"I'm staying," he said. "And don't worry. I won't touch you."

I rose, cleaned up, and put my T-shirt and sweats back on. When I climbed back into bed, the silence loomed heavy between us.

It took a really long time for me to fall asleep.

*****

It was still dark when William shook me awake. I turned the bedside lamp on and saw he was dressed and ready to go. "What time is it?"

"Four-thirty," he said. "I'm going to the gym."

"Okay, I'll text you later."

"Good."

The tension was still there. I could have killed Jeremy.

"William, I'm sorry about last night—"

He leaned down and kissed me lightly. "I'm not angry, Catherine. You have the right to say no. I shouldn't have persuaded you."

"It wasn't all you. I didn't really want to say no. I didn't say no. And afterward—I'm sorry."

"Get some sleep. We can talk later." His finger trailed along my cheek, and he turned off the light. A few minutes later, I heard him close the door and lock it.

I touched my fingers to my lips, where he'd kissed me. I had the distinct impression he was disappointed. I wished he was angry rather than disappointed, because disappointed was a lot worse.

I closed my eyes and drifted back to sleep.

A few hours later I woke again and headed to the shower. After I dried my hair, I heard Jeremy moving around and figured I'd better let him know I was out so he could shower and be ready in time for his conference. I would have rather buried my head under the pillow. I was mortified at the possibility he'd heard William and me, but I forced myself to leave the bathroom and find him. When I came out to tell him the rest of the hot water was all his, he was sprawled on the couch, flipping channels on the TV.

"Hey, I'm out of the shower. I tried to leave you some hot water."

"Thanks."

I took Laird out then came back in and fed him. When I returned from the kitchen, Jeremy hadn't moved. "Don't you have to get to the conference?"

"Sure. But I don't have anything until later today."

"Oh. What time is your first event?"

He waved a hand. "Later."

Later. That was vague. "Where is the conference? One of the hotels? McCormick Place? Do you want me to give you a ride or did you arrange for a cab?"

"It's downtown. The Palmer House, I think. I don't need a ride, but I could use some food. I raided your fridge, but some things never change. How about we go out for breakfast?"

"Ok—if you think you have time."

"I have time." He stood and headed for the guest room, presumably to shower. "You know, I could just blow off the conference. We could spend the whole day together."

I was getting a sick feeling in my stomach that there wasn't any conference, but I didn't want to call Jeremy on it yet. Maybe I was wrong. Maybe I was jumping to conclusions.

"Let's just focus on breakfast for now. I'm starving."

Jeremy got ready and then we walked the few blocks to Toast, which was the best breakfast spot in Lincoln Park and had the most incredible stuffed French toast. We ordered and chatted about the weather and Chicago in winter. Or, more accurately, I listened as Jeremy bitched about how fucking cold it was. "Jace would have hated it here," Jeremy said. "He hated being cold."

"It takes a while to get used to it."

"You really like it here?" he asked.

"I do."

"I always thought you were a California girl through and through. You surfed like you were born on a board."

We chatted some more and even though it was still awkward, Jeremy wasn't a bad guy. He really wasn't, and I *had* always liked him. I could admit now that I missed having him in my life. Jace and I had hung around with Jeremy a lot. Even though the two brothers had very different personalities, they were best friends, and Jeremy was the one other person who had known Jace as well as I had.

"Was Napa the first time you'd been back since you moved? Your parents are both still in Santa Cruz, right?"

"They're still there. I should visit more, but it's hard for me to be there," I said. "I miss Jace when I'm there. I miss him here, but it's worse when I'm there."

"Yeah." He nodded. "I get that. Sometimes I drive by the beach or a restaurant, and I remember a day we surfed or a meal we ate. Guess you don't have to deal with all the landmarks here."

I shook my head. It was easy to forget that other people missed Jace as much as I did. I wished Jeremy and I could have been there for one another—*really* been there. I wished we hadn't fucked everything up with sex.

But we had, and as nice as it was to talk about Jace with someone, something was off. The law conference was obviously bullshit.

"Want to tell me why you're really in Chicago?" I asked as he finished his eggs.

His eyes, so much like Jace's, met mine. "You know why, Cat. When I saw you in Napa, it was like…" He frowned and ran a hand through his hair. "I still have feelings for you and I think you still have feelings for me too."

He looked at me again, the question on his face. I shook my head. "No, Jeremy. I'm sorry."

"It's okay." He began to rise.

"Jeremy, wait. Let me explain, okay?" I felt the sting of tears and sipped my coffee to give myself a moment as he waited for me to compose myself. "Jace was my everything. Those first months after he was gone, I was really messed up. I was hurting so badly, and you were so kind. But what happened between us never should have happened. It was wrong and I've regretted it every day since. It wasn't fair to you. *I* wasn't fair to you."

He was staring at me with hurt in his eyes. I had to make sure he understood. I wouldn't keep hurting him. "I don't love you, Jeremy. I never did. Not like that. There never was an *us* and, deep down, I know you know that. And there's never going to be. Ever. I'm so sorry I hurt you. Really, really sorry. It was the last thing I ever wanted to do. You deserved a goodbye from me at the very least and the way I cut you off and stopped talking to you was pretty cruel. I know that. I'm so sorry."

Jeremy's face was expressionless. This was so uncomfortable, but I couldn't stop now. "I just want you to move on and be happy, and I want to love you like a brother."

He snorted. "A brother."

"Yes. I've always felt that way about you. Besides, I'm in love with someone else."

"William?"

"Yes, William."

"You're sure?"

"One hundred percent."

"Well, good for you. And him," Jeremy said, slumping back in the booth and sighing in resignation. "I had to try, you know? But I get it. Way to let a guy down easy, Cat," he smirked, "but thanks for being honest. I needed to hear it."

"I wish I'd been brave enough to tell you before."

"Me too. But you've told me now, so I'll get out of your way. I'll head back to San Francisco on the next flight."

I felt so relieved. Maybe my stupid Cat Ryder mistakes were finally going to stay in the past where they belonged. "Can I drive you to the airport?" It was the least I could do.

"Thanks, that would be great."

We walked back to my condo, and Jeremy didn't bitch about the weather this time. He was quiet. We went up, and he collected his luggage. He hugged Laird goodbye. Laird whined, as though he knew this was the last time he'd see Jeremy. Great. Even my dog was sad. I showed Jeremy where I'd parked my Volvo, and he stowed his bags in the back. After I closed the tailgate, I turned to give Jeremy a smile, and he pulled me into a hug. It was a friendly hug, and when he pulled back and kissed me, I didn't object. He was saying goodbye, and I realized this might be the last time I ever saw him. I kissed him back.

He pulled away slightly and held my face between his hands. We looked at each other for a long moment, and then I gave him a tentative smile as my eyes filled with tears. We were each other's realest connection to Jace and we both knew we were likely saying goodbye to that too.

We didn't talk much on the way to O'Hare. Jeremy spent most of the drive on the phone, booking a flight home. He found one leaving in a few hours, and I dropped him at the terminal. I didn't get out of the car, but he leaned in the window and said, "Bye, Cat. If you're ever in San Francisco, give me a call."

"I will," I said, though we both knew I wouldn't.

FIFTEEN

Of course I got stuck in traffic on the way home. I kept looking for some sort of accident, but it was the usual gridlock, there for no apparent reason except that everyone wanted to be in the same place at the same time. I was at a complete standstill, and I fumbled for my bag on the passenger seat, thinking to text William that Jeremy was headed home and maybe to ask how his day was going.

I dug in my purse for a good minute, then pulled it into my lap. My phone wasn't inside. Damn. I remembered setting it on the table while waiting for Jeremy to get his stuff. I must have forgotten to grab it. I'd call William when I got home.

Someone behind me honked impatiently, but we weren't going anywhere.

Back at my condo more than an hour later, I found my cell sitting right where I'd left it—on the kitchen table. I'd missed two calls, and I pulled up my voicemail, hoping one was from William. But the first was from one of the execs at Fresh Market. As soon as I heard it, I jumped up and down and let out a scream. They'd loved the work I'd done and wanted to book Beckett and me for more of the Fresh for Spring campaign. We'd discuss details later, but they needed to know if I was available.

Of course, I was available! I did a happy dance with Laird, who let out a few excited barks and bounded up and down with me. Then I called Beckett. My enthusiasm dwindled only slightly when he didn't pick up. I left a message for him to call me right away.

There was a voicemail from my mother too. I was glad I hadn't had my phone with me when she called. I would have felt obligated to answer, and then I would have had to make a lame attempt to be vague about what I'd been up to since we last talked. I really sucked at lying. My mother could always tell when I was hiding something. I wasn't ready to explain Napa to her, or who I'd been with, or who I'd just dropped at the airport and why. I mentally kicked myself for being such a bad daughter. I'd call her later and listen attentively. I didn't want to be surprised when she ended up in Tahiti or the French Riviera with her latest rich boyfriend.

I didn't have a voicemail from William, but I had a text.

In meetings all day. Miss you, beautiful girl.

I smiled, my insides turning a little mushy. Maybe he was over last night's disappointment and really wasn't angry with me. Even though I freaked out before and after, I had to admit that *during*, things had been pretty spectacular. And thank God Jeremy hadn't mentioned that he'd heard us, though I was still sure he had. I'd bet me calling out William's name at the height of ecstasy was what finally clued him in that his chances with me were zero. I texted William back.

Miss you too. XOXO

My heart was still thumping happily. Between Jeremy leaving, Fresh Market, and getting back on track with my stormy-eyed, hotter-than-hell boyfriend, it was turning out to be a banner day.

I kept myself busy with work for a while then fielded a call from Emmy Schmidt at Hutch Morrison's office. We set up a time and date for my meeting with Hutch, and once again, I immediately wanted to share the great news with Beckett. But what was with the silent treatment? I checked my phone and he still hadn't responded to my earlier call.

It was Monday and I hadn't heard from Beckett since last Thursday, before the weekend. We never went that long without checking in with each other. I had a moment of panic, wondering if he was sick or if something horrible had happened to him. Some best friend I was, given that I was realizing the awful possibilities only now. I had a key to his apartment, so I could just go check on him...

Or maybe Beckett was avoiding my calls for a reason. Maybe I'd done something to piss him off and he was being a bitch about it. It wasn't like we'd never gotten on one another's nerves before, but he'd always just told me to fuck off for a day or two and then everything would be fine. Even though I'd just left him a voicemail, I texted him to please call me immediately. I put *immediately* in all caps and added,

I'm getting worried!

I tried to do more research on Hutch Morrison and then clear out my inbox, but my thoughts were way too scattered. My attention bounced from Beckett to Hutch to Fresh Market to William to Jeremy. Finally, I gave up and just sprawled on my couch, which Laird took as an invitation to lay on my feet, trapping me and keeping my toes cozy. I stroked his fur and closed my eyes.

I was seriously elated the Jeremy chapter in my life was done. Hopefully, he'd go back to Amy, marry her, and live happily ever after.

In California.

Far, far away from Chicago.

Last night would have been so much worse if William had known Jeremy and I had slept together. Beckett was absolutely right that no good could come of me telling him, especially now. So I was going to keep my mouth shut, move forward, and try not to think about it.

I checked my cell again, thinking maybe I'd missed a text from Beckett, but still nothing.

I knew William was in meetings, so I texted to invite him over for dinner. I could tell him all my news, then we could enjoy a night alone together and pick up where we'd left off before Jeremy had showed up. Seeing William with his aunt and uncle, going through those photo albums with him and seeing his vulnerability—that was the William I loved, the William I wanted. It might take weeks for that piece of wreckage recovered in Canada to be authenticated and the waiting must be agony for him. He needed me to be the supportive girlfriend I should have been from the start, and I was ready to be that and more.

William texted back a minute later—Beckett should have taken notes—and I frowned at his response.

Working late. Can't tonight. Tomorrow?

That was weird. First Beckett and now William. Of course, I wasn't being entirely fair to Stormy Eyes. He was hugely successful, intent on world domination or something like that, so he probably had to put in a few late hours once in a while. But it meant we would spend another night apart.

Sounds like a plan. Can't wait. Still miss you. XOXO

It was after six when Beckett finally called. "I was about to call missing persons," I teased him. "Where have you been?"

"I'll tell you all about it tonight. Are you up for drinks—or do you have plans?"

"No plans. Tell me where and when."

We agreed to meet at Revolution Brewing in Logan Square. Like most of the trendy places in Logan Square, Revolution Brewing was in an old refurbished warehouse. The hardwood bars and barrel-wood walls were rustic, and the pub advertised that the benches were constructed from 100-year-old beams salvaged during construction. It was a fun place to drink, especially if you liked beer. I was no enthusiast, but I didn't mind a beer once in a while. Revolution Brewing brewed their own and served food too, everything from steak to tofu. Beckett loved the bacon fat popcorn. I liked their fish and chips.

I forgot all about food when Beckett gave me a hug and handed me a cold pint to try. "This is the Coup D'Etat. Good, huh?"

I sipped. "Great. How are you?"

"Good. Cat, is it just me or have you gained a little weight?"

I blinked at him. "First you don't call, now you say I'm fat. Are you trying to end our friendship?"

"No, no!" He held his hands up in surrender. "It looks good on you. You looked like a scrawny waif before. William must be feeding you well."

I looked down at my skinny jeans and long-sleeve, vintage Black Flag T-shirt topped with a black and purple argyle thrift-store cardigan I'd worn with my favorite motorcycle boots. My jeans still fit, though there might be a fraction less room at the waist. I hadn't thought too much about it when I pulled them on. Looking at my shirt, I could see it was stretched a little tightly over my breasts. I decided I'd pass on the fish and chips and think about a salad instead.

"So Fresh Market," Beckett said. "They want you back. Isn't it great?"

One look at Beckett's big grin and I realized he knew before I did. "Why didn't you tell me? Why didn't you call me instantly?"

"It wasn't like that, Cat. But I can't help it if my *lover* can't keep a secret." His eyes were sparkling mischievously as he looked at me and I knew I wasn't the only one caught up in the excitement of a new relationship. Of course Beckett had found out first; Alec was the assistant art director at Fresh Market and part of the team for the Fresh for Spring campaign.

"Just because Alec and I are dating doesn't mean you didn't earn this, Cat. Those cherry shots looked incredible. Alec thought so and so did his bosses. You rocked it. And guess what's next? Fruit and berries! How sexy is that going to be? Red, juicy strawberries at the peak of ripeness, plump clefted peaches glistening with nectar…so hot!" Beckett mocked fanned himself and fluttered his eyelashes.

"Oh my God, you are such a food perv!" I laughed, but I loved that he seemed as excited about doing more work for Fresh Market as I was. It felt great, too, that things seemed back to normal with us.

We kept talking and I told him all about Hutch Morrison and my upcoming meeting with him. Beckett promised to come over and help me get ready beforehand. I never knew what to wear and he had such a great eye for what looked good on me. He had absolutely saved me from numerous fashion disasters. If he hadn't been a pastry chef, he could easily have been a stylist.

By the time we'd hashed out our plan, Alec had joined us. He went to get a beer, and I took my last chance to grill Beckett. "So really, why haven't you called me lately? What's going on?"

He shrugged. "Oh, you know. The usual."

Actually, I didn't know *the usual*. Why was Beckett being so weirdly evasive? "Is it your secret project again?"

No answer.

I tried again. "You've clearly been spending a lot of time with your new *lover*." I reached over and squeezed his arm. "I'm really happy for you. Alec is a lucky guy."

Beckett's face lit up. "I'm loving every minute of it. Cat, Alec is amazing. Seriously amazing."

"Should my ears be burning?" Alec asked, returning with beers for all of us.

"No, Beckett was just saying how amazing you are."

Alec smiled. "In that case, don't let me interrupt."

By eleven I realized I'd drank one or two too many pints of Coup D'Etat, so I started on water. I took a cab home and stumbled in, almost tripping over Laird, just after eleven-thirty. I wasn't messy drunk, but I was definitely buzzed. And I missed my man. Why did William have to work tonight? Why wasn't he here for me to ravish? After a few drinks, I was most definitely in the mood.

I took out my phone and frowned at it. No calls or texts. He worked way too hard. He needed to have a little fun. Maybe I could help him with that.

I stripped off my jeans and T-shirt, shimmied out of my underwear, and pulled on a lace-trimmed, silky black robe and lace thong William had picked out for me. I hadn't had a chance to wear them yet. When I reached up to pull my hair back into a ponytail, the silk felt cool and sleek against my skin. I'd definitely be wearing this again. I grabbed my tablet, propped some pillows behind my back, and got comfortable in bed. With a grin, I called William on my videochat app.

He answered right away, looking serious and professional with a pair of glasses on his nose. Glasses? I didn't even know he wore glasses. And was he in his office? I looked down at my watch. I wasn't wrong. It really was almost midnight. What was he still doing at work? Didn't billionaires get to sleep?

"Hello, Catherine," he said. His silky voice vibrated through me, sending heat straight to my core. I squirmed, pressing my thighs together.

"Hi, yourself. It's been so long since we've seen each other that I forgot what you looked like. Love your bifocals, Grandpa."

He sat back and grinned. "They're not bifocals. I wear them for eye strain after long hours on the computer." He pulled them off and tossed them on his desk. I'd been in his office once before, and now I remembered that his desk itself seemed to serve as a tablet. He must have a webcam set at an angle so anyone who video-conferenced with him would look directly at him.

"Likely story," I joked.

He smirked—yes, it was definitely a smirk—and said, "What have *you* been doing tonight? Not staying home, I take it."

"I was out with Beckett and Alec at Resolution—no, that's not right—*Re*volution Brewing."

His brow rose. "Catherine, are you drunk?"

"No," I said a little too forcefully.

His eyes narrowed slightly.

"Okay, just a little." I waved my hand. "But that's not why I'm calling. It's 11:42, William."

"It's 11:53, actually."

I rolled my eyes. "Whatever. The point is that I'm supposed to look at my watch at 11:42 and think about you touching me."

He paused for a minute before answering. "I do remember something to that effect. But I believe I said every day at 11:42 *a.m.*"

I giggled. "Well, whatever time it is, I'm thinking about you touching me now."

His dark, hooded eyes smoldered on my tablet screen, and his smirk changed to a hungry grin. He was liking my game. "How am I touching you?" His voice was lower now, seductive. "Show me."

That had been the idea all along. I propped my tablet on the bedside table, angled it, and ran my fingers up and down my neck. "Like this. I love it when you kiss my neck, especially when you haven't shaved. Your stubble tickles my skin and makes me shiver…" I could hear my voice turning breathy as my fingers traced my flesh, mimicking William's skilled lips caressing my neck.

"Where else, Catherine?"

I heard the arousal in his husky voice. I wanted him to feel as turned on as I was, to want me as badly as I wanted him.

"Here," I said, opening my robe slightly, giving him a peek of bare skin, just enough to tantalize. I stroked my fingers up and down, from the base of my neck to the curve of my breast. I glanced at him from under my lashes, feeling bold. "I know how much you love my tits, William." Oh, I was definitely feeling bold. *Tits* instead of *breasts* seemed way dirty to me, and William's eyes were molten grey now. He liked it when I talked dirty, and tonight I wanted to be a little naughty.

Or maybe a lot.

"Open your robe wider."

I slowly pulled the material aside, inch by inch. William didn't speak, but he was riveted to the screen. I pulled one side of my robe open, then the other, and allowed the material to slide down my breasts, tantalizing them with the silky material and exposing them to William's hungry gaze.

"Touch your breasts for me, Catherine," he said softly.

I palmed them, their heavy weight aching for him. Leaning back, I arched my back and plucked and rubbed at my nipples until they were dark pink and hard, needy points.

"How does that feel?" he asked.

"Mmm, that feels *so* good. I wish you were here now. I want your mouth on my tits. Do you like it when I say *tits*?"

"It's fucking hot. I love your tits." His voice sounded breathy and hoarse.

Still circling my swollen flesh, I purred, "I love it when you suck my nipples. Hard." I looked at the screen directly. "Like you did on the jet, William."

"I know you do. Show me where you feel it when I suck you."

"I can feel it all the way..." I stroked down my abdomen.

"Lower," he ordered.

I stroked my hand across the front of my thong, slowly. I had imagined me seducing William, but I was slowly losing control of this seduction. He was taking command, telling me what to do, and I loved it.

I kept rubbing my fingers across the scrap of lace between my legs. "I'm wet for you already. I can feel it through my panties. Just thinking about your mouth does that to me."

He groaned and shifted in his chair. His right arm moved, and I smiled. I had a pretty good idea where that hand was going and I thought I heard the sound of a belt unbuckling and then of a zipper. "You look so unbelievably sexy right now, Catherine. Show me where else you want me to touch you."

"Are you hard for me, William?" I teased. "Are you thinking about me touching you? Are you imagining me stroking you, running my hand up and down your big, thick cock? I love your cock, you know."

"Fuck," he hissed. "I'm rock hard for you. Don't stop. Tell me. Where else do you want me to touch you?" His breath came in pants, and my own was just as ragged.

"Here." I feathered my fingers across my lace panties again.

"Show me."

I pushed my thong aside and slid a finger over the moist skin. "I'm so hot here. So swollen," I panted, pressing my finger to my clit.

"Think about my tongue on you. You know you love it when I lick you hard and make you squirm and scream."

"Yes." I closed my eyes and could easily imagine his mouth there, imagine him teasing me to climax. I moaned as a shiver raced through me.

"Move your tablet," William demanded in that deep voice that made me weak. "I want to see you."

"Now who's being naughty," I said, though I felt my cheeks heating. I might be embarrassed about this in the morning, but I couldn't refuse him. I moved my tablet so it was pointing more toward my lower half. "But then you're always naughty."

"Open your legs a little," he said, and it was like he was in the room with me.

"Why?" I asked, wanting him to say it.

"You know why," he growled. "Tell me, Catherine."

"You want to see my—you want to see me?" I was so turned on now and my heart was racing as I parted my legs.

He grinned at me, eyes so large and dark I could hardly make out their color. "I want to see what's mine. More."

I opened my legs wider and ran my fingers along my clit. "Is this good?"

"That's perfect. Now show me what just thinking about me does to you."

I was panting now, hardly able to hold the orgasm back. Still, I knew I wouldn't let myself come without his permission.

I closed my eyes again and I reached down and rubbed, sliding one finger inside. "I'm so wet for you. I want you inside me."

"Use two fingers." I let his voice caress and command me.

I dragged two fingers down, slid them inside. "Like this?"

"Just like that. Don't stop."

My hips were writhing, and I could hardly remember to speak. I slid my fingers in and out, in and out. I could imagine him stretching me, filling me, pounding me. I let out a low moan. "I'm so close, I want to come for you," I said between gulps for air.

"Not yet. Keep touching yourself for me. Tease me. Make it last, Catherine."

My hips pivoted, my body moving in the rhythm he and I knew so well. Finally, he said, in a strangled voice. "Come for me. Now."

My hips bucked, and I pressed my hand hard against my sex as my muscles shuddered around my fingers again and again. "That's right," he said in approval. "Come for me, beautiful girl."

A few minutes later, I opened my eyes. I must have dozed off for a sec. I looked at my tablet screen and he was still there, watching me and looking just as satisfied as I felt. I smiled at him. "I'll have to call you again at the real 11:42 a.m."

He laughed. "I won't get any work done, waiting for your call. And I'm definitely not going to get any more work done tonight."

"You should go home and get some sleep," I said as I yawned. I needed sleep too. I was totally exhausted and I could already feel the effects of my buzz wearing off.

"I will. I'll talk to you tomorrow." His warm, velvety voice wrapped around me. "Good night, girlfriend."

I smiled lazily. "Good night, boyfriend."

His face was the last thing I saw before I fell asleep.

SIXTEEN

I heard a buzzing sound and pried my eyes open. Sunlight blazed into my bedroom, and I squinted and reached for my phone, the source of the sound that had woken me. I had a text from William.

Good morning, video vixen. You were incredible last night. Can't wait to see you later and sample your cooking.

I groaned and pulled the pillow over my head. I was never drinking again. Not only was I hung over, I was mortified. What had I been thinking? Drunk dialing William? Or had it been a drunk booty call? It wasn't even a call. It was an e-booty call. The whole incident was sort of a blur, but some details were definitely very, very clear. I groaned into my pillow again.

I had never done anything like that before. Clearly the alcohol had relaxed—no, *eliminated*—my inhibitions. Had I really—?

I pulled the pillow tightly over my head and wished I could go back to my peaceful drunken slumber. The things I'd said! I couldn't believe I'd been so...well, dirty. But I also couldn't believe how hot it had made William. How hot it had made me. Maybe if I could summon the nerve, I'd try it sober.

I pushed the pillow off my face and texted William back.

Excited about tonight too. XO

And I was excited. Tonight was finally going to be the night I said *I love you.*

After a shower and a very large cup of coffee, I called Beckett. I hoped he was feeling better than I was. He'd promised to help me with dinner for William tonight. I hadn't been drunk enough to think I could cook something edible without a little—or a lot—of help. Beckett answered right away, which I took as a good sign. "Hey, how are you feeling today?" I greeted him.

"Great! How about you?"

"Not as great. You will not believe what I did—"

"Hold on a second, Cat."

I frowned. Usually Beckett was all about juicy tidbits from my life—or anyone else's. He had a subscription to the *National Enquirer.* I heard what sounded like a timer going off and a clatter of dishes. Was Beckett cooking?

"Hey, I'm back," he said. "Sorry."

"Is this a bad time?"

"Um, yeah. Can I call you later?"

I felt a nervous flutter in my belly. "Yeah, but I'll see you this afternoon, right?"

He hissed in a breath. "Uh…"

"Oh, no! Beckett, you cannot bail on me." The nervous flutter escalated to mild panic. I felt flushed and my heart thumped.

"Cat, I'm so sorry. Something came up, and I can't get out of it."

I waited for him to explain or elaborate.

"You'll be fine. Just make something simple. You can do this, Cat."

So he wasn't even going to explain? "Beckett, seriously, I don't care about dinner. What is going on with you? What's with all the secrecy?"

There was a long pause. "I told you. I can't talk about it yet."

"Did I do something? Are you pissed off at me?"

He laughed. "No. Not at all. It's just work stuff. I can tell you soon, and it'll be good for both of us. You know I always look out for you."

That was true. "I'm trying to look out for you too, Beckett," I said. "I don't understand why you can't tell me. I can keep a secret."

"Just be patient. Everything will be revealed in time," he said in an overly dramatic voice. "In the meantime, I have to go. Have a fab dinner!"

That wasn't likely without Beckett's help. I laid my head on the table, hoping it might stop aching for a few moments. I needed water. I needed a plan. I was so not a cook. Why had I told William, Mr. Gourmand, that I would cook for him? Why was I even pretending I could cook something more than a Lean Cuisine? I sat and downed another gulp of coffee, trying to ignore the way my stomach rolled. Cooking was not rocket science. I could do this. I just had to figure out what to make.

Pasta? My throat tightened, and I swallowed back nausea.

Okay, maybe Mexican. My stomach clenched in revolt, and I had the feeling I'd have a distinctly greenish tinge if I looked in the mirror. I doubted much was going to sound very appetizing to me this morning. William knew I wasn't a cook. He wasn't going to expect a three-course dinner.

And then I had an idea. I almost smiled—except my head hurt too much. I really thought it would work, but I was going to need help. Beckett was doing his James Bond routine today, so I was going to have to go with my second choice: Minerva.

I pulled on a sweatshirt and shoes and headed downstairs. The Himmlers, Minerva and Hans, lived in the condo under mine. I hadn't seen much of them lately, but other than Beckett they were my best friends in Chicago. Minerva had been an opera singer in her day, but it was her talents in the kitchen I was after right now. I knew first-hand that Minerva's desserts would curl any man's toes.

I knocked on Minerva's door, and she answered a few minutes later, looking like she was ready for her close-up in a long black silk robe with feathers at the neck and wrists, her hair in a neat chignon, and her make-up perfect. She looked like she belonged in Hollywood. A delicious aroma wafted into the hallway through her open door.

"Catherine! How lovely. I just baked some Pfeffernüsse, traditional German cookies. They're Hans's favorite. You will have one with coffee, *ja*?"

She cooked in that outfit? Obviously, I had come to the right place. "Actually, Mrs. Himmler, I was wondering if you might be able to help me with something today." I explained that William was coming for dinner, and I wanted to make him something wonderful for dessert.

"Smart girl," she said with a nod. "The way to a man's heart is definitely his stomach. Come inside. We will decide on a recipe sure to make him fall in love with you."

"Thank you!"

Minerva's condo was laid out much like mine, but hers had a very European feel and was filled with antiques and memorabilia from her opera career. Hans sat in a comfortable chair by the fire reading the paper. He looked up and smiled at me, but Minerva waved him back down when he tried to rise. "We will be in the kitchen."

I gave Hans an apologetic look and followed Minerva. We perused a few of her cookbooks, which were all written in German, but I could study the pictures. We decided on a *Schwarzwälder Kirschtorte*, which was several layers of rich chocolate cake with whipped cream and cherries between each layer, decorated with chocolate shavings and more cherries. It looked decadent and delicious and Minerva promised me it would make William my slave forever. I made a list of the ingredients, and Minerva and I agreed to meet back at my condo in an hour. She wasn't about to pass up an opportunity to use my AGA.

I'd barely unpacked all the groceries when Minerva showed up, wearing a frilly apron to protect her black slacks and red blouse. She bustled into the kitchen and got right to work. I helped with the simple things like sifting the flour and measuring the dry ingredients, but Minerva handled the whipping and mixing, and the stirring and folding. As she worked, she hummed happily, the tune undoubtedly from some aria she once sang on stage in front of thousands of adoring fans. I knew the look of contentment on her face. I'd seen it on Beckett's a hundred times. On William's too.

"So how is your William?" Minerva asked, as though reading my thoughts. "You are cooking for him, *ja*? That is a good sign. He's handsome, that one." She smiled almost dreamily. I loved that even my nearly eighty-year-old neighbor wasn't immune to William's charm and good looks.

I didn't have the heart to tell her the torte was going to be the only thing I cooked. It was the thought that counted, right?

When the torte was in the AGA, I made Minerva a cup of coffee and we leaned on the kitchen counter. "So are the two of you in love?" she asked.

I felt a flush creep up my cheeks. "Am I that obvious?" I asked.

"Only because I know you. You would not cook for just anyone. It must be love."

I wanted to believe that. "How did you know you loved Mr. Himmler?"

"Ha. Some days I'm not certain I *do* love Hans. The man can be infuriating."

I thought of Hans in his brown cardigan, sitting in the chair by the fire, quietly reading the paper. He didn't look infuriating.

Minerva continued. "Is love something you know, Catherine, or something you decide? Your heart"—she touched her chest—"has made its decision. Now your head stands too much in the way. You young people think love is something you feel all the time. What is it you say? *I fell out of love.* No." She shook her head. "When it is *true* love, you make a decision to love no matter what comes. Do you know how long Hans and I have been married?"

I shook my head.

"Last week we celebrated fifty years."

I blinked. "I didn't even know. Congratulations. I should have brought you a gift."

She waved my suggestion away. "Thank you, but we have everything we could ever want. The point is, do you think I have been in love with Hans every day for the last fifty years?"

"Yes?"

"No! There have been many days, sometimes entire years, when I was not in love with Hans. I didn't even *like* him! "

I couldn't imagine fifty years with William. It was a lifetime. "What kept you married during those years, then?"

"I made a decision to love, Catherine, *ja*? I made it here." She touched her temple. "And here." She touched her heart. "You cannot trust *feelings*. Relationships are like those carnival rides." She made a wave motion with her hand.

"Roller coasters?"

"*Ja*. Some people get scared when they speed too fast or go upside down. They never see how the ride ends. They jump on another ride, only to abandon it also when they grow bored or restless." She leaned close. "Decide to stay until the end of the ride. Yes, it will not always be pleasant, but frightening twists are worth the exhilaration at the end."

I saw far too much of myself in Minerva's analogy. Whenever my relationship with William frightened me, I jumped off. He, however, was steady. He never seemed to doubt his feelings for me. Tonight was my chance to tell him I didn't doubt mine for him. I had decided to love, no matter what.

*****

I didn't hear from William for the rest of the day, and I finally texted around five to make sure he was still coming.

Be there at seven.

His message seemed a bit abrupt, but I figured he was probably in the middle of a meeting. A half an hour before he arrived, I set a beautiful table with a white tablecloth, candles, and the flowers I'd picked up at the corner store. I had pizza from this little place I loved warming in the AGA. I knew pizza wasn't quite on par with salmon mousse or Warm Oysters with Champagne Sabayon, but it was edible. Not to mention warm and gooey with a crispy thin crust. It smelled delicious.

I'd also picked up a six-pack of beer and two bottles of red wine. I made a salad—okay, I opened one of those bags of salad mix and poured it in a bowl—and I had my pièce de résistance, the chocolate torte, on a pedestal in the kitchen. Or perhaps I was the pièce de résistance. I'd changed into the sexiest lingerie I could find, which happened to be a set William had brought back with him from California. I had on crotchless black lace panties, garters and black silk-stockings, and a leather bustier. I'd pulled on a short black skirt, high black leather heels, and a little cardigan. The bustier pushed my girls up and out, and I didn't think I needed anything more to attract William's attention.

I felt a little naughty in the crotchless underwear, but I felt sexy too. William was going to love it.

He buzzed at two minutes to seven, and then was upstairs and knocking on my door moments later. Laird woofed, but I waved him back and opened the door. I stood for a moment, framed in the doorway, but he barely glanced at me. He leaned in and gave me a kiss on the cheek. "Hello, Catherine."

Okay, so maybe the leather didn't do it for him. I stepped aside to allow him to pass, and watched as the delicious smell of pizza hit him. "Smells good," he said. "What are we having?"

I smiled. "Pizza."

He gave a short laugh. "Pizza? Great."

Something was obviously bothering him. Maybe work hadn't gone so well. Or maybe something new had surfaced with the Wyatt situation. "Can I get you a beer? There's wine too," I added. "I thought we might have that with dinner, but I can pour you a glass."

"A beer would be fine."

I felt his gaze on me as I walked to the kitchen. He looked great in dark jeans and a leather jacket. He'd probably shaved before he'd come over. He didn't have a five o'clock shadow, and his hair was smooth and perfectly in place. When I returned to the living room, he hadn't moved or taken off the jacket.

I handed him a beer and he drank without even looking at the bottle.

"I hope it's okay that I got pizza. There's this little Italian place around the corner. They make everything from scratch."

"It's fine. Take-out is fine." He shifted and then his gaze met mine. My heart seemed to slow and slam into my chest. His eyes were a cold blue, no trace of warm grey in them at all. "I need to tell you something. Show you something."

He reached into his leather jacket and pulled out a large manila envelope. He opened it and slid a photo out. I stared at it for a long moment, not certain what I was seeing. And then I gasped. It was a black and white photo of Jeremy and me standing on the street in front of my car. Jeremy was kissing me.

For a moment I didn't understand. Jeremy hadn't kissed me...and then I remembered the goodbye kiss. It hadn't meant anything. It had been completely innocent, but it didn't look that way in the picture. It didn't look that way at all.

"Want to tell me exactly what's going on?" William asked, voice cold.

I shook my head. "It's not what you think." It sounded so cliché, like I was some sort of philandering husband. I tried again. "That picture. It's not...Listen, don't read anything into it. It was just a kiss. It wasn't...how it looks."

"I'm not stupid, Catherine." He threw the photo down, and I watched as the image of me and Jeremy fluttered to the floor. Oh my God, this was bad. Very bad. William wasn't stupid. How was I possibly going to explain? "That guy wanted you. I knew it that night, and I know it now. All the picture does is bring into question your feelings. Do *you* want him?"

How could he even ask me this after last night? Didn't he know by now how much I wanted him? Did he think I had e-sex with just any guy? "No, I don't want him." I shook my head. "Not at all. Not even a little. That kiss? It *so* doesn't matter."

He was watching me, his expression dubious. He didn't know if he believed me. That was fine because I had my own questions. "Want to tell me how you came by this picture? Do you have me under surveillance or something?" I couldn't help but think of the dossiers I'd seen in William's office. Photos and records of women he'd dated or planned to date. He'd said he'd never made one for me. But what was this? If he wasn't keeping tabs on me, where had this come from?

"You haven't answered all of my questions yet," William said.

"I did answer them. I told you this photo is nothing. I want you to answer me. Are you having me followed? Are you having George or one of your other henchman make a"—I didn't want to say *dossier*—"file on me?"

"I think you're avoiding talking about that kiss." He pointed to the photo on the floor, and I wished I could jump on it. Tear it up. Crumple it and throw it in the fire. But the image was in William's mind now. It was too late.

"You want to know about the picture?" I said, hands on hips. "Then tell me about who took it and why." God, I hoped this was just a turn in Minerva's figurative roller coaster ride because right now I really didn't feel so in love with William. Right now I wanted to smash him over the head with that beer bottle.

We stared at one another for a long moment. I wasn't backing down. I wanted answers. Finally, William set his beer on the coffee table and sighed. "I've been having you trailed by security since Napa."

"Since Napa? Oh my God!"

He closed his eyes. "I have my reasons. This latest Wyatt incident has made me uneasy. You're mine, Catherine." His gaze met mine with a look that made me go molten, even though desire was the last thing from my mind. "I haven't hidden that fact, and I protect what's mine. I said at my aunt and uncle's that I had stepped up security. If it's any consolation, I've had coverage on them and my cousins for the past week too."

My head was reeling. "And were they as in the dark about it as me?"

No answer.

"Right. Of course they knew. Why didn't you tell me?" Again! He was doing this to me again! "What is it with you, William? Why do think I can't handle anything? Why don't you think you can be upfront with me?"

He turned away and threaded his fingers through his hair, mussing it. "I don't want to upset your life." He rounded on me. "I don't want my shit to derail your life."

"What? Your shit is part of my life. If something is going on, I need to know."

He shook his head, and I wasn't even certain he'd heard me. "This is all because of me," he said, almost to himself. "I couldn't bear it if anything happened to you because of me." His hands closed on my upper arms, his grip light but possessive. "You're precious to me, Catherine. I just want to protect you."

I wanted to fall into his arms then. I knew he was telling me the truth, or his version of it. I loved that he wanted to protect me. I didn't love that he treated me as though I was a small child who couldn't know about the dangers in the big, wide world. "I don't understand. I get that you want me to be safe, but why keep me in the dark?"

He swallowed and his eyes hardened. "Because I can. And sometimes it's better that way." He turned away from me, and I stared at him. Was that really all he was going to say? Did he actually think that was going to satisfy me?

"It's better? For who? For you! How are we ever going to make this work if you're making all the decisions?"

His shoulders stiffened, but he didn't turn to look at me. Didn't respond.

"What haven't you told me?" I demanded. "Are we really in danger? Have there been threats? Are they against your family? Against me?"

William reached for the beer on the table, drank again, and paced the room. I watched him. He looked like some sort of caged panther. Why did he feel so trapped? Why couldn't he open up to me?

Finally, he looked at me again. "I've told you everything I can at the moment. Now it's your turn."

"Fine." I threw my arms out to the side. "You want the truth about that photo? It's *nothing*. We were just saying goodbye."

He looked at me, his eyes hard, his face slack. He was completely impassive, waiting for me to go on. When I didn't, he said, "Are you certain it meant nothing? It sure as hell doesn't look like nothing."

"I drove him to the airport. He gave me a quick kiss goodbye before we got in the car. End of story."

"Is it?" William's pacing stalled and he turned, heading for me. "He obviously came here to see you. It's a long trip from San Francisco, and you just saw him in Napa. What exactly was he expecting?"

My insides felt cold. I shook my head. "I have no idea." But I knew that wasn't going to fly. I had to say more. I shrugged. "We kind of had a falling out. I guess he wanted to try and make it right."

William's eyes narrowed. He was close enough now for me to smell the leather of his jacket and that other scent that was his alone. "I thought he was supportive after the accident and stuck by you."

"He did. Yes, but…it got…complicated."

His gaze bored into me. "How so? Did he hurt you?"

"No, nothing like that." I had to say more. I had to, but I didn't want to go there. I didn't want to go into it. I'd promised myself the whole thing was over. William didn't need to know. I closed my eyes. "He didn't hurt me, but I hurt him."

There was a long pause, and I finally opened my eyes. William was watching me, his face expressionless. I felt as though we were in merger negotiations, and I was on the losing side. "There's obviously more to it than that, Catherine." His tone was icy, his speech clipped. "Are you going to tell me or not?"

Now was the moment. I could tell him. I could reveal my deep secret. He might be pissed that Jeremy had been here and that we'd kissed, but he'd see it really was nothing. But it *wasn't* nothing to me. What I'd done was unforgivable in my mind. It was shameful. I didn't want to share it with him. And Beckett was right. Telling William wouldn't change anything. It wouldn't undo what I'd done. Finally, I put my hands on my hips. "Do you really want to talk about this?"

They were the same words William had said when I'd asked him about his history with Anya. He glared at me so long and so hard that I had to turn away. "It was a long time ago," I said, more to myself than to him. "It doesn't matter now."

He said nothing, and I sneaked a peek at him. He was still glaring, his face a mask of stone. Finally he said, "Tell me."

I looked at him, and I thought about Minerva and Hans and their fifty years. I thought about William as the little boy who had lost his family. I thought about what I'd wanted for this night, and how I'd planned to tell William I loved him. I still loved him. And I couldn't tell him this. There were some things too awful, some secrets too shameful to share. I bit my lip to stem the tears burning behind my eyes. I did not want to cry on top of everything else. I drew a deep breath and raised my eyes to William's. "There's nothing more to tell. You need to trust me on this."

How many times had he said that to me? How many times had he demanded I trust him without explanation? Now I wanted that same privilege. He could make all the demands he wanted, but I wasn't budging. I had a right to my privacy too. I wasn't going to be swayed by his orders and commands. This was it. I had to stand up for myself. "You have to trust me on this," I repeated.

William sighed. "I wish I could."

He turned without another word, strode to the door, opened it, and walked out. The door slammed closed behind him with a final thud.

Seventeen

I stared at my door for a full minute without moving. I couldn't believe he'd really left. What had just happened? This was supposed to be our romantic dinner, but somehow everything had gone wrong, and we'd ended up in a fight. Again.

But this wasn't our typical fight. Just thinking that made me cringe. How pathetic was it that we'd been together less than a month and I could already label our types of fights? This time William was the one demanding answers, and I was the one hedging. I was the one not ready to open myself up completely. I was the one who'd been left. Usually I walked away from William—more like ran away, actually. Tonight he'd walked away from me. My stomach churned and heaved, and I suddenly felt too warm. I stumbled to the kitchen table and collapsed into a chair before my knees could give out.

Were we really over now? He'd never looked so hurt. Abigail had told me he had a tender heart and I'd seen it on full display tonight. He'd been devastated that I wouldn't answer his questions about Jeremy. My stomach churned again, and I felt my heart sink. The last thing I wanted was to wound William any more than he'd already been hurt. I should be the one buoying him up, not bringing him down. Maybe I just didn't know how to be sensitive enough to him. I closed my eyes, seeing the pain in his gaze again. The look I remembered on his face sliced through me like a razor blade. In that moment, I hated myself. He'd told me often that he didn't deserve me. Clearly, I was the one who didn't deserve him. I was the one who kept fucking things up between us, so many times now it was almost laughable.

But I was heartbroken too. I couldn't believe he was having me watched and had neglected to tell me. Who the fuck does that? I did know he had increased his security, but I'd had no idea that it had been extended to include me. His intentions might have been good, but it still felt like a total invasion of my privacy. Why couldn't he tell me? Why couldn't he trust *me* for once? I *knew* there was more to it than William was letting on and that scared me. What was so awful that it made him feel he had to keep me in the dark? I'd never underestimate him, but that didn't mean I had to justify more bad behavior from him.

I went back and forth about it for what seemed like hours. Finally my head felt like it was about to explode. My stomach growled. There was no point in wasting perfectly good pizza. I nibbled on a slice, drank half a glass of wine, and blew out all the candles I'd lit. The smoky darkness in my condo matched my gloomy mood.

I brought my plate into the kitchen and caught sight of the chocolate torte on the pedestal. I wasn't even sure William had seen it. He definitely hadn't tasted it. Minerva would be so disappointed. All of her hard work for nothing. The smell of rich chocolate wafted toward me and, as always, I thought of William. But the cake reminded me of something Minerva had said too. She'd admitted there were times she didn't even like Hans, but what kept them together was the commitment she'd made to love. No matter what. Had Hans ever walked out on Minerva? Had he had her followed without telling her?

I didn't think so, but I was willing to bet both of them had made mistakes. They'd made a commitment. I wanted to commit to loving William like that, but it seemed like either he or I kept getting in the way. Maybe we just weren't meant to be.

I lifted the torte, pulled the trash out of the pantry, and dumped the whole thing inside.

With a flick of the lights, the condo went dark and I crawled into bed alone.

*****

I snapped awake when my phone dinged, alerting me I had a new text message. I glanced at the time, just before seven in the morning, and then read the text. I already knew who it would be from; no one else would text me this early. No one else I knew was awake this early.

Are you up?

No, but I needed to get up anyway. I hit Send and sat, pushing the hair out of my eyes. I really hadn't expected William to text me. Maybe things between us weren't over. But I just wished we could figure out whether we were together or not. I was so tired of wondering where I stood with him.

Are you okay?

My finger hovered over the phone as I thought about my reply. Was I? Not really. I was frustrated and heartbroken and missing him already. I wanted him back, but I was tired of the drama. I started to type, changed my mind, and decided to be honest.

I don't like fighting with you.

Neither do I.

I took a deep breath. Might as well get to the point. *I don't like being shut out.*

My words seemed to hover on the screen forever. Finally—

I understand.

I shook my head. *Do you really?*

Yes, really.

I wasn't quite sure if I believed that. Maybe William thought he understood, but I wasn't certain our two interpretations meshed. But should I push it more now? He decided the question for me with another text.

I don't like you kissing other men.

He was doing his own pushing. I sighed and typed.

It didn't mean anything. It hadn't meant anything more than goodbye, but I guess if I saw a picture of William kissing someone else, I wouldn't have liked it either. I waited for his response. And waited. And waited. Finally, his reply appeared on my screen.

I know. But I still hated seeing it.

Apparently he had decided to believe me. Before I could type a reply and mention *how* he had seen it and that we really needed to talk about that, he texted again.

Your torte looked good last night.

Ah, so he was changing the subject and *had* seen my dessert. I smiled. That was William. Steering the conversation the way he wanted it to go and always thinking about food. I had other things on my mind. *So did you. I threw the torte out.*

Heresy. Another cake wasted. I should have stayed.

Was he regretting walking away now? If he'd stayed, maybe we could have worked everything out before it got to this point.

I missed waking up with you.

I sighed again. He always knew how to melt my heart. *Me too.* But before he thought all was forgiven, I typed, *I'm still mad at you.*

Ditto. Truce?

I hesitated, and he must have sensed it because his next text came fast and furious.

I want you in my bed tonight. No talking. No fighting. Just us. You're mine, remember? I need to remind you...

I knew what that meant. I closed my eyes as a delicious shiver ran through me. How could I say no to that? *What time should I come over?*

*****

I lounged in bed for a while longer, then got up and showered and took my time getting dressed. I was meeting with Hutch Morrison in a few hours and I wanted to look chic but effortlessly so. I checked the weather and the day was supposed to be sunny and cold, so I went with a short black metallic tweed pencil skirt, a black silk blouse, black tights, and these cute stretch, suede, over-the-knee black boots I'd picked up on sale but hadn't worn yet because of the snow. The boots had a high heel and I knew I'd regret it if I had to walk on any icy patches, but I liked how they made me feel powerful. I put on my makeup and had just finished straight-ironing my hair when I heard a knock on the door.

"Amazing," I muttered to myself. For the first time in days, Beckett hadn't bailed on me. By the time I reached the door, Beckett already had it open and had stuck his head inside.

"Anybody home?"

"Come in," I called, while Laird greeted him with yips and excited jumps.

"Look at you," Beckett said, nodding appreciatively. "You look ready to break some hearts. Love the boots."

"I was going for sophisticated and powerful."

"You nailed it. I'm impressed". Beckett eyed me from head to toe. "You look sexy and on trend and not at all like a substitute math teacher. You've been paying attention. Very good."

"You're such an ass sometimes. You know that, right?" I laughed in response as I twirled around so he could see my back.

"Honey, someone's gotta tell you like it is and stop you from leaving the house looking like a retiree gearing up for a hot night of bingo. That's my job, and I won't ever let you down." He smiled broadly. "But you don't need me this morning, Miss Thing. You did this all on your own, and I don't think you can help it if you break a few hearts today. You look great, Cat. Hutch Morrison's jaw is going to *hit the floor* when he meets you. Oh yeah."

As hot as Hutch Morrison was, I wasn't trying to attract him. Much. "Maybe I should go with pants and a sweater instead?" I said. "I do want him to look at my work, not me."

Beckett shook his head, making his way into my condo. "No way. He's already seen your work, and he's impressed. Now he wants to meet you. Trust me, Hutch Morrison is a real charmer, a ladies' man. You'll get further with him if he thinks you're hot." He glanced around my living room, a scowl crossing his face. "Cat, you haven't even touched the mail I piled up for you when you were in Napa."

I looked at the coffee table. "That's not true. I put more mail on top of it." I waved a hand. "I'll go through it later. I've been busy. You know, with my *lover* and everything. I'm sure you can relate."

Beckett had been about to sit on my couch, but he paused. "What's that supposed to mean?"

"It just means you've been pretty busy yourself lately. You know, with your new boyfriend and your big secret, you haven't had much time for me."

I knew the moment I said it that it was the wrong thing to say. Beckett's smile faded, and his eyes turned hard. "Seriously, Cat? You're calling *me* selfish?"

I bristled. "And you're not? How many times have you cancelled on me in the last week or so? I had to order pizza for William last night after you bailed on helping me cook."

"Poor William. That must have been horrible for him."

"It wasn't, because we got in a fight and he left before eating it."

"Of course you did. More Cat drama to add to the mountain. Grow up, Catherine. If anyone is selfish, it's you."

"Excuse me? How am I selfish? I ask about your life all the time. I care about you. You're the one who won't share with me. You're the one with the *big secret* you can't tell me. I don't keep secrets from you, Beckett."

"And we're back to you." Beckett ran a hand through his hair. "Guess what, Cat? Not everything is about you. How many hours of my life do you think I've spent listening to your problems? I've heard you go over the thing that happened with Jeremy a thousand times. At least!"

My jaw dropped. "Well, maybe after Jace died, you should have just told me to snap out of it and I wouldn't have gotten together with Jeremy in the first place!"

"That's where you're wrong. Jace dying was a big deal, Cat, but the thing with Jeremy wasn't. It's long over and done with. Why are you still holding on to it?"

"I'm not." But my face must have betrayed me because Beckett raised a brow.

"Oh really? What did you and William fight about last night?"

"Fuck you," I said. Sometimes I hated it when Beckett was right.

"That's what I thought. This Jeremy thing has never been the big deal you think it is, Cat. You've turned it into something it's not so you can feel bad about it and give yourself another reason why you don't deserve to be happy."

I stood there, stunned, breathing hard and feeling my chest constrict. I clenched and unclenched my fists as I kept my gaze on

Beckett. There was no hint of a smile on his face, and I could tell he was really angry with me. I was mad too. It had been a long time since we'd had a fight like this.

Beckett was standing right in front of me now, his eyes blazing, his body tight with tension. "You complain about William not opening up, but you know what Jeremy is? He's the excuse *you* use to keep *yourself* closed off, to keep yourself emotionally protected. You're terrified of anyone knowing the real you. The real you who makes mistakes but doesn't think she deserves forgiveness. The real you who can't admit she wants to be loved."

"That's not true," I whispered. But it was. I knew, deep down, that Beckett was right. He always saw straight through me.

"It is true. You spend so much time convincing yourself that you're so awful and that you don't deserve to be loved that you push the people who do love you away. You know what I think? If you really think that way about yourself, then you should spare us all the pain of prolonging this relationship and end it with William Lambourne now."

"What? I can't believe you're saying this. That's not what I want."

"Really? Are you sure about that, Cat? I'm saying it because I see what you don't. William really cares about you." Beckett nodded even as I shook my head. "You're torturing him. And what you're doing to him isn't fair. "

"What *I'm* doing isn't fair? Like *he* tells *me* everything? Why are you defending him anyway? You're supposed to be on my side."

Beckett grabbed my shoulders lightly. "You are such an idiot sometimes."

"Let go!"

He ignored me. "There are no sides, don't you see that? I'm trying to help you understand how lucky you are." He shook me gently. "Do you get how lucky you are? I mean, most of us struggle to find love just once. But you—" He released me and stepped away, then pointed at me accusingly. "You've got a second chance! What are you thinking? That the *third* time will be the charm? I don't think those odds are very good."

I shook my head. My thoughts were spinning now, moving wildly. Beckett was starting to make a lot of sense. And what did that say about me? That I was an idiot? That I was selfish? But maybe, I thought, because I had found love before I knew how it should feel, what it should be. "I do think I'm lucky," I said to Beckett.

"Well, hallelujah! An epiphany," he sang mockingly.

I scowled at him. "But that doesn't mean I have to excuse William when he completely shuts me out."

Beckett put his head in his hands and shook it. "Shut up! Just shut up, Cat. Your issue is that he's keeping secrets? So what? We're all adults, Cat. We *all* have pasts. We *all* have baggage. You don't hold the exclusive rights to that."

"And I've shared a lot of my shit with him, Beckett. All I get from him is him telling me I have to trust him. If this relationship is going to work, he has to trust me. Shouldn't that be a priority in any relationship?"

Beckett folded his arms across his chest. "You want to talk priorities. Okay. Have you ever wondered what William Lambourne does all day? I mean, how exactly does a billionaire noted financier, philanthropist, vintner, restaurateur, and man about town spend his days?"

I could see where this was going, and I took a step back. My knee hit the couch, and I sat down hard.

"Working, Cat. *Working*. He's got a lot of shit going on. Shit you couldn't possibly know about. But you're not a priority, right?"

I looked away.

"You know he's done nothing but make you a priority in his life since the moment he met you. And what's your response? You whined because he left you alone in his fabulous Napa Valley mansion for two days. With staff! I mean, cry me a river, Cat. He's told you time and time again that he hasn't felt like this with anyone else, ever, but that's not enough for you. What does he need to do to make how he feels about you any clearer? I mean, for God's sake, Cat, he took you to meet his family. It's pretty apparent to just about everyone else that you *are* his top priority."

I sat back and closed my eyes. I didn't know if Beckett was right or not, but he'd definitely hit a nerve. I felt awful. I bit my lip to keep tears from falling and ruining my make up, and when I finally felt as though I had control, I opened my eyes. Beckett was kneeling in front of me.

"I'm saying this because I love you. You know that, right?"

I nodded. I knew Beckett loved me, and I knew he was saying what he thought I needed to hear.

"If your friends can't tell you the truth, who can?"

I nodded again.

Beckett's arms came around me, and he pulled me into a hug. "I just want you to be happy. It's okay to choose happiness, Cat. No matter what you do, there's always going to be risk. You just can't let that hold you back anymore."

Beckett rose and looked down at me. "Sorry if I upset you before your meeting with Hutch. You're going to be great."

I smiled weakly and nodded a third time, then watched as Beckett made his way to the door, exited, and closed it with a quiet click. This was not the morning I'd expected.

Laird came and put his head on my knee. I petted him and gave him a quick hug, heedless of the dog hair getting on my clothes. I felt pretty shitty about everything at the moment—my relationship with William, Beckett, my past. Even my future wasn't looking too great. "We'll go for a long walk later, okay?" I told Laird as I scratched him behind the ears.

I wished I could just lie on my couch for the rest of the day and sulk, but right now I had to get moving. I didn't want to drive and mess with parking, which meant I had to hurry to catch the L if I was going to make it to my appointment with Hutch on time.

I went in the bathroom, freshened my makeup, and brushed my teeth. I swiped my face with powder and added a dab of lip gloss to my lips, then grabbed my coat and my bag, pausing when I passed the stack of mail on my coffee table. Beckett had been considerate enough to consolidate it all for me, so I might as well start going through it. I'd have time to read on the train.

I grabbed a couple of catalogs, a magazine, and a large envelope. It didn't have a return address, so I figured it wasn't a bill. Probably another catalog. I stuffed the mail in my bag, shrugged into my coat, and headed out. I pushed open the door to the building as a guy carrying a toolbox slammed the door of a white van and jogged up. "Hey, hold the door!"

I leaned back on the door, holding it open and juggling my bag and mail.

"Sorry," the guy said. "Plumber. Leaky pipe on the first floor, and I'm already running late. Thanks!"

He breezed past me, and I started to walk away but then turned to look back at him. Something about him was familiar. Had I seen him around before? Nothing about him stood out. I just had a weird, *déjà vu* feeling. I shrugged it off and let the door close behind me. I had a meeting with sexy Hutch Morrison to make.

EIGHTEEN

Morrison Hotel was located downtown in the South Loop. It was usually a pretty quick ride on the L, but today the train was crawling along and lingering at every stop for much longer than normal. I had plenty of time to think about my fight with Beckett.

We hadn't fought very many times during our friendship, but the few times we had had been epic. The last big fight I could remember was after Jace had died, when I wanted to give up photography. I couldn't bear to take surfing pictures anymore, and I thought that was all I could do.

We'd argued about it casually over the phone for months, but once I told him I was starting to look for jobs—I didn't care what I did at that point, I just needed to pay the rent—Beckett lost it. We had a huge fight and Beckett told me he would never speak to me again, especially if I took the receptionist job at Discount Tire Warehouse I'd been offered. He was serious. He had more faith in me than I had in myself at that point and he'd argued I could make anything I photographed exciting—even radishes. Then he'd basically dared me to come to Chicago and give it a try. I was so pissed at him, I didn't speak to him for over a month. But I did turn down that job. We made up and eventually I took him up on his offer. Of course, once I'd come to Chicago, I'd decided to stay. And Beckett—damn him—had been right about the radishes. And about me.

He tended to be right about pretty much everything, which meant I could either be pissed at him for a week and then admit he was right—that I hadn't exactly been fair to William—or I could admit it now. If I admitted it now, it would cut out a few steps.

Fine. So Beckett was right. I was selfish. I really never thought about everything William had to juggle to fit me into his schedule. And I also knew that all the annoying secretive shit he pulled, like having me followed or leaving me in Napa, he did because he cared about me and wanted to protect me. Was it so bad having a boyfriend who wanted to keep me safe, even I didn't know what, exactly, he was protecting me from? The world he inhabited was so completely foreign to me—what could I possibly know about what he dealt with on a daily basis? I should just be happy he cared about me enough to go to all the trouble.

As for Beckett's argument about Jeremy, I still wasn't convinced sleeping with my dead husband's brother wasn't a big deal. I could work on forgiving myself for it though, especially now that I had squared things with Jeremy as best I could. Maybe my shame would fade over time. Maybe.

But I did know one thing for certain. I loved William Maddox Lambourne. I loved him so much it hurt when we weren't together. Our texts this morning had been nice, but it was killing me that we were still fighting.

I reached into my bag, looking for something to take my mind off the state of my relationships, and pulled out the stack of mail. I had several thick catalogs—Pottery Barn, Williams Sonoma, Restoration Hardware, Chefs Catalog…that one was for work. The last piece of mail was the large envelope. I looked at it more closely and noted it had only my name and address on it. It had been mailed in Chicago just a couple of days ago.

I ripped it open and pulled out three proof sheets. I hadn't even considered Fresh Market might return the proofs of my asparagus and cherries shots with comments. I flipped the sheets over and gasped. These weren't pictures I'd taken. I stared instead at pictures taken of me.

They were candid shots of my everyday activities—images of me walking alone, walking with Laird, running by the lakefront, juggling bags as I got out of my car, walking up the front steps to my building. They looked like they'd been taken on different days and at different times—I could see the varying amounts of snow in the background, indicating whoever was watching me and snapping away had been doing so on a regular basis.

I tried to remember if the envelope had been in the pile Beckett amassed during my days in Napa or if I'd pulled it from my mailbox and, if so, when. But I couldn't remember at all. Maybe William had intended to tell me he was having me followed and this was how he'd planned to share it with me. But what was the point? To show he was having me watched even during the mundane, routine parts of my life? To demonstrate that he could keep tabs on me *because he could*? What the fuck. Didn't he have anything better to spend his money on? And what did this prove anyway—other than he was a bit obsessive? I stuffed the photos back into the envelope and sighed. We were only going to work if this kind of shit stopped.

I arrived at Morrison Hotel only three minutes late for my meeting with Hutch, which had to be some kind of record for me. The restaurant was housed in an ordinary-looking, two-story, red brick store front. *Morrison Hotel* was arched across the front window in big white letters drop-shadowed in red. I stepped inside and squinted slightly until my eyes adjusted to the dark. It was small and intimate, and I had a view of the entire layout from the entrance. It appeared empty, but I could hear voices and sounds coming from the kitchen, which I could see was in the back.

I studied the sleek, modern lines. The exterior of the building didn't suggest the interior at all. The floors were stone throughout and the tables were polished dark wood. Some had already been set in preparation for dinner with crisp white tablecloths and wine glasses. Tables lined either side of the center aisle framed on one side by plush banquettes and by simple metal and cushioned navy chairs on the other. The ceiling, ornamented with wooden and metal arches, was open, and sleek industrial lighting spotlighted the tables, while circular fixtures gave the entire restaurant a soft glow.

I had only been standing in the entrance for a moment when a leggy brunette in a tight black skirt and a white blouse walked toward me. "You must be Catherine Kelly," she said, heels clicking on the stone as she crossed the restaurant.

"Yes." I still had my hands in my pockets to keep them warm, but I took one out and she shook it. "I'm here to see Hutch Morrison."

"He's waiting for you. I'll take your coat."

I wasn't quite ready to give up the warmth of my coat, but I shrugged it off and let her hang it on an antique coat rack near the door. She led me into the restaurant, and I figured she was taking me back to the kitchen to meet Hutch. But as my gaze swept the room, my spine began to tingle, and when we neared a booth that had been hidden from the entrance by a dark blue partition, I knew right away the man seated there was Hutch Morrison. He looked exactly like his picture—cocky, confident, and sexy as hell. He was blond, tan—interesting since it was deep winter in Chicago—and heavily inked. As I neared, he gave me a slow, sexy smile, which made my heart thunk in my chest. For a moment I was a bit dazed.

Hutch stood, unfolding his long, lean body and easing to a standing position right in front of me. And then it struck me why I was reacting to him so strongly: he reminded me of Jace. They were about the same height, and had a similar build and coloring. I might be with a tall, dark, and handsome man now, but blond and ripped had always been my type. Jace's hair had been naturally blond, and Hutch's looked more light brown with blond streaks from the sun, but the two men really did bear a resemblance. Of course, with all the tattoos, Hutch looked a whole lot edgier and more than a little dangerous. He wore a close-fit black v-neck t-shirt, and I noted the tats peeking out on his upper chest.

I took in his corded, defined arms, also covered in tattoos. I could imagine those arms braced on either side of a woman as he knelt above her in bed. I took a shaky breath and tried to banish the image before I looked too closely and had to admit the woman I pictured him pleasuring was me.

"Thank you, Madison," he said, dismissing the woman. His eyes never left my face. "Miss Catherine Kelly?" His voice was the same one I remembered from the phone, slow and soft. The way he said my name, in that Southern accent, was completely disarming.

"Hi," I said. *Hi*? That was so not the way I began business meetings. If Beckett were here he'd be sniggering already. "I mean, yes. I'm Catherine. You must be Mr. Morrison."

"Sweetheart, I told you on the phone. Mr. Morrison is my daddy." He took my hand and led me to the booth. "You can call me Hutch."

"Alright, Hutch. It's nice to meet you in person."

"Likewise. Let me take a look at you." He gave my hand a little tug before I could sit on the cushioned seat. "Black." He grinned at me. "My favorite color. I hope you have that tight little body from working out and not starving yourself. I intend to feed you, Catherine."

"I"…" I wasn't quite sure how to answer that. I should probably have been offended, but I found myself smiling. "I'm not really hungry, but I wouldn't mind some coffee."

His smile turned mischievous. "Oh, that's sacrilege. You can't come into a chef's signature restaurant without an appetite."

I flushed, embarrassed I'd been so careless with my words. He was right, of course. I didn't mean to offend him before our meeting even began. I started to apologize. "I'm sorry. That's not what I—"

"Don't worry about it, darlin'. I *know* you're hungry. *You* just don't know it yet. But you will." He winked at me. "Wait until you try my cooking." Before I could answer, he tugged me toward him. I realized he hadn't ever released my hand. He did now, moving a hand to the small of my back and holding me against him as we made our way into the kitchen. We were so close that I felt like we were long-lost friends.

I also felt his body against mine. It wasn't only his arms that were muscled and defined. I was pretty sure he hid hard washboard abs and a tight chest under that t-shirt. And there was something so intoxicating about the way he smelled—woodsy and smoky.

The kitchen was just a few steps away, and it was seriously awe-inspiring, even for a novice like me. It was big, much bigger than the kitchen at Willowgrass. It was completely open too, so diners could see just about everything that was going on. Cooking as theater. It was bright and spotless, the stainless steel appliances gleaming, the white surfaces immaculate. It looked meticulously organized and like a perfect stage for Hutch's brand of elegant, refined cuisine. A chef in a white coat and black trousers nodded when we entered. He was at the other end of a long, gleaming, stainless steel center table finely chopping vegetables, likely the *mise en place* for the night's service. Above the table, cylindrical light bulbs hung in glass cases, reflecting softly off the steel.

"This is majorly impressive," I said.

Hutch smiled at me. "This is home." But for someone who was home, he looked a lot more serious than he had in the restaurant's seating area. He moved confidently around the counter where food was expedited and toward the ovens and stove tops. He looked completely at ease and also completely focused. I could tell he was a man who was intensely passionate and dedicated to his art.

At the other end of the prep table, Hutch began to mix ingredients, and while I sort of paid attention to what he was doing, mainly I watched the way the muscles in his arms flexed and released.

"What are you making?" I asked.

"A little sampling from our upcoming menu. Brown sugar and cinnamon beignets with a simple blueberry compote and café au lait with chicory. Sound good?"

"It sounds fantastic. Now I understand why it's so hard to get reservations here."

He glanced up at me. "We don't take reservations, honey," he said. "We sell tickets." He moved toward the stoves, heating the oil to cook the beignet dough he'd just prepared.

"My friend Beckett mentioned something about tickets. He's a food stylist and a big fan of yours."

Hutch looked over his shoulder, a knowing grin on his face. "I bet. So you haven't eaten here?"

"No."

He turned toward me. "For shame, Miss Catherine. We'll have to change that." He moved to the prep table again and began doing something with blueberries. "The way Morrison Hotel works," he said, never taking his attention from the food, "is that you buy a ticket to one of my food *events*. Right now the theme is 'London Calling.'"

"So what kind of food is that?"

"It's *my* kind of food. I was really interested in exploring the French influences in Marrakech and I also love London pub fare. You know, fish and chips, bangers and mash, mussels, roast beef. Really hearty, traditional English food. I explored the different flavor profiles and textures and came up with some of my own techniques for combining them, then I made it all work. That's what I do."

Hutch gave me a satisfied grin as I stood there, speechless.

"The upcoming theme is 'Sticky Fingers,' and that's going to be Southern and Creole fare. Much more down home for me. A little simpler too. I'm from Alabama, you know, just outside of Mobile."

"Thus the beignets."

"Yes, ma'am. I'll be exploring the food of my youth for a while, but I'll move on to something else in three months or so. I decided to go with tickets because I knew reservations would be impossible to get anyway. This was going to be the hottest restaurant in Chicago the minute the doors opened."

"That's pretty cocky," I said before I could think.

"I'm only cocky about three things, Catherine, and those are things at which I excel. One is cooking. When you taste this little snack, you can be the judge as to whether I've oversold myself. But back to the restaurant." He moved again to the stove, working on his beignets. I had forgotten he was even cooking. He was so relaxed and confident. He reminded me a lot of William in the kitchen.

"If you want to eat at Morrison Hotel—well, not you, darlin', you can be my guest anytime—you buy a ticket for the theme. It's going to cost you about a hundred and fifty bucks or thereabouts, depending on what we're serving and whether you want wine pairings. You pay in advance, and your place is reserved. You don't have to wait to be seated. You don't have to flag the waiter down at the end of the meal and ask for the bill or face that awkward moment when no one is sure who is going to pay. That's all taken care of. You just bring your appetite and sit back and wait for the show."

I leaned my elbows on the prep table and watched his back as he removed the beignets and dusted them with cinnamon and brown sugar. He turned, placed them on the table, and drizzled the compote beside them. They smelled so delicious, I wanted to reach over and tear a piece off. "Sounds like a good system," I said. "What about people with dietary restrictions? Vegetarians or gluten-free?"

He scowled at me and then reached for two large coffee cups. "We make it pretty clear we don't accommodate that sort of thing."

"Really? Why not?"

"Because every dish on the menu has been carefully constructed and prepared so that it's the best. People come here to experience my vision, Catherine. If we start taking out ingredients and substituting others, it's not my vision any more, it's theirs. That's not what Morrison Hotel is about." He handed me a cup of coffee, which smelled better than any coffee had a right to. "Don't tell me you're a vegetarian."

"No," I said.

"Thank God. I heard you were from California." He gestured toward the restaurant, and I led the way. Behind me he balanced his cup of coffee and the plate of beignets. "I never considered you might be one of the granola eaters. Not after I saw those cock kebabs."

I felt my face heat. I didn't know why. There was no reason his verbiage should embarrass me. Beckett called them cock kebabs too, and I didn't blush with him.

We sat at the booth where he'd been before, Hutch on one side and me on the other. The beignets were between us. "So tell me about the project you want me to work on," I said.

"Oh, no, sweetheart. Pleasure before business. These beignets aren't going to taste as good if they're cold. Eat up." He lifted one and raised it to my lips, so I had little choice but to open my mouth and bite. As soon as I tasted the brown sugar and cinnamon on the flaky warm dough, I closed my eyes.

"This is delicious." I licked my lips to catch the sugar on them with my tongue.

"I do like watching you eat. Now try it with the compote."

I opened my eyes and watched as he swirled the beignet lightly in sauce. With William I would have obediently opened my mouth again, but this time I took the beignet from Hutch and tasted it on my own. "Mmm. Interesting. I wouldn't have thought of pairing blueberries and beignets."

"It works, doesn't it? My grandma used to make something like this and it reminds me of summer, of foods of my youth. Sometimes simple *is* perfection."

"It's amazing."

He sat back and sipped his coffee, looking satisfied. I sipped my own coffee and then had to have another sip.

"You like?" he asked, brow raised.

"It's perfect. Just the right amount of sweet and strong."

"You definitely have to come back and dine with us, Catherine. If you agree to work with me on the book, you'll dine here often."

I smiled and sipped the coffee again. It was really good. Way better than the instant stuff I made or the lattes I consumed at Starbucks.

"That was your cue, darlin'. We can talk about the book now."

"Oh! Sorry." I sat straight and leaned forward. "So tell me about it."

"I'm going to do an e-book with a narrative about the restaurant, and I want fabulous pictures to accompany it. I told you our next theme is 'Sticky Fingers.' I want you to photograph it all: the restaurant, my team, the process of creating and assembling the dishes, and the food. That's the important thing. I want the food to look fucking awesome. That's why I need you."

I was intrigued and a little intimidated. "It sounds fabulous, but it's also a really big job."

"I don't do anything halfway. It's a huge undertaking and it's going to get a lot of attention, but I think you've got the right eye for it. I didn't pull your name out of a hat. I asked around. I did my research."

"Then you know I haven't done anything like this before."

He sat forward, arms on the table between us. "I know you're the person I want. I've seen good things. I've heard good things. I'm impressed, Miss Catherine Kelly, and I don't impress easily. I know Ben Lee. He's the one who first suggested you."

"Ben was really sweet to take me on at the last minute. I owe him."

Hutch shook his head. "Take a look at your photos in *Chicago Now*. Those figs were damn sexy, Catherine, almost pornographic. Then take a look at the waitlist to get into Willowgrass. Your debt is paid."

I felt my face heat again. I had the feeling Ben's cooking, more than my photographs of his raw figs with blue cheese and drizzled with warm, spiced honey, was the reason Willowgrass was so successful. But Morrison Hotel was on a whole other level. It would be huge to have my name associated with it and with a chef like Hutch. He was internationally revered and what I'd seen from him in the kitchen reminded me of what I'd seen in so many of the best surfers. Determination, razor focus, absolute dedication. Hutch would not be an easy man to work with. "I'm definitely interested," I said.

"Good. Take your time and think about it. Ask your Mr. Lambourne his opinion. He's been in here more than once."

I blinked in surprise before it occurred to me that Ben might have mentioned my relationship with William. Still, I hadn't expected the conversation to move to him—to William. "He's not *my* Mr. Lambourne," I said. William wasn't anyone's to claim, least of all mine at the moment. Hutch cocked an eyebrow.

I gestured futilely. "William and I...we're..." I faltered. What exactly were we now?

"Now this *is* interesting. He's a lucky man if he has you, Catherine, but I kind of like the odds better if he doesn't." He winked at me.

I almost laughed. Hutch had a way of flirting that was more fun than predatory. He was a lot different from William in that way. But if he and William were in business together, I needed to know that up front. "Is William an investor in Morrison Hotel?" I asked.

"Oh, no, darlin'. Lambourne is a good guy, and he definitely has his hand in eateries all over town, but this ain't one of them. Morrison Hotel is all mine. I don't want you in order to get to him. I want you because you're the best."

"Alright. What do you need from me? A proposal?"

"You read my mind. See, we work well together already. And Catherine, I'll want that ASAP. I want to move on this."

Sensing the meeting was over, I rose and Hutch, always the gentleman, followed. "Any questions for me before you go?"

"Not really." I should have left it at that. I knew I should. But I didn't. "You mentioned you were cocky about three things. One is cooking and I have to admit, those were the best beignets I've ever had. What are the other two?"

We paused at the entrance, and he gave me a lazy grin. "Are you sure you want to know?"

I nodded, not sure at all.

"You aren't going to find anyone who can cook, play guitar, or fuck better than I can. I'm cocky, but I live up to the hype."

I didn't have a response, but was saved when Hutch leaned forward and kissed me on both cheeks. I caught his scent again and a glimpse of the tattoos that began on the side of his neck and snaked downward. Just what artistic wonders lay under his shirt? I blushed and stepped away.

"Call me, beautiful," he said, seeming to know exactly what I'd been thinking. "I'll be waiting."

*****

I stepped out of Morrison Hotel and into the bright sunlight, made even brighter by the contrast to the dark interior of the restaurant. I only paused for a moment to get my bearings because I knew exactly where I was headed—to WML Capital Management. I figured it was about a thirty-minute walk up Michigan Avenue, but I didn't mind. The sky was clear and it was brisk, but not windy, plus I needed the time to get my head on straight.

The project sounded great and Hutch Morrison was hotter than hell. Though he wasn't really a temptation, I wasn't completely immune to his playful flirting, and that made me want to be with my boyfriend. The boyfriend I was lucky to have. The boyfriend I was madly in love with. The boyfriend I was ready to tell whatever he wanted to know about me.

I thought about what I was going to say to William. Whenever I was in his presence, he tended to overwhelm me. He wanted me in his bed tonight but today, I needed to have a calm, rational, adult conversation with him. No fighting. No stand-up sex in front of his floor-to-ceiling windows overlooking all of downtown Chicago—at least not right away.

I walked quickly, passing men and women in heavy winter coats, enjoying the rare sunny day in early February. For the moment, I was one of the faceless and nameless in the crowd, caught up in my own thoughts as I strode purposely toward my destination.

William and I had shared incredible chemistry from the moment we'd met. He'd pursued me, and though I'd resisted, I really didn't mind being caught. He was gorgeous and thoughtful and really, really, *really* amazing in bed. I never even had a chance.

The fact that he could give me more orgasms than I could count in the space of a couple of hours didn't make me fall in love with him. I fell in love with the man who loved to cook, who sang off-key, who made wine, and who still held on to a hope for his family, even though all seemed lost. He was loyal, protective, and tender.

Deep down, I knew I could trust him. I trusted him with my body, and I could trust him with my secrets and my heart. And I wanted to be with him. No matter what. Yes, he drove me crazy when he took off without letting me know. Yes, all of his money got in the way of our relationship sometimes. But I loved him, and that meant I would take the good with the bad. I just hoped he would give me the chance.

I wasn't prepared to let everything slide, however. This stalker thing—having me followed on the sly and sending me the photo proofs—that had to stop. If he felt better having his security team look out for me, fine. But I wanted to know about it.

As I crossed over the Michigan Avenue Bridge, I took a deep breath of the cold air. My cheeks were tingling and my fingers, even inside my coat pockets, were numb from the cold. I was so lost in thought, I almost passed William's building. I caught myself in time and entered through the revolving doors. The elevators were straight ahead, and I waited with several men in business suits until one arrived. I could see myself in the reflection of the elevator doors. My cheeks were pink from the cold and my hair was windblown. I didn't smooth it or straighten my scarf. This was who I was.

Finally, I stepped in and pressed the button for the top floor. A couple of the men glanced at me curiously, but I moved to the back and didn't make eye contact. I remembered the first time I'd come here. I'd been with William then, in his private elevator, and he'd pushed me against the wall and kissed me savagely, taking my breath away. The memory of his hard body pressed against mine, his tongue thrusting between my lips, his hands in my hair was enough to make my legs weak and my breath come in short gasps. I curled my hands into fists, eager to see him, to touch him, to kiss him.

After we talked, I reminded myself. I had the envelope with the proofs in my bag. We needed to talk about those before we touched or we'd never have the conversation.

I was alone in the elevator for the last few floors, and when I stepped off, the floor was hushed and quiet. A handsome older woman sat at a circular desk guarding the doors to the inner office area. She gave me a cautious smile as I approached.

"May I help you?"

"I'm here to see Wil—Mr. Lambourne."

"Do you have an appointment?"

"No. I…Just tell him Catherine Kelly is here."

The woman's brows shot up and her eyes quickly perused my hair and clothes. Maybe I should have brushed my hair.

"Just one moment, Miss Kelly." She lifted her phone and spoke quietly into the receiver. Then she replaced it and smiled at me again. I shifted from one foot to another, feeling awkward until the door behind the receptionist opened and Parker emerged.

"Miss Kelly. I'm so sorry not to meet you. I wasn't expecting you."

"Hi, Parker. Call me Catherine, please. I'm here to see William. Does he have a minute?"

"Come back with me." She gestured for me to follow her into the inner offices. She keyed in a code and opened the door. This was the area where William's private elevator opened. Obviously he had extra security to keep unauthorized individuals out.

I followed Parker to William's outer office, and she spoke as she walked—or teetered—on black stilettos. I wondered if her feet hurt by the end of the day. "Mr. Lambourne isn't expecting you. He's in a meeting right now, but I'll let him know you're here."

She gestured to one of the fancy modern chairs near her desk. Dutifully, I sat, unbuttoning my coat and unwrapping my scarf now that I was warming up. Parker lifted the phone and spoke quietly. I heard my name but not much else.

A moment later, she replaced the receiver and said, "May I get you something—a latte or a bottle of water? Whatever you like."

I wasn't thirsty, but I sensed Parker wanted something to do. "Water would be great," I said, looking around the reception area. Like William's office, the décor was minimalist, but here and there Parker had managed to add a bit of color. A red pillow on one chair, a small colorful abstract print above her desk.

She disappeared around a corner and returned a moment later with a cold bottle of water. She also held a glass filled with ice. I took both but set the glass down and drank from the bottle. My hands shook slightly, and I didn't want to spill.

I waited. Parker waited. She tried to look busy, but we were both just biding time. Finally, her phone buzzed and she snatched it up. "Yes. Very good." She replaced it and stood. "Right this way, Catherine."

I jumped up and had a moment's hesitation about what to do with the water bottle. I left it on Parker's desk and gathered my bag. Parker opened the door to William's office, and I stepped inside.

It was exactly as I remembered—stark and stylish—and I looked toward William's desk as Parker closed the door behind me. He was seated behind it, and immediately my mind flashed to our video chat from the other night. He'd been behind the desk then too, but he'd been wearing glasses. There was no sign of the glasses now, but I could still envision him behind the desk, watching me as I touched myself on screen. I felt my cheeks flame and took a step inside. I wasn't feeling as brave as I had on the way over. I felt very much the intruder.

William stood up, his expression unreadable, but I saw a flicker of something in his eyes. His gaze snapped to the chair before his desk and then back again. I followed his look and noted we weren't alone. The man in the seat across from William faced away from me, showing only the back of his head, but there was something familiar about him nonetheless.

Something very, very familiar.

NINETEEN

The man turned, and I gasped. It was Beckett.

For a moment I couldn't process it. Everything was strangely surreal, like a scrambled image that made no sense. Why was Beckett in William's office? Beckett didn't belong here. Beckett and William had nothing in common except…

Me.

Oh my God. I stumbled back a step. I took a deep breath, forcing oxygen into my chest, which felt tight with panic. Beckett had just accused me of thinking everything was about me. So maybe this wasn't about me. That didn't mean it wasn't weird—my best friend and my boyfriend. Why hadn't they told me about this? Was this something else they were hiding from me? Something bad? Had something happened to a friend? Someone in my family?

"What is this?" I blurted out, looking from William to Beckett. "What's going on?"

Neither man answered. My heart pounded even harder in my chest. What was wrong? What couldn't they tell me? They would have said if it was my family, so it had to be something else. "Is this what you've been so secretive about?" I asked Beckett. I looked at William. "Is this another thing you can't tell me?" Still neither one of them spoke.

I looked from Beckett to William and felt tears burn my eyes. I had to get out of here before I started crying. "I'm sorry. I can see I'm intruding. I'll get out."

"Cat—"

"No, Beckett. It's okay. I'll just go." I looked at William. He looked concerned, and I didn't want his concern at the moment. I just wanted to run before I started sobbing. The paper of the envelope brushed my arm, and I reached into my bag and yanked it out. "Here, you can have these. Maybe we can talk about it later when you're...not so busy." I tossed the envelope on the table in the center of the room and turned to leave. Before I could reach the door, William was beside me. He took my arm and swung me around to face him.

"Catherine, calm down. This is not what you think. There's nothing secret about this." He gestured to Beckett, who had risen now.

"Really? Nothing secret? *I* didn't know about it."

William's hands rested on my upper arms, holding me firmly in place. I didn't fight him. I was still holding back tears, but it was difficult to resist those stormy-grey eyes, especially when he had his gaze leveled directly on me. "Beckett has been wanting to tell you about this since the beginning. He stopped by this afternoon to ask if he could. He said he told you he signed an NDA."

"So?"

"My big secret," Beckett said. "Remember? I told you I was working on something but I wasn't allowed to talk about it yet?"

The puzzle rearranged itself again. So this meeting was about Beckett and William doing business? Together? I glanced at Beckett again. He was dressed in a suit. Of course it was a slim pastel blue suit with tight trousers, much different than William's classic charcoal wool Armani, but like me, Beckett tended to dress *creatively*. If this was business, the suit made sense.

"What does he have to do with the NDA?" I asked, pointing at William.

But William answered before Beckett could. "I'm a financial backer in a new restaurant venture."

"Cat, I'm going to run a bakery," Beckett said. "That's the big news. And it's not just any bakery."

I stared, trying to take in what Beckett was saying. This was huge. "Do you remember Emil LeClerc?" William asked.

"No." The name sounded familiar, but I was still reeling from the news that Beckett was finally going to get the chance to bake. He would finally achieve his dream.

"Emil LeClerc catered the Art Institute dinner we attended," William said.

I remembered that dinner very well. It was my first date with William and my absolute worst date ever. William had been sweet and charming in the car on the way there but had changed completely once we arrived. He'd been cold and distant and completely ignored me. I'd ended up walking out without even saying goodbye. But I remembered William had praised Chef LeClerc, and I'd wanted to try his food. I'd run into Ben Lee that night, and Ben had remarked that he'd trained in France under LeClerc. Ben had given me a bite of a blini, but other than that I'd mainly drank my dinner. I never got the chance to eat much of the beautiful food.

"I do remember," I said. "Ben said you'd backed LeClerc's New York City restaurant." Suddenly my heart clenched. "Beckett, you're not moving to New York, are you?"

"No. LeClerc is opening a restaurant in Chicago."

"Not quite," William added. His hands were still on my arms, and his thumbs were moving in circles, sending waves of warmth through me. "LeClerc is the name behind a French bistro concept restaurant that I and several other investors back. We'll be rolling it out in Chicago in a new luxury boutique hotel opening in Lincoln Park. Bistro LeClerc will be in the hotel, and next door to Bistro LeClerc will be Patisserie LeClerc, a bakery."

"Pastries, Cat," Beckett added. "Just like Paris." His eyes shone brightly, and his face was flushed with excitement. I couldn't help but smile.

"The kind of delicacies you're so good at making," I said.

"Exactly. And the patisserie is going to have a storefront and offer lots of fabulous confections. But we'll also supply the bistro with all of its bread and desserts."

"And what Beckett has been wanting to tell you is that he's been tapped as the head pastry chef for Patisserie LeClerc. If the concept succeeds here, similar outlets will open in Las Vegas, Miami, and Los Angeles. Beckett will oversee all of that."

"Cat, I've been dying to tell you," Beckett said, moving toward us. "I'm so bad at keeping secrets, especially from you. But I couldn't take the chance I'd fuck it up." He held his hands up. "Not that telling you would fuck it up, but I had to sign the NDA, and I'd never signed one and was paranoid. Everything happened so fast."

"Once we knew LeClerc wanted Beckett, we moved quickly," William added.

"Forgive me, Cat?" Beckett pled. "It's not the same if I can't celebrate with you. Don't be mad, okay?"

"Oh, Beckett." I stumbled away from William and gave Beckett a huge hug, my eyes welling with tears. I was so glad things were okay between us again and so happy for Beckett. I squeezed him tightly. This was an amazing opportunity. I could see that quite clearly. It was exactly the kind of opportunity I'd always wanted for Beckett and the kind he had never dared dream of. He was so talented, though, and he totally deserved this. I pulled back and looked Beckett in the eye. "I'm so happy for you. I'm sorry I was such a complete ass. Again. Let me make it up to you. I'll throw you a huge party to celebrate. It's going to be awesome."

"No parties yet," Beckett said. "Technically, I still can't talk about it. But I really wanted to tell you, and that's why I came to William's office. I just signed the contracts at the lawyer's offices a few blocks from here. I came over to plead for leniency."

"Beckett, you're completely forgiven. We'll party in a few weeks."

"As soon as PR makes the announcement, you should be good," William added.

"PR!" Beckett squealed. "I've never had PR people—I mean, technically they're LeClerc's people. He's the star, but I don't care. Next I'll be lunching with my *agent*."

"It won't be long before you're a star too." I squeezed his arm. Both of us were grinning like idiots.

"See, this is why I had to tell you. William told me he thought it would be okay right before you got here. I was going to call you the minute I got home, but you beat me to it. Champagne at my place later?" Beckett winked, clearly thrilled beyond measure.

"Absolutely," I said. "I can't wait."

He gave me another hug, then looked at William. "And I think that's my cue to depart stage right." He moved to shake William's hand. "William, thanks for everything. Catch you later, okay?"

"Later," William said with a bemused smile.

Beckett moved toward the door. "Cat, call me..." He held his hand to his ear in a phone gesture. He gave me a meaningful look, opened the door, and then he was gone.

William and I were alone. Suddenly, flutters erupted in my belly. I was so nervous. It was one thing to imagine telling William I loved him when I was a half a mile away. It was another when he was standing right in front of me, his smoldering gaze raking over me. It was all the more nerve-wracking because he looked so fucking hot in his suit. It fit him perfectly, and he looked completely cool and powerful in it. But I also knew he looked as good out of it as he did in it. We were standing there, saying nothing, and I had to be the one to break the silence. "I'm so happy for him," I said, gesturing to the door. I was pretty sure William knew how happy I was for Beckett—he'd been right there when I'd burst into tears—but I rambled, just to keep talking. "I've always thought that all of his talents weren't being utilized in food styling. Part of me worried that he was just doing it for me, so I could get work."

William nodded, listening with the same intentness I imagined he showed everyone from world leaders to little old me. Suddenly, I felt so unsure of myself. And the more insecure I felt, the more I babbled on, telling William more things he already knew. "Beckett has been my best friend for a decade. He's been such a great friend. He's the most selfless person I know. He deserves this. He's really talented. You know that, right?"

"I do," he said, saving me from babbling on. "Catherine, you have nothing to worry about. I met Beckett because of you, and I did recommend him. But he landed this on his own." As usual, he seemed to understand what I was saying even though I hadn't spelled it out. "Beckett impressed LeClerc," William said, putting a hand on my back and leading me toward his desk. "And that's no easy feat. Beckett's an immensely talented pastry chef, and you're right—he deserves this and more."

I felt some measure of relief. I didn't want there to be any rumors that my relationship with William had garnered Beckett this opportunity. He'd earned it on his own. "Thank you," I said.

He moved so his arms were around my waist. I could smell his cologne, that special scent that was uniquely William Lambourne. "And now I think we have something to discuss."

"We do?" I whispered.

"You came to me," he pointed out. "Not that I mind. I'm always glad to see you, but I assume there was something you wanted."

"Besides accusing you of conspiring with my best friend?" I gave him a sheepish grin.

"Yes, besides that."

We did need to talk, and I wasn't going to be able to keep my thoughts straight if I was standing so close to him. All I could think about was touching my lips to his and pressing my body against his. I wanted to strip off that suit—perhaps leave the red power tie—and feel him skin to skin. Exercising more willpower than I thought I possessed, I stepped out of his embrace.

"This must be serious," he said, looking as displeased as I felt.

"It is. We need to talk."

"Alright, but I don't want to do it here. Too many interruptions."

He moved to his desk, swiped his hand across it, and tapped something.

"Yes, Mr. Lambourne." It was Parker's voice.

"Tell George to bring the car around."

"Yes, sir."

"And reschedule my afternoon appointments."

Pause. "Right away."

He tapped the desk again.

"How do you do that?" I asked, gesturing to his desk. "It just looks like glass from this angle."

He grinned. "It's magic."

"I'm not five."

"I'll show you the technology some other time. It's nothing more than a tablet on a larger scale."

And, I imagined, with a much larger price tag.

He walked toward me and gestured to the door. "Ready?"

"Yes. Where are we going?"

"My place. Is that okay?"

His territory. Was that an intentional power play? I could have fought the decision, but I was reluctant to have our discussion at my condo. Right now it held too many memories of our last fight. "That's fine." I followed him to the door. "Oh, wait." I dashed to the table where I'd thrown the envelope and picked it up, stuffing it back in my bag.

"What's that?" he asked.

I gave him a puzzled look. Was he really going to pretend he didn't know? Or maybe he didn't want to discuss it until we arrived at the penthouse. "Let's talk about it at your house."

We took the private elevator down. William didn't move to kiss me, but he did hold my hand all the way down and out of the building. George was waiting out front with the black SUV. He held the door for us, his head held high. He didn't even glance at me, just murmured, "Good afternoon, Mr. Lambourne. Miss Kelly."

Some things never changed. We climbed in the back of the car, and William raised the privacy screen. I wondered if he would pull me onto his lap, kiss me, run his hands up my skirt…but he merely held my cold hand in his large warm one. "No gloves?" he asked. I gave him a look, daring him to say anything.

He grinned and squeezed my fingers. In a way that was comforting, and his restraint meant I could keep my thoughts focused on the conversation ahead.

I loved him.

I was willing to be totally honest with him.

The stalker shit had to stop.

As soon as I covered those topics, I could jump him.

"What are you smiling about?" William asked.

"I'll tell you later," I said.

The drive to William's penthouse at the pricey State and Walton location didn't take long at this time of day. We arrived and George opened the car door for us. William led me through the foyer and into the elevator. My heart pounded against my ribs. This was it. I was going to bare my soul. I could only pray William accepted me.

The elevator doors opened on the fifty-sixth floor, and we stepped into William's marble lobby. Beyond the small entryway, the floor-to-ceiling windows showcased the Chicago skyline. The bright sun glinted off the glass and metal, and the dark blue expanse of the lake extended as far as I could see. William led me into the living room and shrugged off his coat, laying it neatly on a chair. I watched him remove this outer layer and took a deep breath. It was impossible not to think of the last time I was here—the night William had surprised me with the naked sushi. I could remember him whispering in my ear, "Are you still hungry?"

I had been then, and I hungered for him now. I didn't know if I would ever have my fill of William Lambourne. I shivered, thinking about that night and the way William had touched me, caressed me, fucked me…

"Do you want to sit down?" he asked.

"Maybe in a minute," I said, pulling the envelope from my bag. "First I want to talk about this."

TWENTY

"What is that?" William asked, moving to stand beside the chair. He was angled so that when I looked at him I also had a glimpse of my black and white surfing photo hanging on his wall. I couldn't help but stare at it and think about that time in my life. That time—*all* of me, my past and my future—were part of William's life now. If there was another way to show that more plainly, I couldn't think of it. He was displaying his commitment to me on the wall for all to see. My art was part of his home. He wanted me here with him—he had just dropped everything he'd planned for the afternoon to be with me. I'm sure it wasn't easy for Parker to reschedule all of the meetings and conferences with big shots this afternoon, but William hadn't even seemed to think twice about it. I was part of his life now. I was one hundred percent included. I was the priority. Finally, I got it.

I wanted to show him I felt the same way. I dropped the envelope and moved toward him. At the same time, he opened his arms and enclosed me within them, pulling me against him. As soon as I touched him, my determination to talk wavered. He smelled so good, comforting and enticing all at the same time. I buried my face in his chest, inhaling his scent and feeling the steel of his muscled torso. I could hear his heart beating, could hear the way it quickened when I wrapped my arms around him. It felt so good to be in his embrace, like sinking into your own bed after a long vacation. I felt *right* here.

His hand brushed down my hair, twirling it around his fingers and tilting my head back gently. "I hate fighting with you." His voice was soft and serious.

"*I* hate fighting with *you*. This," I squeezed him tightly, "this is what I like."

"Mmm. We can agree on that." He lowered his mouth and brushed his lips over mine in a slow, tantalizing stroke. My lips tingled and tickled as I strained to close the distance between us. He still held my hair, and he used that hold to keep me from capturing his mouth as he darted his tongue out and ran it lightly over my upper lip.

I closed my eyes, feeling my whole body simmer with a heat that I knew would build and build until he made it bubble over. His tongue now licked lightly at my bottom lip and then he sank his teeth softly into the flesh. "I've wanted to do that since you walked into my office," he murmured. "I want to see you bite your lip when you come."

I shivered and took a shaky breath. I had to remember what I'd wanted to accomplish. I was getting sidetracked. It was very difficult not to when I touched William. "We need to talk," I said.

"Dirty talk? I like it." His eyes sparkled down at me as he tried to contain a grin.

I couldn't help but smile in return. He was in one of his playful moods. I loved those, but I couldn't afford to indulge it at the moment. "You know what I mean."

He sighed and released my hair, but he didn't step back. He was going to make me break the contact between us. I gritted my teeth and forced myself to release him. "I—" I cleared my throat and tried to think how to begin.

"I haven't been a very considerate host. Would you like something to drink?"

"I…yes. That sounds great." I could use the time to formulate my thoughts, but instead of leaving me to grab me something to drink, he took my hand and tugged me along with him into the kitchen.

It was as cold and stark as I remembered. The cabinets and counters were sleek white, and the stainless steel appliances gleamed under the expensive spotlighting. My counters were littered with empty water bottles, random pieces of camera equipment, and half completed to-do lists. William's counters were bare and spotless. Hutch Morrison didn't have the monopoly on meticulous kitchen organization, it seemed.

We stopped in front of the refrigerator—a ridiculously oversized SubZero—and he opened the white cabinet next to it, which concealed a wine cooler. He paused for a second as he surveyed the contents, then pulled out a bottle. I had a peek inside before he closed the door. The bottles were organized perfectly by variety, turned label up, and stacked in neat rows. I shook my head. "Sometimes I wonder what you're doing with me."

He raised a brow as he slid out a drawer, produced a corkscrew, and began to open the bottle of wine. "Why would you say that? It's me who doesn't deserve you. You're talented, smart, beautiful, and great in bed. How lucky am I?"

Well, when he put it that way… My cheeks flushed, but I made myself accept the compliment. "Thank you. I just meant that I'm such a mess, and you're so organized." I watched as he effortlessly pulled out the cork and then grabbed two wine glasses from an upper cabinet. He poured, filling each with a deep pink liquid that I immediately recognized.

"Is that the same rosé we drank at Casa di Rosabela?" I asked. The rosé that he was so proud of, the rosé which had inspired my safe word. I could feel my blush deepen across my cheeks.

William smiled broadly as he handed me a glass. "Very observant. It is. See, I'll make a wine connoisseur out of you yet, Catherine. Cheers." We touched glasses. I sipped the wine, dribbling a bit on my bottom lip. I lifted my hand to catch it before it ran onto my chin, but he grabbed my hand and shook his head. His eyes were dark and intense. My breath hitched.

"Messy can be sexy," he said, touching his finger to my mouth. "Very sexy." He dipped his head and licked the drop of wine from my bottom lip. At the taste of him mixed with the bright yet delicate flavors of the rosé, my thoughts flashed back to Napa, to our night with the honey and handcuffs and his scorching hot kisses between my legs. My arms came up and I wrapped them around his neck, pulling his mouth to mine for a deeper kiss. He didn't resist, and this time I pushed him back, pinning him to the counter and pressing against him.

"I thought…you wanted to talk," he said, his voice husky and breathless with need. I loved that I could do this to him, that I could make him want me so much.

"Talking can wait," I muttered. "I've missed you too much."

His lips were on mine again, and his hands cupped my cheeks, then tangled in my hair, angling my head to deepen our kiss. He stroked my mouth with his tongue, filling me in the same way he would with his cock. My core throbbed as heat rushed between my legs. I could feel that I was already hot and slick and ready, and I reached for the button to his trousers.

He caught my hand. "Not like this," he said firmly.

I blinked, the haze of my desire making his words confusing. "What's wrong?"

"We're not going to fuck in the kitchen. Not this time. I'm going to do this right."

I frowned. "You always do it right." I moved to kiss him again, but he blocked me.

"As flattering as that may be, I am determined." He bent and swept me into his arms, one hand behind my knees and the other around my shoulder.

I gasped. "What are you doing?"

"Carrying you to the bedroom. Grab the wine." And he really was. He was carrying me through the penthouse, heading for his bedroom.

"William! I'm too heavy for this," I squealed as I tried to balance our wine glasses and the half-full bottle of rosé while settling into his arms.

"Do I look like I'm having trouble?"

I had to admit he didn't. He moved almost effortlessly, as though my weight was nothing. When we reached the master suite, he lowered me on the large platform bed that dominated the room. The drapes to the huge windows were open, and he didn't move to close them. I watched as he stood over me and removed his tie. He unbuttoned his collar, and I sat and reached for my boots.

"Let me." He knelt and took one boot in his hands, unzipped it, and pulled it off my foot. "These are very hot, by the way. Very dominatrix," he purred wickedly as he repeated the gesture with the other boot. He was kneeling at the side of the bed, but soon rose and knelt beside me, placing his hand behind my head and lowering me gently to the pillow. He kissed me tenderly, tasting my lips and then moving to my neck and my earlobe. His hands remained cupping my face, but I wanted to feel him touching me all over. I arched, trying to tempt him, but he continued to kiss me, making sure he teased me with the slowness of the way he moved down my neck.

"William," I moaned. His mouth and hot breath on me tickled deliciously, and I shivered all over.

"Patience," he said, his lips trailing to my collarbone. I arched again and realized his knee was between my legs. I scooted down, causing my skirt to ride up slightly, and pushed my sex against him.

"Catherine…" he said in warning, but he didn't move away. I wondered if he could feel the heat blazing through my panties and the thick tights I wore. He unbuttoned my blouse and kissed the skin he bared while I pressed against him, moving slowly up and down. Another button loosed and he kissed the tops of my breasts. He was paying such careful attention to me, worshipping me in a way that was both sweet and incredibly erotic.

Another button and he smiled when he saw the black lace bra I wore. "Also very hot," he said appreciatively. Then he kissed my hard nipples through the lace, and I couldn't stop my hips from rocking as I rubbed against him. I moaned softly as he licked and sucked my nipple. Then he pulled the lace aside and took my bare point into his mouth, sucking hard while he increased the pressure of his muscled thigh against me. The pull of his lips sent a shock wave through my entire body and I moaned again, louder this time.

"Don't hold back, beautiful girl. Let it happen," he breathed as his lips found my other nipple and began to coax it to a hard peak. I couldn't believe I was going to come. I was still dressed. We both were. But my body tightened and I dug my fingers into his back as I shattered into a million pieces and cried out in ecstasy.

Finally, when my pleasure subsided, he moved back to look at me, his hand tenderly cupping my face. "You look so beautiful right now," he said, eyes still hungry. "I love to see you glow. But I'm not done with you."

I laughed softly. "Ok," I said. I was ready for more and ached for his touch even though he had just made me come. It didn't matter;

I couldn't stop wanting him. I expected him to roughly strip off my clothes and plunge himself into me, but instead he took his time and undressed me. Slowly, he unbuttoned the rest of my blouse, raising me with one hand behind my shoulders and pulling my top off. Then he unhooked my bra and discarded it as well. We didn't speak and the only sound was our ragged breathing and the rustling as he removed my clothes and tossed them to the floor.

When he reached for the button on my skirt, I couldn't contain my moan. He was moving so languidly, so reverently. When his fingers brushed my skin, he must have seen my reaction because he smiled but he didn't stroke me, didn't fondle. Somehow this benign neglect made me want him all the more. He pulled off my skirt, then tugged my tights down, freeing one leg and then the other. Then he reached for my black lace panties.

I lifted my hips as he tugged them off and dropped them on the floor. I was naked, and his gaze seemed to feast on me, to drink me in. "You're so lovely," he said. "You have the most beautiful skin, Catherine. I don't know what I did to deserve you. And I can't stop wanting you. I can never get enough." His hands moved to the buttons on his shirt, unfastening them slowly, never taking his eyes from my body, my face. When he reached for the button to his trousers, I couldn't stop my legs from spreading slightly. He drew in a slow breath as he slid his pants off, baring his black boxer briefs and the tent his erection made within them.

I parted my legs farther and when he tugged off his last piece of clothing and revealed his rigid beautiful cock, I pressed my fingers against my swollen sex. "No." He shook his head, then leaned in to grasp my hand and move it away. "I want you soft and ripe and ready for me."

I was so hot for him. I was clenching the sheets and writhing with anticipation. "William, please. I want you so—"

He straddled me, this time keeping his legs on either side of mine. His hands imprisoned my wrists lightly and he kissed me, trailing his lips down my body, tasting every inch of me. Finally, he released my hands and gently pushed my legs apart. "I know, beautiful girl, but let me take care of you." I felt his fingers brush up my thigh to my sex. He parted my swollen folds and gently trailed a finger around my entrance and then slowly slid just one thick finger inside. "You're so wet already," he said as he slowly moved his finger in and out. I could feel the pressure building, the heat coalescing in my core as he looked at me and added another finger. He slid down my body and positioned himself between my legs.

"Oh God," I groaned. I leaned my head back and closed my eyes. His fingers felt so good inside me as I rocked my hips in rhythm with his hand. When he slightly curved his fingers up, hitting that sensitive spot on top, I jerked and involuntarily clamped down on him, the pressure I felt inside instantly increasing. My toes began to curl. "William, William," I muttered as I reached my hand down and ran my fingers through his thick, dark curls.

"Not yet," he whispered as his fingers kept up their gentle-yet-firm assault. Then his head dipped and his mouth was on me, swirling my clit with just the tip of his tongue. I cried out as the involuntary tremors of an orgasm started to unfurl through me, not quite releasing in full, but fluttering almost painfully in the background. "Good girl. Now your reward." His fingers slid out of my slickness and he licked me again, his tongue hot and hard, trailing down and thrusting in and out of my entrance. His thumb moved to my clit and pushed firmly against that swollen bundle of nerves and I heard him, from far away. "Come now, Catherine. Come in my mouth."

The orgasm ripped through me, my body shaking, my breath coming in long, surrendering moans. My head whipped back and forth and my grip on the duvet was vicelike as William's mouth stayed firmly on my sex, each contraction and shudder of pleasure an offering to his lips.

Just when I thought the pleasure was finally bearable, he moved up my body and slid into me hard and fast. He thrust into me over and over again, filling me so completely that the pleasure was almost pain. And then like a lightning bolt, I was coming again, pulling him deeper into me with my every shudder.

He stilled inside me until the waves finally quieted, until I could focus. I looked into his face. His body fully covered mine and his forearms were flat on the bed on either side of my head, caging me as his hard cock waited inside me. Our eyes locked for a moment, then he bent and we kissed deeply, our tongues tangling and mating as he began the slow, steady rhythm of claiming me. Deeper and deeper he drove into me, my hips arching to meet his movements as I yielded to him and let him in to my very center. Our mouths stayed connected as our bodies moved in slow, exquisite harmony. My whole being flooded with an ecstasy I'd never felt before and I became lost in the sensation of us becoming one.

I could have kept kissing him for hours, could have stayed in our glorious embrace for days, but William pulled his mouth away and lifted up on his arms. He looked at me so intently that I closed my eyes and tilted my chin up, signaling I wanted his mouth back. "Catherine, look at me," he said softly.

I opened my eyes and my gaze met his again. I smiled, and felt him twitch and pulse inside me. "I love you," he whispered, and then he thrust again and lowered his head, groaning against my neck as he came.

*****

We lay entwined together on the bed for a long time. My heart was bursting and my head spinning. Had I heard him correctly? He loved me. William Maddox Lambourne III loved me. And he had beaten me to it. He'd told me first. I was elated and could feel the choke of tears in my throat. I couldn't speak.

Finally, he rose on his elbows and looked into my eyes. I gave him what I hoped was a not-too-shaky smile. "Did you hear me?" he said. "That might not have been the best timing—"

"You said you loved me," I whispered.

"You don't have to say it back. I've been wanting to tell you since before we went to Napa. I couldn't keep from saying it any longer. I love you, Catherine." His beautiful eyes framed with all those thick dark lashes weren't stormy now. They were a warm silver grey, shining with what I hoped was anticipation and excitement. And the kind of love that might last a lifetime.

I smiled. "William." I wrapped my arms around his neck. "I've been wanting to tell you since before Napa too, and now I'm afraid you'll think I'm just saying it because you did."

"What have you been wanting to say?"

I smiled, tears of joy coming unbidden now. Sometimes he was like a mischievous boy, teasing me until he got his way. I tilted my head back and looked at him. "I love you, William Maddox Lambourne," I said. "I love you, I love you, I love you. God, I love you!"

He laughed heartily and then kissed me tenderly but deeply. The kiss was so sweet I had to take a deep breath to keep from tipping into full-blown weeping.

We lay in each others' arms for what seemed like hours, kissing and repeating the words we'd both longed to hear and speak. Then we made love again and again. I would never get enough of William.

*****

It was early evening when my stomach rumbled loud enough for William to hear, prompting us to take a break for some dinner. When I finally rolled out of his arms and rose from the bed, I instantly missed his warmth and his lips. Dinner sounded great, but we did have some other things to tend to. "We still need to talk, and we should probably do it now."

"Alright. Let's get cleaned up first."

A few minutes later, we met back in the living room. He wore a light blue T-shirt and a pair of navy drawstring pajama pants slung low on his hips. I was clad in the dress shirt he'd discarded earlier. As soon as I entered the living room, he hissed in a breath. "You might want to talk fast," he said. "You're fucking hot when you wear my shirts."

The look in his eyes was definitely motivation to begin—and end—the discussion. I glanced at the chair where I'd dropped the envelope earlier. It was still there. Waiting. "First, I want to say I'm sorry. I'm sorry for last night. You asked me about Jeremy, and I shouldn't have been so evasive. It wasn't fair and I should be as open with you as I want you to be with me. From now on, I promise I will be. My life is an open book. Anything you want to know, I'll tell you."

William stared at me, looking a bit wary. I'm sure he was wondering what I expected in return, and I rushed to reassure him. "I don't need anything in return from you. Yes, I want you to feel like you can tell me things, but I understand if you can't right now. I accept you no matter what. I'm not going to fight with you about that anymore. I trust you. I trust you unconditionally. I love you, William."

He closed the distance between us and took my hands. "I love you too, Catherine. And I trust you. But you have to understand, sometimes I keep information from you for your own safety."

"I know that's your justification," I said, "and if you don't want to tell me, then I'll deal, but the stalking has to stop. From now on, if you want to know something, just ask. I'll tell you whatever you want to know. No secrets. The photos were too much. You made your point."

William's eyes narrowed. "What photos?"

I slowly reached down and picked up the envelope. Did he really not know? I didn't think he was playing a game with me. He wasn't like that. My hand was trembling now, and I held the envelope out to him. He took it, opened it, and pulled the photos out. He glanced at them, turned the envelope over to look at the address, and then slowly looked up at me.

His eyes were an icy blue now, cold and dangerous. "Where did you get these?"

"They came in the mail," I whispered. "I thought they were from you."

"No. I've never seen these before. God, I wouldn't do something like this to you. Send something like this." He flipped the envelope around again. "Was there a note, any sort of correspondence?"

I shook my head.

William dropped the photos and the envelope on the chair and took my hands again. He looked at me so intensely it scared me. "Think, Catherine. Are you certain? This was all that was in the envelope?"

I nodded, starting to feel very uneasy. What the hell was going on? "I just opened it today on the L. I don't even know when it came. It was in my mail stack. I thought…" I shook my head. I would be apologizing to William forever at this rate. "I know you're having me followed. I want you to call off your spies. It's creepy to see pictures of myself like this."

William stood still for the space of three heartbeats then let go of my hands and raked his fingers through his hair. He walked slowly to the windows overlooking the city and Lake Michigan. He didn't speak for a long time, and just as I was about to say something, *anything*, he said, "First of all, I understand why you think I had these taken. You saw the file I had on Jenny Hill, and I know doing elaborate investigations on women I dated or might have dated was fucked up on some levels." He spoke without looking at me, his hard eyes on the city's skyscrapers. "But I tried to explain to you that that approach has been necessary for my protection. I've been a target ever since my family died, and that's the only way I knew how to protect myself and the women I've dated from those who might seek to"—he paused and took a deep breath—"exploit my weaknesses."

It was difficult for me to imagine he had any weaknesses, though he must have thought he did. He thought he was at risk enough to justify spying on me. "Listen, I understand someone in your position has to be careful," I interrupted, "but that doesn't mean—"

"No, you don't understand." He rounded on me, folding his arms across his broad chest as he stood framed by the Chicago skyline. "That's the problem. Believe me when I say—again—I have never, *never* had a dossier on you. I had you under surveillance to keep you safe. But I only know what you've told me about yourself. I'm flying blind with you, and it scares me. Loving you scares the hell out of me because it makes me vulnerable."

I'd never seen him like this, so emotional. He seemed to be fighting to keep his feelings in check. I wanted to reassure him. "William, loving me doesn't make you vulnerable."

"Oh, yes, it does, and I question my decision not to make a dossier on you every day. Not because I don't trust you, but because I need to keep you safe, Catherine. The more I know about you, the more effectively I can do that. I'd never forgive myself if anything happened to you because of me." He stalked to the chair and lifted the photos again. "These are the evidence that you're not safe. These aren't messages to you from me. They're messages to me about you. He's showing me he can get to you."

I shook my head. "Wait. *Who* can get to me?"

"I didn't have these photos taken."

A chill ran up my arms and across my back. I suddenly felt ice cold. "If you didn't have them taken, then who did?" My voice sounded hollow and far away, and much calmer than I felt.

William was beside me in a moment. He gathered me in his arms, warming me with his body and maneuvering me to the couch. He sat beside me and looked me in the eye. "There are things I haven't told you. I didn't want to scare you, didn't want to alarm you. Truthfully, I didn't want to scare you away from me. But it's too late for that now. You need to know that you could be in danger."

I wasn't processing what he was saying. Danger? How could I be in any sort of danger? My gaze darted to the photos again. Suddenly, I saw them in a new light. I was unprotected, unaware, an easy target. But from whom?

"Someone is making threats," William went on.

Somewhere in the distance I heard a familiar ringtone. My cell. I ignored it and focused on William.

"The threats are why I wanted you in Napa with me. I wanted you out of Chicago and under my protection. It was the only way I knew how to keep you safe once I thought you might become a target."

The ringing stopped, and I assumed the call had gone to voicemail.

"So this started before we even left Chicago? You've known about it for how long then?"

"For a few weeks." He looked sheepish and I watched him steel his shoulders and lift his chin. He was obviously struggling with telling me all of this, but he seemed determined to nonetheless.

"Is this connected to the Wyatt thing that's going on, with the wreckage?" I asked, my voice dead and flat as the words tumbled out of my mouth.

"I think it's all connected. We just haven't been able to figure out how. Yet. George is on it now, as are other members of my security team. We're thinking about notifying the FBI, but I've held off. Until now."

The FBI? This was much more serious than I realized. The steep chill on my spine deepened.

"I've received an envelope like this too," he said. "Several, in fact. They contained newspaper clippings about Jace's accident, the two of us at the Art Institute, a mention of you in conjunction with the opening of Willowgrass. The first one arrived while we were broken up and you were sick. I told you I was going out of my mind with worry then and I was. Because you were sick, but also because I was so afraid that something was going to happen to you. And you wouldn't see me or talk to me."

I looked at him and my heart shattered. I'd had no idea. I couldn't imagine what kind of hell I had unwittingly put William through then.

"And I've received photos taken of me" He gestured to envelope I'd brought. "I didn't have these pictures taken. Whoever is watching me is also watching you."

My cell began to ring again, and I ignored it. "So I'm in danger? There's some creep out there who might hurt me to get to you?"

But he wasn't looking at me anymore. He was staring at my bag on the couch behind us. "You'd better answer that."

I blinked. "What?"

"Your phone. It's been ringing non-stop."

Concerned now, I grabbed my bag and rifled through it until I found my phone. I saw on the screen immediately that the caller was Minerva. My heart clenched in my chest. Why would Minerva call me? I felt William take my hand and realized I was shaking. But he was beside me. He was giving me the strength and support of his love.

"H-hello?"

"Catherine? Thank God. Where are you?" Her voice was high and shrill and I felt the first stirrings of panic creep in.

"I'm at William's. What's wrong, Minerva?"

"It's your apartment. Someone broke in."

"W-what?"

William's hand clenched over mine. He must have heard Minerva's voice carry through the phone.

"The police are here, dear. You had better come home right away. They want to talk to you."

My entire body shook now, and I was so cold my teeth were chattering. "O-okay. I'll be there in a few minutes." I glanced at William. His face reflected dread but also determination. I knew without a doubt he would do anything to keep me safe.

"Do hurry, dear," Minerva said. "And, Catherine, there's one other thing."

My hand clenched painfully around William's.

"We can't find Laird."

I ended the call with Minerva and looked up at William. I couldn't stop the tears from flowing now, and he pulled me into his arms as I sobbed. I was so scared and overwhelmed by how things were quickly spiraling out of control. And Laird. Laird! I looked down at my watch and it was nearly six. It was dark out. Laird wore a reflective collar with ID tags, but the nighttime Chicago streets in winter were no place for my dog. I needed to start looking for him. I pulled back from William's embrace and wiped my sleeve across my runny nose. "Listen, can you have George drive me home? I need to talk to the police, then I need to start looking for Laird. The sooner I can start walking through the neighborhood, the sooner I can find him.

My cell number is on his tag, so if someone finds him first, maybe they'll call me—"

"Catherine." William looked down at me. "I'll take you to your condo so you can talk to the police. And I'll help you look for Laird. But you can't stay there."

"What do you mean I can't stay there?" I looked up him and he wore a stern expression. "Where else am I supposed to go? That's my home! I'm not going to let some stupid break-in scare me off. Minerva didn't even say if anything is missing."

"Catherine," William said again, this time in that dark and dominating tone that meant he was determined to have his way no matter what. "I love you and there is no way in hell I am letting the woman I love spend the night in what is currently a crime scene. No way, no how. We'll go over there and talk to the police. Then you can pack a bag to bring back here. Then we'll look for Laird. No arguing."

I stared back at him, my gaze hard on his, and let out a deep sigh. He was right. He was only thinking about my safety and my well-being. He loved me. And I loved him too.

"Ok," I said. "Let's get dressed and go."

"See, was that so hard?" he asked as he grabbed my hand and pulled me along to the master suite to find our clothes.

I sat on the edge of William's bed buttoning up my blouse and watched as he pulled a heavy cable-knit sweater over his T-shirt. He'd already put on a pair of tight faded jeans that did wonders for his ass. He starting talking while he was lacing up a pair of rugged hiking boots. "I'll talk to George and ask him to pick up the envelope and proof sheets and have them analyzed. We've already sent all of the other stuff I've received to the lab, but so far it's all come back clean. No prints, no identifying markers. Maybe we'll get lucky with yours."

"Yeah. Well, let's hope so," I replied. I felt like I'd landed in an episode of *Law & Order*.

"Are you sure that envelope came in the mail?"

"I assume so. It was in the mail pile Beckett made while I was in Napa, but I don't know. I guess we can ask him if he remembers it."

"Have you noticed anything unusual around your building? You know, weird cars outside, odd people hanging around? Anything unusual?"

I thought for a minute. "No, not really. It's pretty quiet around there and Minerva and Hans are almost always home. If something was up, I'm sure they'd know about it."

I sat for a moment, my mind whirling. Something was there, a thought that was hazy and just out of reach, kind of like déjà vu. *Oh shit, déjà vu*. William must have noticed the stunned expression on my face, because he quickly asked, "What is it? Did you remember something?"

I looked at him, my heart racing. "This morning, when I was leaving. There was a plumber who was walking up as I was walking out. He was just shutting the door of a white van parked out front and he asked me to hold the building's door. He said he was there to fix a leaky pipe on the first floor. You don't think..." my voice trailed off.

"Well, we can find out." William looked around and saw my phone on the bedside table. He picked it up, looked at it, pressed a button, and held it to his ear. "Mrs. Himmler, this is William Lambourne, Catherine's boyfriend."

Even through my shock I thrilled a little at hearing William call himself my boyfriend. He was more than that to me now. My lover, my friend. My protector. Boyfriend couldn't possibly encompass all of those things.

"Yes, she's fine, thank you. And thank you for calling earlier. I have a question. Did a plumber come today for some work in your condo?" There was a pause and I saw him nodding. "Alright, thank you. We'll see you soon. We're leaving in a just a few minutes. Ok. Good-bye."

William looked at me, his expression dark and weary. "She didn't have a plumber come today, Catherine."

"Oh fuck," I replied. "Do you think I unwittingly let whoever broke into my condo in? I basically showed him the door?" I felt sick. If I really was in danger from whoever was threatening William, it was entirely possible that I'd literally walked right past him this morning and let him into my building.

"Do you remember anything? What did he look like, how old? Anything noticeable? Think!"

I ran the entire scene over in my head, closed my eyes and tried to remember. "He was mid-30s, I guess, kind of tall." My voice trailed off. There had been something so familiar about him. Had I seen him around before? He reminded me of something…of someone. Then it hit me. I looked up at William.

"I remember now. Why I had that déjà vu feeling when I saw him. He reminded me of someone."

"Who?"

William was standing close enough for me to touch him, his face hard and impenetrable but his eyes filled with worry and concern.

I reached out and put my hand on his arm. I looked at the face of the man I loved, looked into his beautiful stormy, blue-grey eyes. "He reminded me of you."

TO BE CONTINUED…

Catherine and William's story continues in

A FEAST OF YOU
THE EPICUREAN BOOK 3

Available now!

ABOUT THE AUTHOR

Sorcha Grace is an adventurous eater, beach lover and author of scorching contemporary erotic romance. She is also the nom de plume of a nationally bestselling author who publishes in another romance genre. Find her on Facebook and Twitter.

www.facebook.com/SorchaGrace
Twitter: @SorchaGrace

Printed in the USA
CPSIA information can be obtained
at www.ICGtesting.com
JSHW031703140824
68134JS00036B/3498